He Went With
John Paul Jones

This edition published 2022
by Living Book Press

ISBN: 978-1-922919-05-2 (hardcover)
         978-1-922919-04-5 (softcover)

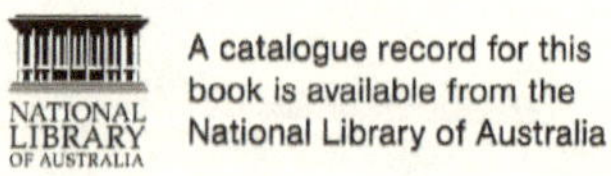

A catalogue record for this book is available from the National Library of Australia

He Went With

John Paul Jones

LOUISE ANDREWS KENT

ILLUSTRATED BY

VICTOR MAYS

Living Book Press

CONTENTS

CHAPTER 1

UNDER THE COUNTER

"NICK! YOUNG Nick! Nick Young! Wake up—time to get up—six o'clock—six o'clock..."

Nicholas Young Caryl half opened his weary eyelids. Then, for a moment that was like a dive into green water, he drifted back into sleep. Yet he still heard the river noises—wind chuckling over the water, gulls screaming, sails being hauled up, oars clanking in rowlocks.

He thought: Those must be the oars of the barge. That's Richard Dale calling. This is the morning we're going fishing... my birthday, June 5... 1767... twelve today... fishing on the island... barge waiting... get up, must get up... foggy morning, I reckon. Cold too... sleep a minute longer...

"Nick—Nick Young! Six o'clock..."

The voice was getting louder and harsher. No Virginia voice was ever like that, Nick thought, yet there was still a moment when he expected to open his eyes in the big, airy bedroom of his Uncle Nicholas's house in Portsmouth, Virginia. The tall magnolias between the older Nicholas Caryl's house and the Dales' house would be in bloom; white flowers bigger than teacups opening out of great silky, furry buds. The mist from the Elizabeth River would be dripping off the shining leaves. Redbirds would be crimson flashes among the flowers. At the plantation, roses would be in bloom.

"Nick Young!"

He knew the voice now. *It was Mr. Gribble's.* He could hear those heavy feet starting down the twisting stairs.

Nick rolled out from under the counter into the dark shop. He could smell cheese—not roses. The river outside was the Thames. This was England. This was London—not Portsmouth.

"Coming, sir, coming," he called.

He tugged Pambo by the collar and dragged him out from under the thin, tattered blanket that was their only covering. Pambo felt the cold even more than Nick did, so Nick always made the Negro boy sleep next to the wall of the counter. After all, if it had not been for Pambo (short for Palambo, which was short for Paul Ambrose Caryl) Nick would, he remembered with a shiver, be sleeping next to his brother Sandy in the graveyard of the English Caryl family. But he must not think of Sandy's grave or of the night he died. Not now. Not with Mr. Gribble's buckled shoes and fat legs in thick gray stockings already showing on the stairs. The end of the grocer's cane showed too.

Of course they were beaten. They were beaten most mornings but usually not until after breakfast. Mr. Gribble never struck in anger, he always said. He must do it, Nick supposed, for the exercise. It was the only kind he ever took. This time the beating came before breakfast. Nick was so used to it that it was no longer very painful, but it annoyed him. He considered it undignified to be beaten by a fat little man whose face grew as red as his waistcoat and who wheezed at every stroke.

Pambo howled when Mr. Gribble hit him. As he pointed out to his master, that was what the little old robin wanted. Pambo was always obliging.

"He hits you much more than he does me, Mistoh Nick Young. Because you stand there so quiet and proud. You ought to yell a little, Mistoh Nick Young."

Back in Portsmouth, Virginia, everyone always called him Nick Young to distinguish him from his uncle, Nicholas Tabor Caryl. The night Nick and Pambo ran away from the house of Nick's English cousins, the boys had agreed it would be safer for him to drop the name of Caryl. London was a vast city. Here, in this narrow, dark street that twisted away from the Thames, they were miles from Lawrence Caryl's house in Bloomsbury and from the garden with the graveyard at the end of it. Still the name of Caryl was not a common one. Somehow it might come to his cousins' ears that Nicholas Young Caryl was still alive, in which case, as Pambo remarked, they would not be alive long.

They had told Mr. Gribble that they came from Jamaica. This was true. It was off the coast of Jamaica that his Uncle Nick's ship, the *Pocahontas*, carrying tobacco from the Caryl plantation on the James River, had been wrecked.

In Jamaica, Nick had noticed, people sounded more English than they did in Virginia.

We must sound as English as we can—Nick had told Pambo—in case we meet anyone from Jamaica.

On the whole Pambo did better than his master. Only he always said "Mistoh" instead of "Mistah" like the waiters that night at Lawrence Caryl's. Pambo certainly did not sound English this morning as they pumped water into the wooden trough in the yard back of the grocer's house so they could get washed.

Nick said rather crossly—he was shivering from the cold water and the blows from Mr. Gribble's cane still stung—"Don't call me Mistoh. I've told you seven-eight times that it's silly for a grocer's boy to have a servant. Even old Gribble might think of that after a while. You call me Nick—hear?"

"Yes, Mist—Yes, Nick," Pambo said. "We'd better go and sweep the floor or we won't get any of that dee-licious breakfast, Nick. None of that moldy bacon that I smell cooking, Nick; not any of that tough old cold bread, Nick, left over from breakfast that morning King Charles got his head cut off, Nick. None of that chocolate they make with so much of the tasty water out of the Thames, Nick—"

"And don't you call me Nick every minute either," Nick said.

He was smiling now. Nick was never mad with anyone long, as Pambo knew. Indeed Mistoh Nick, as Pambo still called him in his mind, had hardly ever spoken harshly to Pambo in the nine years since Pambo had become Nick's servant. Pambo had been a present to Nick on his third birthday. Pambo was then seven years old.

He could remember Nick's uncle saying, "Now, Paul Ambrose, you are going to be Mistoh Nick's boy. You look after him. Don't let him fall in the river. Stay right with him, hear?"

So Pambo had stayed with Nick and here they were, eating moldy bacon and drinking watery chocolate under Mr. Gribble's sharp black eyes. They were a mighty long way from Caryl's Maze, Pambo thought. Nick thought about Caryl's Maze too, and about the ruffled shirt he had on. It was getting too small for him. Wrapped up in another shirt were the book in which he wrote his journal, his box of colors, and his brushes. There was also a purse, netted of light green silk.

Cherry had hemmed the ruffles for the shirt and netted the purse. Cherry and her mother lived at Caryl's Maze on the James River. Caroline Ashton was Cherry's real name. They called her Cherry because of her bright pink cheeks. Her father, who had been captain of one of Uncle Nicholas's ships, had been lost at sea. Mrs. Ashton and Aunt Dorothy Caryl had gone to school together in England. They had learned to speak French so that anyone who had learned to speak French in England could understand it. They had learned to net purses and make quill-work mirror frames and do embroidery and paint on ivory.

Luckily, Nick remembered, they also knew how to smoke hams and pickle oysters and spice beef and make almond cakes.

"Nick Young," Aunt Dorothy would say, "you and Pambo take this basket and go out in the henhouse and find me twenty eggs, hear?"

Ambrosine, Pambo's mother, was a fine cook but Aunt Dorothy had a lighter hand with an almond cake. When she tucked back her sleeve ruffles and covered her dress with a linen apron, even more wonderful things than usual were carried from the big kitchen along the colonnade into the dining room.

Mrs. Ashton and Aunt Dorothy tried hard to teach Cherry to cook and speak French and to color engravings. Cherry preferred sailing on the river, playing bowls, and chasing through the boxwood maze. For some reason she had taken a special dislike to paintbrushes, so Nick, who was happiest with a brush or a pen in his hand, used to do the hard parts for her. She could manage trees and sky and grass but when it came to faces and brocaded petticoats, she would groan loudly and pass the picture over to Nick. Cherry never learned to draw anything more complicated than a house with smoke coming out the chimneys. Often the smoke blew one way out of one chimney and the opposite way out of another. Nick would hurry through his fencing lessons—he hated the sight and sound of a foil—and rush back to his painting table.

Cherry would have liked to fence. She could bowl better than Nick. She could walk as neatly as a cat on the rail fence around the paddock. She was a fearless rider and the only girl Nick had ever seen who would take a fish off a hook without squealing. She was not afraid of mice, either. On the whole, Cherry was less tiresome than most girls. Some people might even consider her pretty, especially in her green silk with a pair of cherries hung over her ears for earrings. Nick did not think she was pretty. He liked blue eyes; Cherry's were green. Her hair was no special color, just a warm brown with a lot of gold in it. Unlike the ladies in the engravings, she had a short, slightly turned-up nose. Her mouth was not the perfect cupid's bow Nick was in the habit of painting. It was also too big. She ran around in the Virginia sunshine so she had freckles.

Her mother and Aunt Dorothy were having a hard time making a lady of her.

I wonder, thought Nick, as he and Pambo finished their chocolate and started taking down the shutters of Mr. Gribble's shop, how they are getting on.

He had plenty of time to think about Caryl's Maze that morning. After the beatings were over, the morning was rather quiet.

Pambo had gone off to his work in the storeroom behind the shop, saying cheerfully, "Nice man, Mr. Gribble; saved us the trouble of dusting our clothes, Mistoh—I mean—Nick."

Mr. Gribble had already left for his favorite coffee house farther up the street, growling as usual to his wife: "Send for me at *once*, immediately, if any important customers come in." There had not been many important customers since Nick and Pambo had been working for the grocer. Mrs. Gribble waited on the kind of customer who wanted a pound of cheese or a jar of marmalade. It was only when some sea captain came in to order stores for the ship's cabin that Mr. Gribble was sent for.

It was Nick's turn that cold, rainy June morning—it was his thirteenth birthday—to stay in the shop. He must open the door when the knocker clanged, call Mrs. Gribble, be ready to run out into the rain for Mr. Gribble. It was Pambo's turn to help squeeze lemons for Mr. Gribble's specialty, a concentrated lemon juice, and to paste labels on jars of black currant jam.

Before Nick and Pambo came, Mr. Gribble had had only one boy who helped in both the store and the shop. His name was Duncan and he had run away to sea as Mr. Gribble's shop boys often did for some reason. Mr. Gribble, an economical man with names as well as with other things, often called both Pambo and Nick "Duncan." If they did not answer promptly he naturally hit them with his cane.

What Mr. Gribble would like, Nick thought as he got out his drawing paper and began to draw a redbird on the branch of a magnolia, would be a clockwork boy. He would wake himself up every morning. His name would be Duncan. Nick had taken a dislike to Duncan because Mr. and Mrs. Gribble both spoke so well of him. Duncan, it seemed, jumped briskly out from under the counter every morning without being called. He preferred his bacon and his straw moldy. He liked his tea weak. Duncan minded neither cold nor heat. He loved cabbage. He did not play the fiddle, as Pambo did, keeping the maidservants from their work. He did not, like Nick, greet the customers with paint on his fingers. Duncan's appearance was always neat.

Nick knew, because he had seen himself in the only looking glass available—the outside of the shop window—that his own figure could well have been used for frightening the crows who pulled up the young corn shoots at Caryl's Maze. He had grown a couple of inches since they ran away from his cousins' house. He was a head taller than Pambo now. His bony wrists stuck out from under his sleeve ruffles. His green suit, the one made by William Paul, the tailor at Fredericksburg, the first suit of his that was not made at home, was too small for him everywhere. There were holes in the stockings his aunt had knitted for him. The only thing that fitted him was his beaver hat. It had been a fine hat, three-cornered. It had cost thirty shillings. Nick wished he had even one of the shillings now. There were only pennies in the silk purse that Cherry had made and they belonged to Pambo, who had earned them playing his fiddle in the street. Mr. Gribble, of course, did not pay them anything. Their food was a great expense as he often pointed out, usually adding that in the kindness of his heart he had taken them off the street and given them a home.

If it had not been for the kindness of his heart, Mr. Gribble often asked, how would it be possible for two poor boys from Jamaica to be sleeping dry and safe and warm under the counter of a shop near London Bridge?

It was true at least that they were dry, Nick thought, shivering a little. How long they would be safe was another question.

THREE-CORNERED VOYAGE

WHEN NICK thought back over the events that had led him from Caryl's Maze in Virginia to Mr. Gribble's shop in London, he always began with his twelfth birthday and Richard Dale's voice calling. Nick and his brother Sandy were orphans. Their father and mother had died of smallpox when Nick was a small boy. Sandy, who was nine years older than Nick, was heir to the plantation on the James River called Caryl's Maze. Nick lived at the plantation but he often spent the night at his Uncle Nicholas's house in Portsmouth next door to the Dales'. His uncle was losing his eyesight and growing a little deaf. He liked to have Nick, whose voice he could always hear, come in from the plantation and stay. Nick would read the *Virginia Gazette* aloud to him in the evening and in the morning go with him to the office of Caryl and Company on First Street and read him long lists of the goods that traveled in Caryl ships to faraway places.

That June morning Richard Dale was calling from the top of the big magnolia tree just outside Nick's window. Richard was always climbing something. He was getting in training for life on a ship, he used to tell Nick. He was planning to run away to sea before long and make his fortune. He fell out of a good many trees in the course of this training but usually managed to land right side up.

Nick stumbled out of bed when he heard Richard's voice and went yawning to the window.

"Coming, Richard, coming!" he called.

Richard Dale swung down out of the tree and strolled over to the pier. Nick dressed quickly. He did not need to do much washing because he would be swimming later at the island, he told himself. He glanced out the window again as he pulled on his stockings.

Through the mist, which was thick that morning, he could just see the barge at the end of the pier. The red flag with the white anchor and star on it, the flag that all Caryl ships carried, hung in limp folds. The gilded carving on the bow hardly shone at all. The red and white striped awning looked wet and dark. The Negro rowers, singing while they waited, were standing on the pier. They had on their blue coats with the red facings.

Pambo and Dickson, the butler, came out carrying baskets and put them into the barge. There would be fried chicken and ham and a big wedge of fruitcake, Nick knew. The barge would take them to the island and then go back for Nick's uncle and for Dickson. Later in the day the barge with Dickson and his uncle in it would pick them up and they would all go to the plantation for supper.

The mist turned into hot steam and burned off as they rowed up the river. The goldwork began to shine in the sun. Nick sat in the stern and steered. The Negroes sang to the beat of the oars. It was a wonderful day—the best day of his life. The rockfish were biting near the island. Pambo made a fire and they cooked their fish with bacon for breakfast. They cooked spoonfuls of scalded corn meal in the pan. Hush puppies, Pambo called the crisp brown cakes. He said that was because when dogs whined for something to eat you threw them a corn meal cake and said "Hush, puppy!"

Nick didn't care what they were called or why. Nothing ever tasted so good.

They caught more fish. They swam in the clear water near the rocks and baked themselves dry in the hot sunshine. Then they fished some more but the fish had stopped biting.

"Mosquitoes haven't though," Nick said to Richard, slapping one on his wrist.

"They never bite me," Richard said.

"Too tough probably," said Nick "I was over in Dismal Swamp last week. They about chewed me up." He brushed one away from his forehead and said, "Let's explore the island. We might find some buried treasure."

"Where?"

"Why, anywhere. Don't you know pirates used to come here? We might find a skull and crossbones cut on a pine." No pirate had been so obliging as to cut any marks on any of the pines they saw. All Nick acquired was more mosquito bites. Both boys were hot and tired when they came back to the beach where Pambo was sleeping in the shade. He woke up and spread out the dinner from the baskets. There were all the things Nick had expected and more too.

They were just finishing the last of the fruitcake when the barge came back for them. Uncle Nicholas could still see enough to steer, or perhaps it was Dickson who steered. Nick did not know because he and Richard slept as the barge moved over the miles between the island and Caryl's Maze.

The plantation was on a creek that ran into the James River. The sun was going down in a sky of hot red and gold as they came around the bend and saw the house. The bricks of the south front were rose red. The white columns of the porch looked pink. The boxwood maze was dark behind it. The breeze from the shore brought the scent of box and roses and hot rolls baking.

Aunt Dorothy came out of the kitchen. She handed her apron to Ambrosine and they laughed at something the cook said. She started along the colonnade. Then she saw the barge and started running across the green lawn to the wharf.

"Cherry!" she called. "Cherry—they've come!"

Soon the wharf was full of people. The Negroes were shouting "Happy Birthday, Mistoh Nick Young! Good evenin', Mistoh Richard!"

And it was a happy birthday for them both, Nick remembered. Richard's birthday was not until November but the family was poor since Richard's father had died and Nick had always shared his birthday with Richard. So there were presents for them both. There were silk purses from Cherry, green for Nick, blue for Richard. There were new linen shirts and silver sleeve buttons for them both from Aunt Dorothy, golden sovereigns to put in the purses from Uncle Nicholas, stockings from Mrs. Ashton, new fishing rods from Sandy in England. Captain Farrand of the *Pocahontas* had brought them.

Nick, even in Mr. Gribble's dark little shop, could still see the long mahogany table with the wax candles in the silver candlesticks and the big silver bowl full of red roses. He could still see his aunt and Mrs. Ashton with their powdered hair, his uncle with his big old-fashioned wig standing up with a glass of champagne in his hand to propose a toast to Richard and Nick. He had Dickson pour a little into Nick's glass so he could drink to Richard, some into Richard's glass so he could drink to Nick. He himself poured a thimbleful into Cherry's so she could drink to both.

"Pretty big thimble," Cherry said. "Ouch, it stings my nose!"

"I hope you didn't give the child too much, Mr. Caryl," Mrs. Ashton said.

"Nonsense, madam! It's a lady's wine. A tankard wouldn't hurt her," Nicholas Caryl said, laughing. "Now, Nick Young," he added, "here comes the best present of all and you shall read it, since these candles seem pretty dim. It's strange how the candles don't give light the way they used to. And I certainly sent out the best spermaceti—well, no matter—read the letter. From what Captain Farrand said, there's good news in it. It's from Sandy."

So Nick stood up—the candlelight was plenty bright enough for him—and read Sandy's letter.

Caryl House, Bloomsbury, near London
April 8th, 1767

To my dear and honored Uncle Nicholas and to all the family,

Thank you, sir, for the money you sent by Captain Farrand. Funds were getting rather low. I have left Oxford. Since I shall be twenty-one next autumn, I think I have learned all the Latin and Greek a tobacco planter needs.

That is what I intend to be, my dear uncle, and I hope you are glad.

At least I can translate the Latin on the sundial—*Non numero horas nisi serenas*: I count only the sunny hours; and the words on the Golden Horseshoe—*Sic juvat transcendere montes*: Thus it was pleasant to cross the mountains. Isn't that about right?

Well, it won't be long before I ride with the Knights across the mountains and count the happy sunny hours around the sundial—for I am coming home!

I know I can best show my gratitude, my dear uncle, by learning to manage the plantation as well as you and Aunt Dorothy have done for me. I shall try to deserve all the kindness you both have given me and Nick Young since we lost our parents. I know he feels as I do and I am happy that we shall soon be together.

Do not worry about my being in debt. I have paid all my bills at Oxford and thanks to your generosity I now have plenty of money. As you see by the address, I am staying with your cousin Lawrence and his sons. You may remember that Gilbert, the second son, was up at Oxford with me. He was sent down last year, not being much more interested than I am in Latin—perhaps not so much. They tried to make a clergyman out of him but that was not much use. Cousin Lawrence hopes his father, Sir George Caryl—I've never seen him, he stays at Caryl's Mount all the time—will buy commissions for Gilbert and Frederick so they can be in the army. Gilbert, however, says he would rather come out to Virginia. He is most interested in our colony, likes to hear about our life there, thinks it must be vastly agreeable. I tell him to come with me and see for himself. He says he will, next time one of our ships makes the voyage. There is something about him that will surprise you. You will see what it is when we come.

I can hardly wait to see you all again. I fancy Nick Young has grown so I would not know him and Cherry must be quite a young lady. Perhaps you would not know me either. My cousins, Gilbert's sisters, say I am "vastly improved." I no longer speak with a colonial accent, they say. Another change occurred only last week. When we were coming down from Oxford a highwayman held up our coach. At such times people here usually hand over their purses but to his surprise I jumped off the box and set upon him with my rapier, wounding him in the arm.

He dropped his pistol—it was not even loaded—and, the other man with me attacking him too, rode off pretty fast I can tell you. Not before he had given me a cut on the forehead with his dagger, though. It was not deep and it is healing well but it will, I suppose, change my looks a little. Perhaps that is the improvement my cousins talk of!

Now you must write and tell me what to bring you from London and the next time one of your ships—I hope it will be the *Pocahontas*—sails from Brown's Wharf past the Tower and leaves the Thames behind her, I hope one of the passengers will be

Your respectful and affectionate nephew
ANDREW TABOR CARYL

P.S. I send two fishing rods, one for Nick Young and one for Richard Dale. Tell them Gilbert and I will sit on the island in the shade and drink that good lemon punch Aunt Dorothy makes while they catch rock for our dinner.

SANDY

A happy buzz of talk followed the reading of Sandy's letter. They played bowls in the moonlight later. The moon was the brightest and most golden Nick had ever seen. There were hundreds of little moons in the river. Fireflies flashed their lanterns along the edge of the woods and over the tobacco fields and all through the boxwood maze. Richard won the game of bowls—he always did.

"I'll race you to the dial," he said to Nick. "Put your handkerchief on the sundial, Cherry, and we'll see who brings it back to you."

"I left it there already," Cherry said. "I knew you'd race tonight."

They had always raced to the sundial on Nick's birthday. Even before they were big enough to see over it, they had learned to follow the turns and twists through the maze. Sandy had taught Nick, first carrying him on his back, then holding him by the hand, and Nick had taught Richard. As they grew bigger Sandy would give them a start, joining in the race himself.

They all had the pattern of the maze clearly in their minds. It was laid out something like the one at Hampton Court in England, only with one or two extra dead ends. Even with a late start Sandy always won. He never hesitated between left and right or found himself in a blind alley. They would hear his swift footsteps on the grass long before they reached the dial. The real race was between Richard and Nick to see who would come in second.

"Well, one of us will win tonight but not after Sandy comes," Nick said.

"Perhaps he's forgotten," Richard suggested.

"When he forgets his name!" said Nick. "Here's the mark. Count for us, Cherry."

"One—two—three—go!" said Cherry and they were gone, lost in the shadows of the box bushes.

It was still hot in the maze. The sweet musky scent of box was all around them. Richard was faster on his feet but he hesitated a second at the third turn, the one to the right, which led after two more turns to a white marble seat with a marble faun with pointed ears beside it. Nick always thought that except for the ears the faun had a look of Sandy, but he did not see it that night. In the second Richard paused, Nick passed him, running faster than he had ever run before. He turned down a short path, right—another short one, right again—a long one this time, then left and left again around three sides of a little square with another seat, another statue. Two more turns brought him to a path that ran almost the whole length of the east side.

He could hear Richard behind him now. Nick did not look back but ran on, taking the proper turns almost without thinking. He passed the last of the blind alleys, smelled roses, ran past a great bush of white ones to the sundial and snatched Cherry's handkerchief.

The moon was so bright that he could read the Latin words Sandy had quoted. There ought to be a moondial tonight, Nick thought, but there would be plenty of sunny hours to count when Sandy came.

Richard Dale's voice said, "Some people seem to be in a mighty big hurry here tonight."

He sat down panting on one of the marble benches among the roses and mopped his face.

"Why I never went out of a walk!" Nick said. "How is it you are so warm, sir? I feel the chill of the evening myself, sir."

Strangely enough it was true. He did feel chilly. His legs ached. So did his head. Did he ever give Cherry her handkerchief? He could not remember. The way out of the maze seemed long. For the next few weeks he still seemed to be wandering in it.

He must have caught a fever on the island or in the Dismal Swamp, they told him afterwards. Wherever he caught it, it was a bad one. The doctor bled him many times, they said, and made him drink water with Jesuits' bark steeped in it besides other medicines, most of them bad tasting, but he still burned with fever and shook with chills. He still seemed to be chasing Sandy through the maze. No matter how fast he ran, he could never see his brother's face. Only once Sandy turned but it was not his face Nick saw. It was the face of the marble faun and the ears were pointed.

At last the fever left him but he still felt ill and listless. He asked for Richard but Richard had gone to sea as he had said, so many times, that he would. He had not run away after all but had gone with his mother's permission. There were younger children in the family and Richard was sure he would win fame and fortune at sea and help them all. He was about twelve and if you were going to follow the sea, twelve was not too young to begin.

"I wish I could have gone with him," Nick said.

His Uncle Nicholas was sitting by the window.

"Would you like to go for a sea voyage, Nick Young?" he asked in his kind, soft voice.

He came over to the bed and looked down at his nephew.

"My eyes are not very good these days but it does seem you look mighty thin and yellow. The doctor says a sea voyage might do you good. Captain Farrand sails next week with a cargo for Jamaica. He'll pick up another there and take it to London; sugar, you know, and rum and molasses. One of his three-cornered voyages so he calls them. Then he'll fetch a cargo home from London. The best part of it will be—can you guess, Nick Young? Do you remember your birthday supper? The letter you read?"

Nick sat up in bed. For the first time the dark clouds seemed to be rolling away.

"Sandy!" he said.

"You are right, boy. Now if you eat your dinner today and the doctor's pleased with you when he comes tomorrow, I'll tell Captain Farrand he'll have a passenger on the first two corners of his voyage as well as on the third."

So the long voyage that had finally landed Nick and Pambo in Mr. Gribble's shop began; for of course Pambo had gone with his master. They all said to Pambo—Aunt Dorothy, Mrs. Ashton, Cherry, Uncle Nicholas—all said: "You look after Mistoh Nick Young. Bring him home safe and well, Pambo, hear?" and Pambo had answered, "Yes, *ma'am*! Yes, *sir*! I'll do that very thing."

The cabin of the brig *Pocahontas* was a pleasant one and Nick passed many happy hours. He had brought books with him and he read them—old books of travels and adventures by land and sea. He read of Drake and the *Golden Hind*, of Marco Polo in Cathay, of how Magellan found the straits that bear his name but died in the Philippines though his ship went all around the world. He learned how Cabral discovered Brazil and how Vasco da Gama first sailed around the Cape of Good Hope to India; of William Dampier who went to a place Nick had never even heard of before called New Holland, of how some people thought it might be part of a great southern continent as big as North America. He would like to go and find out, Nick thought. He read about Captain John Smith who was already one of his heroes. Indeed, it was to please Nick that his uncle had named the new brig *Pocahontas* in honor of the Indian princess who had saved Captain Smith's life.

His Aunt Dorothy told him he was descended from Pocahontas through the Tabors. A Tabor great-great-grandmother had married into the Rolfe family and of course Nick knew how Pocahontas, after she married an Englishman, was Lady Rolfe.

"And you look right much like an Indian yourself, Nick Young," she had said.

Indeed, with his dark eyes, high cheekbones and straight black hair, Nick did have something Indian about his looks, especially now that he was out in the sun and wind again. His skin was tanned to a fine bronze before they had been long at sea. With a feather headdress, deerskins and wampum he might have passed as a young Indian brave even with Lady Rolfe herself, or so Captain Farrand said.

The Captain had many old sea tales to tell—of cruising in the West Indies, of pirates and buccaneers and maroons, of treasure ships sunk, of treasure buried on lonely islands.

After the first few days Nick was no longer content to sit and read or lie on the deck. He wanted to learn about ships, he told Captain Farrand.

"I want to follow the sea," he said, "like Richard. Perhaps when Sandy manages the plantation and Caryl and Company, Richard and I can be his captains. I ought to start learning now."

Nick could see by the way the Captain's blue eyes twinkled that he was pleased. He was a big quiet man who did not have much to say and seemed to have little to do on the ship. He did not even read but smoked, gazed happily at the sky, gave an occasional order in a soft drawl, made punch with lemons and limes in it in the cabin after supper. Perhaps he was a sea captain because he was a little lazy, Nick thought. Nick of course intended to be a more ambitious kind of captain.

"Well," the Captain said in his slow, pleasant way, "at least you know you have to learn. Most folks think they know how to start with. We'll begin with the lines," he added, speaking more briskly. "Maybe I should start you swabbing decks but I reckon we'll put you ahead a piece and begin with the lines."

Nick learned his ropes by climbing all over the rigging with the sailors, furling and unfurling sails until he knew every yard, spar, line and sail the way a cat knows the ivy it climbs to get into a bird's nest. So the days slipped away. Almost before Nick knew it they were sailing in waters Columbus himself might have troubled when he searched for a western route to the Spice Islands and found a new world.

"With good luck we would reach Jamaica tomorrow," Captain Farrand said one evening, "but I'm afraid there's a storm in those clouds. We're running into hurricane season."

It seemed very calm to Nick. The wind had dropped. There was so little breeze stirring that it was too hot to sleep in the cabin that night. Before morning Nick had lived through his first storm at sea. Perhaps because it was the first, he always remembered it as the most violent and dangerous. It seemed to pick up the *Pocahontas* and spin her around like a dry leaf in a whirlpool of ink. The darkness was the worst part, Nick remembered, as they tossed from one foaming black mountain to the next. It was worse than the shrieking wind or the dizzy motion of the ship. The ship's lanterns seemed to give no more light than fireflies in the maze at home. Where would they be blown? How could anyone tell?

Yet, he remembered afterwards, he was not afraid.

Perhaps that was because Captain Farrand was as quiet and easy as if he had been squeezing lemons in the cabin in a flat calm. His voice rang out above the wind now. His orders, no matter how dangerous, were obeyed promptly by the crew. Nick, tugging on a rope with Pambo, felt as if he and the Captain and every sailor were all part of the ship.

A sentence from one of his books flashed into his mind:

"On his ship, the Captain is king: he can do no wrong."

Why that, Nick thought, gazing into the blackness where the waves seemed to foam more fiercely than ever, is purely nonsense.

He had read enough history to know that kings often did very wrong indeed. So could the Captain, any captain, do wrong and if he did all his crew and his ship would go to the bottom.

This quiet man, whom he had thought lazy, would make a better king than most of those Shakespeare wrote about, Nick decided.

Above him a voice from the top cried: "Land, ho! Land to port."

Nick saw it too, darker than the waves, which showed white against it even through the darkness as they broke. They were

running past it safely, he thought, not knowing then that no ship is safe in a storm on a lee shore.

Beneath his feet the *Pocahontas* jerked violently, then shuddered and shivered with a grinding noise.

"Hit something, I reckon, Mistoh Nick Young," the sailor beside him muttered. "Rock maybe. Hope we ain't stuck—no, no, we're clear. Captain'll get us around the island where we can ride it out easy. He's a *sailor*, the Captain is."

They did ride it out safely with bare masts and yards and a sea anchor, but the rock had damaged the ship near the bow. Water was coming into the hold, the carpenter said. Nick took his turn at the pump with the rest but after an hour the Captain, finding him there, sent him to the cabin.

"After all, you came on this voyage for your health," he remarked, "go below, sir! Pambo, see that your master gets dry and warm. He looks mighty blue."

"Aye! Aye, sir!" Pambo said.

Pambo had become very nautical since they had been at sea.

Strangely enough Nick's fever did not come back. He slept better than he had for many weeks and woke to a blue sky and the smell of a tropical island. He could hear the pumps still going. He hurried on deck. The first thing he saw was the sailmaker pushing a big needle as he stitched two pieces of canvas into a large bag. He used a piece of leather on the palm of his hand instead of a thimble. There were heaps of tarred hemp picked into oakum on the deck beside him.

"Good morning, Nick Young," Captain Farrand, who was strolling along the deck, said in his lazy everyday drawl. "Quite a puff of wind last night. We have a little water coming into the hold and we're going to try an experiment. I've seen it done;

works pretty good sometimes. You might be interested. You still planning to follow the sea?"

"Yes, sir, I'd still like to learn."

"We're going to put this oakum and the scrapings from the hencoops into this bag, make sort of mattress of it. We'll quilt it a little so the oakum will stay pretty even. We're going to put a long rope on each side and fasten the other ends of the rope each to a yardarm, one to port, one to starboard. Then we'll cast the bag overboard at the bow and keel haul it under the ship. If we are lucky and strike the right spot—and I think we will be, for we've made the bag right *good*-sized—the force of the water going into the ship will carry the bag into the hole. It will act like a stopper, I hope, and keep out enough water so we can get to Jamaica. Then we'll heave the ship down and make what repairs are needed.

"It may take some time," he added, "and if we can I'll get you a passage with some captain I know who is bound for England. Jamaica is a bad place for fever and I'd rather you were at sea; besides Sandy will be thinking you are lost."

By late afternoon the *Pocahontas* was moving briskly along. They reached Kingston in Jamaica the next morning. The day after, Nick and Pambo embarked on the brig *John*. She was bound for Whitehaven on the English side of Solway Firth.

CHAPTER 3

FIRST COMMAND

IN THE CABIN of the brig *John* a young man was sitting at the table with books and a chart spread out in front of him. The cabin seemed cool after the steaming heat on shore. Green light and a fresh breeze came into it from the water outside.

The man at the table—he must be about Sandy's age, Nick thought—stood up and made the kind of bow Mrs. Ashton had often tried to teach Nick to make. He began to wish he had learned.

"As I understand we are to share the cabin for the voyage, I think we should introduce ourselves," the young man said. "My name is Paul, John Paul from Kircudbright in Scotland."

He pronounced it Kircoobree with fine rolling r's but otherwise did not sound nearly so Scottish as McFarland, the new young overseer at Caryl's Maze.

"I'm Nick Young Caryl from Portsmouth, Virginia, Mr. Paul," Nick said.

"One of my favorite colonies," John Paul said politely. "I spent a most happy winter in Virginia with a relative of mine some years ago."

"Did you come to Portsmouth?" Nick asked. "I feel as if I might have seen you before."

"I saw it only from the water," John Paul said in his deep pleasant voice. "A charming place with the squares and the brick houses and the trees and flowers."

His voice seemed meant for a bigger man. He was no taller, Nick thought, than Pambo who was five feet five and a half. Nick himself was already five feet six when he left Virginia. Aunt Dorothy had measured them both against one of the porch pillars just before he sailed and he felt sure he had grown since. He could almost look over Pambo's head. Nick was two inches taller than Sandy at the same age, as the old marks on the pillar showed.

As he sat at the table over his books, John Paul had seemed bigger than he did standing. His shoulders were broad though somewhat stooped and rounded. His arms were long for his height, Nick noticed, but otherwise he was lightly and trimly built. He had reddish hair and the colorless skin that often goes with it, the kind that burns and freckles easily. He had evidently been exposed much to sun and wind. He had a deep furrow between his eyes. They were sailors' eyes, Nick thought. The kind that change color and, though they may be brownish on land, look gray or green or blue at sea according to the moods of the sea. They looked green that day in the cool, green-lighted cabin. They were large eyes, widely opened, and seemed to notice everything.

"I am afraid I am disturbing you," Nick said.

"Oh, I have the whole voyage to read and study," John Paul said. He smiled suddenly and his face, which had been stern, changed completely. He looked happy, even gay, as he added, "I shall enjoy being a passenger for a change. I have been at

sea since I was twelve. I'll neither take an order nor give one till we sail into White-haven. Then when the cargo's landed, we'll sail across to Kircud-bright. Most of us on the ship are dour Scots from Kircud-bright, Mr. Caryl. We're going home to see our mothers and sisters and to take them the few shillings we've picked up. Maybe a little present or two, though of course we're not foolish with our money. Yes, I shall enjoy my holiday."

John Paul's holiday was short. Anything—as Nick was rapidly learning—can happen at sea. What happened on the brig *John* this voyage was not storm and wreck but fever. The master fell ill first and John Paul at the Captain's request acted as master. He set the course for the ship. He took the sun with the quadrant every day to find the position of the ship. He decided what men should be on watch. After a few days the Captain too came down with fever and asked John Paul to take his place as well.

"Just till I feel a wee bit steadier on my legs, John," he said. "The master will be better soon and so will I but now you are the only one aboard who can navigate."

So John Paul, barely twenty-one years old, acted as captain as well as navigator of the brig *John* and brought her safely into Whitehaven. Both the Captain and master died during the voyage. They were buried at sea, John Paul reading the burial service. His deep voice could be heard clearly above the noises of wind and water.

The prayers for the dead men were read in what Nick thought of as John Paul's English voice. When the young captain gave his orders to his fellow Scots from Kircudbright, it was in what seemed to Nick a foreign language. They were indeed a grimly dour lot of men and Nick felt that they did not like their new captain. Still his orders were promptly obeyed. The brig, which during the early part of the voyage was somewhat untidy, soon looked as trim as the English frigates that sometimes sailed into Hampton Roads or anchored off the marine yard at Gosport. Her deck was scrubbed as clean as the floor of Ambrosine's kitchen. Tarnished metal was polished. Paint below decks was washed clean of candle smoke and finger marks. Melted tallow was scraped off the lanterns.

John Paul studied his books and charts no longer. The charts were of distant coasts—Africa, Java, Bombay. Nick expected that the books would be of voyages of discovery and tales of the sea. To his disappointment he found they were books he had often seen on the shelves of his uncle's library—Addison's *Spectator*, Pope's translation of the *Iliad*, Milton's *Paradise Lost*. There was also something called *The Compleat Letter Writer*. It gave models for every kind of letter Nick could imagine and more besides. There was also *The Young Gentleman's Guide*, which suggested exquisite manners for a number of unlikely situations. Nick did not wish to learn what to say to a young lady if you had the misfortune to spill claret on her new dress. The things he wanted to learn were out on the deck where John Paul was.

"You will be a planter, I suppose, someday," John Paul said to Nick over their dinner of boiled beef and turnips.

Nick blushed, looking slightly more coppery than usual, and said: "No, sir. My older brother owns the plantation. I hope to follow the sea. Captain Farrand was teaching me on the *Pocahontas*. I know my lines, sir, I think."

"Why, we must see if you do," said John Paul, his face losing its almost melancholy expression for a moment. "If you do I'll make a midshipman of you. We need someone amidships."

Nick never forgot what he learned during the days that followed. He put himself to sleep at night with the names of lines and sails.

John Paul would show him a chart and say, "Now, Mr. Caryl, you are sailing into this harbor. Wind is nor'-nor'west. Tide at the flood. You are close hauled on the starboard tack. Man in the maintop calls 'Sail to port, sir!' You can't see her yet. Now, what do you do?"

And Nick would tell him, not always correctly to be sure, but John Paul was endlessly patient and one day pleased his pupil by saying thoughtfully, "I believe you have learned something."

They would study problems over their meals with bits of ship's biscuit for rocks, salt cellars for ships, and a table knife to show the direction of the wind. There was a book of the Captain's that Nick liked much better than he did *The Young Gentleman's Guide*. It told about the organization of a ship.

Just before Nick sailed his Uncle Nicholas had given him a thick volume, bound in brown leather. The gold letters on the back said: "Nicholas Young Caryl, His Book."

"Write or draw whatever you like," his uncle had said.

The first thing that Nick had written in it was an account of the hurricane in which the *Pocahontas* was damaged. The next pages told about how John Paul became captain and master of the brig *John*.

Nick wrote:

I always supposed the master of a ship meant the owner or else the captain. It really means sailing master. On some ships he is called the mate. John Paul says that on a small ship the captain often acts as master too and does the navigation. He says that with an experienced crew, like this one, there is no reason why he should not do both. Indeed, these Scots go about their work well, only in a glum way, often scowling at their new captain and at me. I think they do not like taking orders from him when he is so much younger than they, or me for carrying the orders which I do now because I am an acting midshipman. Most of them come from Kircudbright and knew Capt. P. as a boy.

Perhaps they do not like his being able to speak English like an Englishman or putting in a French or Spanish phrase here and there, or writing verses, or studying *The Young Gentleman's Guide*. One of the ship's boys told Pambo that the Captain was only the son of a gardener to a Mr. Craik and that his uncle was gardener to the Earl of Selkirk at his place on St. Mary's Isle.

"Yet he gives himself the airs of a Lord," said the boy. (He said Lair-r-rd, I suppose, but it's enough I have learned to understand them without writing it down. Pambo speaks broad Scotch now!)

Many of the pages of Nick's book were covered with numbers instead of letters. The numbers were part of a code Captain Paul had taught him.

"It's a grand thing for saving space and for writing down anything private," the Captain said.

Nick had nothing very private to write but he liked the air

of mystery given to the simplest remark about the weather by writing it in numbers. He kept the pages on which the key to the code was written tucked into his best buckled shoes. Captain Paul showed him how he had made the code by numbering words in a small dictionary.

"You could make your own," he said, but Nick preferred to copy down the Captain's.

These were some of the words he had written down:

America—221
Foreign—28
Copy—315
Particular—1600

Sometimes words were broken up and parts of them had a special number. For instance, -tion was 123. Punctuation marks had their own numbers: 1056 for a comma, 1235 for a dash. Nick could soon write it quickly. Like any shorthand or code it was easier to write than to read.

Captain Paul would write down numbers in his small, neat writing and Nick would write the proper words underneath. He soon had pages covered with such statements as:

716—571—1199—1196—396—1508—28—322—1017
We went to the minister of foreign affairs or
1001—840—456—1582—1199—1196—396—1235
I paid my respects to the minister—
922—674—1187—834—698—1600—1582
he receiv-ed me with particular respect

Captain Paul spent no time on unimportant matters but practiced writing to kings and ambassadors.

One day toward the end of the voyage Nick said, "Ought I perhaps learn words for common things—like salt beef or biscuit?"

The Captain turned his stern, melancholy look on him.

"Yes," he said. "If you do not care for glory and honor."

For a moment Nick felt that this short, round-shouldered young man, not much older than Sandy, was really on the road to fame and glory. Then he began to wonder how the captain of a small ship loaded with rum and molasses expected to win distinction. The Captain was called on deck just then and Nick was left puzzling out more numbers.

"Great designs," John Paul had written, "are carried out only through imperturbable coolness and inflexible determination." Underneath he had added: "Oceans are wide but in all their ports men meet"—a sentence Nick was to think of many times. As he finished writing it, Pambo appeared saying in his new blend of Scottish and Virginia accents: "We are not far from Kircudbright, Mistoh Nick."

Nick hurried to the deck. They were sailing past a coast where the rocks rose sharply to ground covered with great oaks and chestnuts. In the distance towered mountains higher than any Nick had seen in Virginia. The Captain told him their names—Saddleback, Skiddaw, Helvellyn. He showed him the mansion of Arbigland and the trees and gardens his father had planted around it. A short distance away was a white spot.

"It is the cottage where I was born," he said. "You can understand that I easily and early became familiar with the sights and sounds of the sea. This coast rises so boldly and the water is so deep below it that ships can approach it within a stone's throw. I used to look down from up there through the trees and see the masts of ships like trees too. I would hear the voices of the pilots giving their commands and the sailors answering. I used to mimic them, my mother says, long before I knew what they meant. My playmates and I would make fleets of ships from sticks with bits of cloth for sails and I would screech out orders in a fine, commanding style, I can tell you... Ah, the wind is shifting. We can run before it to Whitehaven."

The brig *John*, her sails all spread to catch the light breeze, traveled across the Solway Firth towards Whitehaven.

Captain Paul dropped from Scotch into English and said with one of his elegant bows, "You will step on English soil tomorrow, Mr. Caryl."

CHAPTER 4

ENGLISH SOIL

YEARS AFTERWARDS when the name of Whitehaven was on everyone's tongue, Nick wished he had noticed the port more closely. At the time he had compared it unfavorably with the Virginia harbors he knew—Norfolk, Portsmouth, Hampton Roads. There were no king's frigates in Whitehaven. Small vessels carrying coal to Ireland or linen to England used the port a great deal, John Paul said. He added that it was a good harbor and well protected by the forts at the entrance. At least, he said, it would be except that the English guards were drunk and sound asleep every night. No doubt they were so already, he added, since it was growing dark.

"*Quis custodiet ipsos custodies?*" the Captain said, giving the Latin as fine an English sound as Nick's tutor did. In fact, though Captain Paul had said he had never had any schooling after he was twelve years old, he seemed to know the same quotations as Nick's tutor who was a master of arts from Oxford University. Nick knew that the one Captain Paul had just used meant: "Who is going to guard these guardians?"

When did John Paul find time to learn Latin? Nick wondered.

As he said goodbye to him the next morning, Nick felt sorry that they were not likely to meet again and said so.

"Ah, Mr. Caryl, oceans are wide but in all their ports men meet. The correct code numbers, please?"

Nick laughed and gave them to him. He received one of John Paul's infrequent smiles as a reward.

It was a gray English morning when they parted. The fog was so heavy that it dripped off the spars like rain. It had closed in heavily last night. Captain Paul walked along a narrow, twisting street with Nick and Pambo to show him the inn where stagecoaches stopped. He knew every foot of the way even in the fog.

He used his English speech and grand manner to the landlord, telling him that this was Mr. Nicholas Caryl from Virginia who wanted a coach to take him to his great-uncle's estate, Caryl's Mount, over by Coniston Water. No doubt the landlord knew of it.

Yes, the landlord said, he did and there would be a coach in about an hour that would take them within a short mile of it.

He thanked the landlord, who said he was vastly pleased to entertain Mr. Caryl and suggested grilled kidneys and bacon for breakfast. Nick invited Captain Paul to stay but he said he must see to unloading his ship.

"Come to Virginia—come and stay with us at Caryl's Maze," Nick said. "You could sail right to the end of the lawn, you know, sir. Pambo and I would be happy to see you, wouldn't we, Pambo?"

"Vastly pleased, vastly, sir," said Pambo, who, like the Captain, was practicing his English.

John Paul thanked them both. He put Nick's thanks for his kindness aside with one of his best bows and a "Your servant, sir, Mr. Caryl."

He looked very small and slight as he went out into the gray street and slipped away into the fog. In spite of his rounded shoulders he had a quick, graceful way of moving. He had the slight roll in his walk that comes from much standing on a ship's deck but he gave no impression, as sailors often do, of being ill at ease on land. Nick himself was still dizzy from the change and felt clumsy and awkward.

He said so to Pambo, who chuckled as they jolted along in the coach and said he had almost climbed up the wall of the inn, expecting to get into the maintop.

"I wish we could get into it now and see the country," Nick said.

Their places were inside the coach and they were traveling through narrow lanes darkened by high hedges. That was all they could see, for the November morning had hardly lightened at all. The coachman had said that it might be a wee bit misty.

Nick wrapped himself in his new camlet cloak, blue camlet with cape and collar of blue velvet. Aunt Dorothy and Mrs. Ashton had made it for him, copied it from one that Colonel Washington had worn on his last visit to the plantation. The Colonel used to call at Caryl's Maze on his trips to the Dismal Swamp. Parts of the swamp were being drained under his supervision. Cherry had been brought in from fishing one fine morning and set to hemming the heavy linen lining of the cloak. She had a good deal to say about boys who went off to England and had to have clothes made for them, none of it complimentary.

The cloak was warm. Nick went to sleep and dreamed that he and the Colonel were shooting and a great flock of mallards was rising in the morning mist. The sun came through suddenly and their heads were shining bits of emerald. He woke and found the English mist thinning and the coach climbing a steep hill. The sun thrust long fingers of light through the clouds and showed a country of bare hills across a deep valley, silvery lakes, sheep grazing in fields still brilliantly green.

It all looked strange to a boy whose life had been spent on tidewater, though it was beautiful in a way, Nick thought, rather like an engraving in one of his uncle's books. Then the pale sun vanished again and the coach splashed through rain and mud. It was still raining when they reached Coniston Water.

The inn was a small gray stone building not much brighter or warmer inside than out. They did not order food or a room but asked the landlord if they could leave their bags for a while.

"We are going to my great-uncle's, Sir George Caryl's, at Caryl's Mount," Nick told the landlord, and asked if they could hire a carriage to take them there.

There was no carriage. They could travel on shanks' mare, the landlord said. People in Virginia talked about shanks' mare so Nick knew he meant they would have to walk in the mud. He found the man's speech almost as hard to understand as that of the men on the brig *John*. Pambo, however, had no trouble and when the landlord added; "Gae till 'ee see twa cats on t'gyte," told his master promptly that they were to go until they saw two cats on a gate.

"Do you know if Sir George Caryl is at home?" Nick asked.

The landlord laughed and said that Old Father Christmas was always at home at this time of day and he hoped they would enjoy their visit. Nick wondered a little at his familiar tone but decided that his great-uncle was probably a generous man and good to poor people like his twin brother, Nick's grandfather. He remembered his portrait in the library at Caryl's Maze. He could not remember his grandfather but he knew that his

Uncle Nicholas looked much like the portrait, so perhaps his uncle and Sir George were alike. They might be. After all, Uncle Nicholas, though he had never seen Sir George, was his nephew.

Perhaps, Nick thought, he would not feel so homesick when he reached Caryl's Mount. It was strange that he had never been homesick at sea, even in the hurricane, but he had been ever since they left John Paul and the ship.

"What's that, Pambo?" he asked. "I'm afraid I wasn't listening."

"I just said they got mighty funny cats in this country that would sit on a gate in a rain like this. Yes, sir, Mistoh Nick. Does seem like those cats haven't got good sense!"

The cats turned out not to mind the rain. They were leopards carved out of stone and they leered out of the mist from the gatepost in a sly and threatening manner. They appeared again on the coat of arms cut in the stone of the posts. They were holding up a shield with the Caryl thistles and roses.

"This is right, Pambo. Those are the Caryl arms. Don't you know my uncle has them painted like that in his dining room in Portsmouth?" Nick said, his homesickness lifting.

"Family certainly seems right fond of those cats," Pambo replied without great enthusiasm.

The gate was opened for them by an old woman who did it somewhat unwillingly, Nick thought. Either she did not listen to his explanation of why he wished to see Sir George Caryl or did not understand it or did not care whether she did or not. She accepted the shilling he gave her in silence. Nick had no great supply of money, barely enough, after he had paid his passage on the brig *John*, to get them to London. He rather wished he had his shilling back.

Perhaps, he thought charitably, she has toothache.

A good many of the people they had seen today had swollen faces. Perhaps they all had toothache. It might be the chill, Nick thought, pulling his cloak around him.

It was not raining now but moisture was still dripping off the twisted arms of the oaks that lined the avenue. The landlord had not said that it was a walk of another half mile from the gate to the house. The "short mile" they had been promised had become almost two.

The avenue wound upward steeply and at last they saw the house through the mist. It was foolish, Nick knew, to have expected something open and welcoming and warm like the red and white of Caryl's Maze. The house on Caryl's Mount, he thought, shivering a little, was like a prison. It had rough gray stone towers, slits of windows, a door of blackened oak studded with huge nails. Nick imagined it guarded by tall men in armor.

Actually, the butler, who answered their knock by opening the door a crack and peering cautiously through it, looked more like a rabbit than a crusader. Nick was afraid he might pop back into his hole again but the butler listened to their story with interest, saying, "Really, sir, most unusual!" at intervals and rubbing his blue hands together. He left them in the hall, where the stones were colder than wet earth under their feet, where moth-eaten tapestries moved in the draft that blew along the stone stairs, and dark portraits of long-dead Caryls looked down on him. Suspiciously, Nick thought.

The draft also blew open the door of the room the butler had entered.

Nick heard him say, "No, Sir George. The young lad does *not* resemble any of the family. And the boy with him is a blackamoor. However, they speak like Colonials and the one who claims you are his grandfather's brother does indeed resemble a red Indian, sir. Such as I saw when I escaped murder and scalping when I was in the army with General Braddock, sir, and—"

"Well, let's not lose *that* battle all over again, Figgis!" said a high, peevish voice. "Show them in. I don't suppose they'll scalp us."

Sir George Caryl's library had a fire in it, though a small one. After the dank chill of the hall the room seemed almost warm. Its owner was a huge man in a faded crimson dressing gown. Twisted folds of green flowered silk covered his head. He was sitting in a big red armchair with one bandaged foot propped up on a stool. In an age when most gentlemen were clean shaven, Sir George Caryl had a mass of white whiskers covering the lower part of his fat red face. He looked like Father Christmas in an old play that Nick had once seen. He also in a strange way looked like the portrait of his twin brother, Nick's grandfather. Only, Nick thought, it was as if his grandfather had been blown up the way the Negro boys on the plantation blew up bladders for footballs. If you ran a pin into one of Sir George's big red hands or cheeks, he would go *pop* and shrivel up, Nick thought.

The only things that were small about Sir George were his eyes, his mouth, and his voice.

"Well, curse you, why don't you say something?" he asked, his little gray eyes darting from one boy to the other.

"I am your great-nephew, Nicholas Young Caryl. Finding myself unexpectedly near Caryl's Mount, I have come to pay my respects to you. My Uncle Nicholas suggested that my brother Alexander and I should visit you before we go back to Virginia—"

Sir George interrupted him.

"What proof do you have you're my great-nephew? Curse you, Figgis. Don't stand there—get on about your work—"

The butler scuttled off. Nick took a ring off his finger and held it out.

"This ring with the Caryl arms on it was my grandfather's, your brother William's. You have one like it, I see."

"D'you call that proof? Why, you could pick it up in any pawnshop, couldn't you?"

"I don't know, sir. We don't pawn family rings in America."

"Well, we do in England. I wager my grandson Gilbert would pawn it before he'd had it twenty minutes. How do I know what a red Indian from the colonies would do? You are part red Indian, I'll wager."

By this time Nick was a good deal redder than most Indians.

He said, "My mother was descended from Pocahontas, sir—"

"Who's he? Never heard of him."

"She, sir. An Indian princess who saved the life of Captain John Smith. She married Sir John Rolfe and was received at court here in England."

"Never heard of any of 'em. And this blackamoor—he's a prince, too, I suppose, hey?"

"No, Sir George, he's my servant and good friend. May I have my ring back, sir?"

Sir George Caryl held it out.

"Take it, but don't get near my foot. I've got the gout and it's most confoundedly swollen. So, in Virginia, you make friends of your black rascals, do you?"

"No, sir. In our part of Virginia we don't make friends of any rascals, either white or colored."

Sir George gave a sudden, screeching laugh.

'Why, you're a wit! Confound you. I believe you might be a Caryl after all. *Figgis!* Curse the fellow—never here when he's wanted!"

Sir George reached out for an embroidered bell pull and tugged at it.

Nick said, "That bell pull, sir—"

"Well, what about it. Ever see one before? Hey?"

"Yes, sir. You and my grandfather married sisters, named Young. They both made these bell pulls from the same pattern, with the Caryl roses and thistles, for their husbands. My grandfather took his with him when they went to Virginia and it's in the library at the plantation."

"It is, hey? Figgis! Oh, there you are and about time—this is my great-nephew, Mr. Nicholas Young Caryl, Figgis."

"Thank you, Sir George. Happy to know you, Mr. Nicholas, welcome to Caryl's Mount, sir."

"Take this Black Prince out and give him some of the good October ale we brew at Caryl's Mount. And bring some here for Mr. Nicholas."

Figgis led Pambo away.

"Do you brew ale at this place you call Caryl's Maze?"

"No, sir."

"Why, what do you drink, then?"

"My uncle drinks a glass of port or claret sometimes. There's champagne for a party. My aunt has tea or coffee or chocolate for her friends. In hot weather we have a punch with lemons or limes in it. I think my aunt puts peach brandy into it, too. I drink milk or water, myself."

"Well, you'll drink ale here."

Nick found the glass of ale Figgis brought him thin, bitter, and sour but he managed to swallow most of it.

"Well, where are you going now, my young redskin?" his great-uncle asked.

"Back to the inn, sir, and then to London to meet my brother. He is staying at your son's house there. I have the address— somewhere in Bloomsbury."

'Well, you won't see my son. He's on his way here. Curse him! He's sent a letter to say so. He wants money from me, I expect, to pay gambling and racing debts for my confounded grandsons. Do you want money from me?"

"No, sir."

"That's lucky, for I have none to spare. Gold doesn't lie around here the way it does in America. But, I forgot, it's your brother who has the estate there—you'll have to whistle for your living, eh?"

"I'll have to work for it," Nick said. "We have ships. I hope to be captain of one someday."

Sir George gave one of his screeches.

"A beggarly sea captain, a pirate! They're all pirates—don't tell me anything else."

Nick did not tell him anything else and his great-uncle went on, "And your brother? He'll be living in luxury on the estate. How you must hate him!"

"I don't hate him. We don't—"

"I know. You're going to say that in Virginia everyone loves everyone else. That, my boy, is confounded nonsense. Fathers hate their heirs and heirs hate their fathers. Younger sons hate their older brothers. You don't suppose your grandfather loved me, do you? His twin, twenty-seven minutes older, heir to all this—" Sir George waved his fat hand around the library with its shelves of musty books—"and he going across the sea to live with a lot of savages and yokels. And don't tell me you don't have yokels in Virginia!"

"I don't know what you would call our neighbors, sir. Some of the best-known men in the colony are my uncle's friends. Colonel George Washington—"

"Never heard of him," said Sir George, who seemed to think

he thus disposed of Colonel Washington and everything else about which he was ignorant.

"I reckon Figgis has heard of him, sir, if he was with General Braddock. My uncle thinks Colonel Washington is going to be right well known in the colonies someday."

Sir George was not interested.

"If you are going to London, my lad, you'd better be on your way." He tugged at the bell pull again, moved his bandaged foot, swore savagely, was silent a moment and then said in a tone different from any he had used, "Look here, you Honka Pokus or whatever your name is. I like you. I'm going to give you something better than money—good advice. Don't let your brother play cards with my grandsons. Osborne and Gilbert and Frederick have no money to pay anyone anything and I'm not going to give them any. Besides, they always win. Get your brother on your pirate ship and both of you—and the blackamoor—go home."

"We mean to, sir. With good luck we might be there by Christmas."

"Then good luck to you," said Father Christmas.

Figgis showed them through the cold hall and swung the great door open. As it shrieked on its hinges, Figgis looked over his shoulder nervously and held out his hand toward Nick.

He said, "Pambo here says you know Colonel Washington, Mr. Nicholas. He was very kind to me, saved my life from a scalping knife once. For his sake I'd like you to have this sovereign. You might need it on your journey."

Nick said, "Why, Figgis, that's mighty thoughtful but I reckon we have enough money for the journey and when we get to London my brother will have plenty. You keep it and add some more to it and sail across to see us at Caryl's Maze someday. You'll be right welcome."

"Figgis!" came a screech from the library.

Figgis scuttled away, the gold coin still in his hand.

Nick was to wish more than once that he had taken it.

CHAPTER 5

MASQUERADERS

THE JOURNEY to London was long and seemed longer. Hours seemed days. Days seemed weeks. Yet at last they saw the city, wrapped in a vast cloud of smoke and fog. Under the cloud it was dark even at noon. Candles twinkled faintly in the dingy little shops. The roar of wheels along the muddy streets seemed never to cease. Spires and domes of churches and the tops of houses were only shadows in the yellowish, smoky fog. The coach moved slowly in a circle on the edge of which figures would appear out of the fog and melt away into it.

Suddenly Nick felt homesick. Strangely, what he missed was not the big rooms of Caryl's Maze but the small neat cabin of the brig *John*. He remembered asking Captain Paul, who had been telling him about a storm at sea, if he had ever been afraid.

The Captain had smiled and answered: "Never at sea—only on land."

Pambo, however, liked London from his first sight of it. He liked the men shouting, "Chairs to mend!"—the children darting in and out among the horses' feet, the fat women crying, "Mackerel, fresh mackerel!"—the things in the shop windows.

"See those tarts, Mistoh Nick Young! Wouldn't be surprised if that was strawberry jam in those tarts..."

The tarts would vanish into the fog before Nick saw them but Pambo would go on, "Saw little boy, carrying pewter flagon of ale out of a shop. Reckon he's taking it home to his father. Wonder if he'll get there with the foam still on. Reckon it tastes some better than Old Father Christmas's ale..."

It was Pambo who found out, at the inn where they stopped, how to get another coach to take them out to Bloomsbury to Lawrence Caryl's house. It was Pambo, too, who got seats for them beside the coachman.

The fog thinned as they left the center of the city. By the time they reached Bloomsbury, they could see treetops and gardens. Here and there lay an open field. The coachman pointed out fine new houses of red brick that reminded Nick of his uncle's house in Portsmouth. He showed them Montagu House and added that there was a fine place for fighting duels behind it. He spoke as if this was an especially convenient feature of the neighborhood.

Mr. Lawrence Caryl's house was not far beyond the dueling ground. It was older than the houses around it. Something about its many gables reminded Nick of an old house in Virginia called Bacon's Castle. There was supposed to be a ghost at Bacon's Castle.

Shivering a little, he pulled his cloak around him. He remembered that the ghost walked in a garden among trees dark with mistletoe and ivy, that ivy grew thick around a gravestone with a skull cut on it. He shook off a feeling of dread. He would see Sandy soon. They had arrived in time for his birthday. He would give him his grandfather's ring, the one with the Caryl arms. It was all he had to give and Sandy had always liked it.

Before long they would be on the *Pocahontas* and everything would be all right.

The coach rumbled to a stop at a pair of wrought-iron gates in a brick wall.

"There's those old cats again," groaned Pambo as he saw the Caryl leopards, in bronze this time, looking down at him.

From somewhere inside the wall came the sound of voices and a faint ringing of steel on steel. People were always fencing on land, Nick thought wearily. Yet he had enjoyed fencing with Captain Paul on the deck of the brig. It was different in the salt, sunny air, with lines taut, every sail filled above their heads, and the clean deck swaying under their feet.

Like the leopards, grim-looking gatekeepers seemed to be an old Caryl tradition. The London one, a man in rusty black, looked at them suspiciously through the rusty ironwork.

"No," he said hoarsely, "Mr. Alexander is not here. He and Mr. Gilbert have gone into the city. I will tell Mr. Osborne," he added and went off, leaving them outside the gate.

For a minute Nick felt as if he could not bear it. He could stand being cold, hungry, dirty from the journey, with no money to buy a present for Sandy. But not to see Sandy on his twenty-first birthday—Thrusting his clenched fists deep into his pockets and throwing his head back, he clenched his teeth to keep them from chattering.

He thought: Will he know me? Has he changed? Will he be glad to see us?

He looked at Pambo, who was no doubt thinking the same thoughts as he stood there shivering but who managed a smile and said, "It won't be long now, Mistoh Nick Young."

At last the gatekeeper came back, sulkily opened the gates, and led them into the house. There seemed to be no other servants. The house was less gloomy than the one at Caryl's Mount but the diamond panes of the windows were covered with cobwebs. It was a long time since anyone had polished the dark oak of the woodwork.

A black, old table with twisted legs was pulled up close to a dying fire. The remains of a meal were on the table—empty wine bottles, a mutton bone, boiled cabbage. A large brindled tomcat, who had been gnawing the bone, jumped off the table and spat at them from underneath the ragged leather seat of a banister-backed chair. There was a chair like it at Caryl's Maze, only polished with beeswax and with a cushion embroidered with butterflies and flowers.

As the servant limped off to the back of the hall, Pambo muttered, "Cat knows folks from Virginia come thousands of miles, might be hungry. Smart cat, English cat. Thinks we'll get his bone."

Pambo could always make Nick smile. Nick smiled now and said, "If he doesn't look out, I will."

The gatekeeper had left the door at the back of the hall open. Through it they could see a patch of green lawn. Pale sunshine—even the sunshine looked wet, Nick thought—showed rosebushes with a rose or two still in bloom. Ivy was thick on the brick walls and on the ground. Beyond the lawn was a chapel, something like the one at Caryl's Maze—only the stones of this one were covered with moss. The stones in the graveyard beside it were mossy too. Dark yews shaded them. Ivy had begun to creep over them.

On the lawn two men were fencing. As the gatekeeper reached them, they lowered their foils, picked up their coats, waistcoats, and wigs from a bench, put them on and strolled slowly toward the house.

"Good day, Cousin. I am Osborne Caryl," said the one in purple and gold, "and this is my brother Frederick, youngest brother, you know."

"If he knows, you dolt, why tell him?" said Frederick peevishly.

Frederick was in crimson velvet trimmed with tarnished silver and with a good many spots on it. Both were short, fat-faced, fat-fisted young men who would look, Nick thought, like Father Christmas when they were fatter and had the gout. Frederick was more talkative than his brother and swore more rapidly and more often.

Nicholas wrote of this meeting in his book:

I will leave out the oaths my cousin Frederick uses because they would fill too many pages. Everyone in England swears a good deal, I notice, but Frederick swears the most. He has a high, squeaky voice like Sir George's and he talked very fast, telling me that the *Pocahontas* had come and was ready to sail home. They all thought at Brown's (that is Uncle N's agent) that the brig *John* must be lost at sea and I must have been drowned.

He said he supposed I must be myself and not an impostor, that Sandy would know when he came. In the meantime, the blackamoor (I wish they would not say that) could take our portmanteaus upstairs and did I have any other suit? Because there would be a great dinner tonight.

"You know Sandy's twenty-one today," he told me. "Sandy and Gilbert have gone into the town to arrange about it. Everything, wine, servants, food, all will be sent from the Crown and Stars Inn. We don't have servants here, except old Jameson and he's not much of a cook.

"We keep bachelors' hall here, you know," he added. "My mother and sisters live at Bath. Take the waters, you know."

Osborne, who seems kind enough, only slow-witted, kept repeating things Frederick said a little after him: "Great dinner, yes... not much of a cook, no... Bachelors' hall, you know, Cousin." He is the oldest but seems to do what Frederick tells him.

So I went to my room and washed in cold water and put on my best green suit, the one William Paul, the tailor at Fredericksburg, made and one of the new shirts Aunt Dorothy gave me. Cherry hemmed the ruffles. I have grown since the coat was made so the sleeves are now about right. Paul made them long on purpose. Suddenly, while I was putting on the coat, I thought of how Captain Paul used to remind me of someone and I couldn't think who. It was of William Paul, the tailor. He had the same rounded shoulders and deep voice, also the same way of looking at you as if he saw right through to your backbone and out the other side.

I reckon he must be the relative John Paul said he spent a winter with in Virginia once. Of course, William Paul is much older and has not been out in the sun and wind and salt spray, but is pale from sitting indoors cross-legged all day long, stitching. I reckon John Paul was ashamed to say his brother was a tailor.

He talked about being a gentleman—how a gentleman should feel, what a gentleman should do, how he would not sit at table with anyone not a gentleman. Perhaps he would not have talked so much about it if he had been born one; but even if he and William Paul are both only a gardener's sons, I think they are both better gentlemen than my cousin Frederick or his grandfather, Sir George.

I wondered, listening to them as they talked, if Gilbert were like them, too. I asked and they both burst out laughing.

Frederick turned as red as his coat and Osborne as purple as his. Frederick wheezed out, "Hee, hee, hee—you'll see what he looks like, yes!"

I soon found out what they meant.

A coach stopped at the door. Sandy and Gilbert got out of it, and—I could not tell which was which.

They were dressed alike in pale gray and gold. They wore small wigs just covering the tops of their ears. (I wish I could wear a white wig and not this lank old black hair.) They walked alike, talked alike, smiled alike. I looked for the scar Sandy wrote that he had on his forehead.

They both had scars. Both stood there laughing because I did not know which was Sandy. Yet it was not really strange. I had not seen him for more than four years. I was not yet eight when he sailed away. Whichever of the two he was, he was greatly changed, taller, broader, with a deeper voice, and his manners were very grand. He wore a rapier and had a snuffbox set with diamonds. At least they looked like diamonds.

I began to feel dizzy. I knew my chill was coming on. Pambo saw how my teeth were chattering. He said I had better go to my bed. He had to carry me. My legs would not hold me up. After I was in bed, twice either Sandy or Gilbert came alone to my room and each told me he was really my brother and talked about carrying me on his back through the maze. But only one of them was wearing the Golden Horseshoe, of course. Except even now I am not sure which one wore it.

I said to one of them—I think it was Sandy though he did not have the horseshoe—that it was cruel to treat me so. He had been laughing but he stopped and said kindly, "Why, Nick Young, it's only a joke. Your fever must be mighty bad. I didn't know I could fool you. Other people, not you. Feel my scar, it's quite real. Gilbert's is only painted on."

Just as I reached out to touch it, the other one came in and they pretended to dance a minuet, bowing to imaginary ladies, turning and twisting, till I did not know which one had been speaking to me. My fever was very bad by then. There was a big looking glass hung opposite the bed. As they passed it there would be four of them, mocking me. Even after the guests had come and both had left me, I still thought I saw them in the glass. Then for a long time—it was days, Pambo says—I did not know anything at all.

And now I shall never know which was Sandy.

GOLDEN HORSESHOE

ALL THAT Nick knew of that night, Pambo told him. Pambo had tried to tell him before, but in his fever it had been only part of a nightmare.

At last the fever left him and Pambo told him again what had happened.

Pambo had been ordered by Sandy—he was sure it was Sandy—to help serve dinner that night. It was all like magic, he said. The house, which had been so gloomy, suddenly glowed with wax candles. Fires blazed on the hearths. In the kitchen, men from the Crown and Stars unpacked great baskets of food and wine. The dining-room table was covered with white damask. It sparkled with silver and crystal and fine china.

The dinner was good, almost as good as a dinner at Caryl's Maze, Pambo said. There were turtle soup and roasted pheasant, lemon tarts and a great many other fine things. The guests were Captain Briskin, a big, loud-talking gentleman in a scarlet coat, who drank a great deal of wine, and someone they called S'John, a very quiet, thin gentleman in black, who drank very little. Pambo asked one of the waiters who he was.

The man stared and said, "Fancy not knowing S'John!" and

explained that it was Sir John Desmond from Ireland, who had killed five men in duels and wounded no one knew how many more. The other man in black, the jolly-looking one, was Mr. Hallam, the Caryls' chaplain. He lived in the house back of the chapel. He drank a lot, too. The small man in scarlet was a friend of Captain Briskin's, surgeon in the same regiment. Pambo never knew his name.

"There'll be fortunes lost on the turn of a card here tonight," the waiter told Pambo.

"I thought then, Mistoh Nick Young," Pambo said, "that things didn't look right. I felt mighty sure the only one that had a fortune to lose was Mistoh Sandy. Those buzzards, your cousins, didn't have anything and I reckoned the soldiers didn't, either. And from what that waiter said, that white-faced S'John's fortune was in his sword."

After dinner, Pambo told Nick, they all sat down to play cards. Captain Briskin, the chaplain, Osborne Caryl, and the surgeon were at one table; Sir John Desmond, Gilbert, Frederick, and Sandy at the other.

"Everything was right quiet at first," Pambo said. "I was in the kitchen, eating my supper. Waiters didn't bother to wash any dishes. Just bundled plates, silver, a whole ham no one had touched—wish we had that ham now—into those big baskets they had and carried them off in their carts. If I hadn't been gnawing on a pheasant bone, I reckon they'd have taken that, too. The headwaiter sent in the bill and Mistoh Sandy came out and paid it."

"Were you sure it was Sandy? How?"

"First place, he had the money. Second place, how he spoke to me. Easy, friendly, asked me about my mother's rheumatism. That Gilbert didn't know how to speak to a colored boy."

Then Pambo told how the house was suddenly dark again except for the drawing room where the card tables were set. Jameson, the gatekeeper, had given his keys to Osborne Caryl and had gone off to his bed in the attic. Pambo was left in charge of the wine. The first time he went in to fill the glasses everyone was still playing cards. The second time, Gilbert, with Sandy's golden horseshoe in his shirt frill, and Frederick Caryl were standing looking on while Sir John Desmond and Sandy—Pambo was sure it was Sandy—were throwing dice.

"He'd been drinking right much of that port wine, Mistoh Nick Young, and he didn't sound so English any more. He had a big pile of gold in front of him and he kept making lucky throws. I don't know what that Sir John said to him but all of a sudden, just as I opened the door, Mistoh Sandy jumped up and slapped him in the face."

The cardplayers—Pambo said—all jumped up from their table, too. The strange thing was they all called Sandy "Gilbert."

"You shouldn't have done that, Gilbert," they said. Even the one Pambo knew was Gilbert said: "You shouldn't have done that, Gilbert! Ask S'John's pardon."

"It's too late for that," Sir John Desmond had said. "Mr. Gilbert Caryl must answer for it—and at once."

"Certainly, S'John," Sandy Caryl had said. "Though my name's not Gilbert, you know. At your service. Bring the candles, Pambo."

"I tried to stop him but he only pushed me aside."

"You pickle your own oysters your own way, Paul Ambrose," he said.

"It was Mistoh Sandy all right, I know."

There was no wind that evening. The candle flames hardly

flickered at all. The sky had cleared and the moon was full. There was plenty of light on the lawn to murder anyone by, Pambo said.

"For that's what it was, murder. That S'John could have killed Mistoh Sandy any time he wanted. When he got tired of playing with him, he did. Ran his sword right through him. That's all. They still pretended it was your cousin Gilbert got killed. I know better. I saw his ears, Mistoh Nick."

"What about his ears?" Nick had asked.

They had both had their wigs off, Pambo said, Sandy and Gilbert, who was his second.

"Mistoh Sandy's ears were round on top, like anyone else's.

That Gilbert's were pointed, like the ears on one of those statues in the maze. Remember that statue, Mistoh Nick Young?"

Yes, Nick remembered the statue of a faun blowing a reed pipe and smiling a little like Sandy. Yes, he understood now what Pambo had been telling him. It was all planned. The empty house, the hired waiters—and the hired killer, Nick thought bitterly.

Everything Gilbert Caryl needed was at hand. The Captain to report to the magistrates that there had been fair play. The surgeon to say he had done his best but the wound was fatal. Plenty of seconds. Plenty of wine to make them all but Gilbert and Sir John a little drunk. The chaplain to say prayers over the dead man and to see that he was buried quietly and properly in the Caryl tomb. Perhaps the other guests really thought it was Gilbert who was buried. If the masquerade Gilbert and Sandy had carried out had confused Nick, others may have been deceived, too. Perhaps Osborne did not know. Osborne was stupid. Even Frederick, who was brighter, might not know. He might think it was really Sandy—not Gilbert—who was now on board the *Pocahontas*, bound for Virginia.

They were all gone, like the glass and the silver and the waiters in their powdered wigs. Even Jameson had gone, limping fast toward London, leaving his keys with Pambo.

Sir John Desmond had gone to France as he usually did after a duel. The captain and the surgeon had gone back to their regiment. Osborne had gone to Caryl's Mount to announce Gilbert's death to their father. Frederick had gone to Bath to tell his mother and sisters. The chaplain stayed in his house but never came near the big one.

"I told them all you had smallpox, Mistoh Nick Young," Pambo said. "They couldn't get out quick enough. I told your cousin Gilbert you were a mighty sick boy. He came to your door that next morning. I reckon he was going to see if you knew he was not your brother. He jumped back quick as a rat with a ferret after it. Afraid of spoiling that pretty face, I reckon. Though it's spoiled some already."

"What do you mean, Pambo?"

Pambo said that the wound on Gilbert's forehead was real now, not painted on any longer. He had given himself a real gash—with a razor, maybe. It had started bleeding again while Pambo was packing his clothes. He had cursed and wiped off the blood with his handkerchief. Pambo had bandaged the cut with a strip of linen torn from a shirt and some sticking plaster.

The shirt had something pinned to the frill. Gilbert had not noticed it. After he had gone, Pambo had taken it out and had brought it to Nick, who was now holding it in his hand.

It was the Golden Horseshoe.

"It belongs to you now, Mistoh Nick Young. It was your grandfather's and then your father's and Mistoh Sandy had it because he was the oldest son and you are the next. I wasn't going to let that murderer take it back to Virginia with him— No, *sir!*"

Nick had not cried before but he did now. He tucked the hand with the horseshoe in it under the pillow and buried his face so Pambo would think he was going to sleep again.

Probably Pambo knew but he just said gently: "That's right, Mistoh Nick Young, you go to sleep. We must leave here tonight and I have a few little things to attend to."

Nick stopped himself from crying by thinking about the horseshoe. His uncle used to show it to him and tell him the story: how the Blue Ridge Mountains stood like a wall between Virginia and an unknown land until 1716 when Governor

Alexander Spotswood decided to go and see what lay behind the mountains. Among the fifty gentlemen who rode with him was Nick's grandfather.

The roads were so rocky and the horses wore out so many shoes that the riders had to learn to forge new ones. They would take turns at the forge, stripping off their long coats and waistcoats, even their shirts, and going to work like real blacksmiths. Afterwards they would wash off the soot in cold mountain streams and ride upward, always upward. At last they reached the top of a high mountain. They looked over a world of boundless prairies, of forests untouched by the axe, of brooks running west, instead of east, to join great rivers. They named the mountain for King George and drank his health there.

When they got back to Williamsburg, the Governor founded the Transmontane Order. Its members were the men who had crossed the mountains with him. To each he gave a golden horseshoe with garnets for nails and on the back the words *Sic juvat transcendere mantes.* The members were called Knights of the Golden Horseshoe. When a Knight died, his oldest son became a Knight and could wear the horseshoe and the crimson velvet coat of the order. So—as Pambo had said—the horseshoe in Nick's hand had been worn by his grandfather, by his father, and by Sandy. There was little happiness in thinking that it was now his own.

But at least, he thought, Gilbert is not wearing it.

He slept after that.

It was moonlight when he woke again. He heard the watch go by the house, calling, "Past twelve o'clock and a fine, bright night!"

Pambo appeared with a bowl of hot soup and a hunk of

stale bread. "Last of the dinner," he announced. "Made that soup out of pheasant bones. Old tomcat tried to get them. I won. Mighty mad old tomcat."

Nick was suddenly hungry.

"You're a good cook, Pambo," he said. "Must we pack now?"

"All packed, sir. All I dare take. I just buried you, Mistoh Nick Young."

"What?"

"Yes," Pambo said. "I told that chaplain you died of smallpox. He was mighty kind. Gave me an empty coffin there was in the tomb. I put some stones and dirt in it I dug out of the grave. I told him we'd better have a grave and not just put the coffin in the tomb because of the smallpox. He let me dig in the graveyard. Didn't come near me till I got the hole dug and the coffin in it, and covered up. He just sat in his house, drinking port wine. Then he came out and said the prayers, standing up pretty straight. I told him your name and dates and he wrote them down on a piece of slate. Said no doubt Sir George would see to a suitable stone later. I reckon it will be quite a while before Father Christmas spends money on a stone. He said he would write to Mr. Sandy in Virginia and tell him the sad news.

"I told him I would get my things and lock up and give him the keys. I don't dare take your clothes. They might say I stole them. We don't want anyone chasing us. Let me help you dress. Put on your green suit. They'll think you were buried in it."

So when they went out into the moonlit night, Nick took with him only his paints, his book, and one of the shirts Aunt Dorothy had made. Pinned into the ruffle Cherry had hemmed was the Golden Horseshoe.

CHAPTER 7

IMPORTANT CUSTOMERS

Tʜᴇʏ ᴅɪᴅ not travel far that first night. They must not take a coach, Pambo said. Any coachman would certainly remember a colored boy and a white boy traveling together.

"And if they catch us—" Pambo said.

He did not need to complete the sentence.

Nick nodded and they started walking across moonlit fields as fast as his shaky legs would take him. They slept a little while in the porch of a church. Luckily the weather had turned warm. The next day was a pale copy of an Indian summer day in Virginia. Soft golden haze hung over the city. They reached the Thames that day. It was gray and brown near shore but where the breeze ruffled it there were blue lights. Pambo played the fiddle in the streets while Nick sat and watched the wherries crossing the river. Pambo came back with a pocketful of pennies. They ate dinner at a clean little inn overlooking the river and then traveled by wherry down toward London Bridge and the Tower.

Brown's Wharf, where the Caryl ships brought their cargoes, was somewhere below the bridge, Nick knew. He had no idea, until they shot under the bridge and saw the forest of masts rising everywhere around them, what the shipping of the port of London meant. Norfolk and Hampton Roads and Portsmouth were nothing to it. Here were ships from all over the world, battered and dingy from many voyages, or trim and new with brightly gilded carving and freshly painted figureheads. There were sloops, brigs, brigantines, barkentines, frigates, even great ships of the line. Wherries and barges crossed constantly from ship to shore, from shore to ship. Boatmen roared at each other and missed collisions by inches.

Nick asked their wherryman, who was singing "Sally in our Alley," to take them to Brown's Wharf. The man interrupted his song long enough to say he had never heard of it. They had better land at Tower Stairs, he added. They could ask at inns and shops in the streets near the river. He wished them luck cheerfully, picked up a new passenger, and rowed off singing "All in the Downs the Fleet Was Moored."

Richard Dale used to sing it, Nick remembered, and wondered where Richard was and if he would ever hear his voice again. He mustn't think about Richard, he knew. Instead he looked up at the old, gray tower and wondered where Sir Walter Raleigh's window was. Could Sir Walter see the ships setting their sails? Or only hear the shouts of the sailors and silver trumpets blowing? Virginia must have seemed a long way off to the prisoner.

It was late that day when they gave up hunting for Brown's Wharf. They were some distance from the river in a narrow, curving street where the upper stories of the houses almost reached across and touched each other. They sat down to rest on a doorstep. Across the street, Nick noticed, there was a sign in the window of a shop. He walked across and read it. It said Boy Wanted. Mr. Gribble had just put it in the window. It was only that morning that Duncan—the model shopboy, lucky Duncan!—had run away to sea.

As Mr. Gribble was careful to point out, he did not need two boys to do the work of one. Their food would be a great expense. No doubt, he added, they expected a big supper this very evening. Nick said hastily that they had had supper. Pambo had earned it for them by playing his fiddle. All they needed now was a place to sleep.

That was how they came to have their bed under Mr. Gribble's counter.

They never thought that first night that they would still be there when spring came. They had never found Brown's Wharf. Or rather, they had found three of that name but no one at any of them had ever unloaded a ship from Caryl's Maze. Occasionally Mr. Gribble shut his shop and took his wife to see her aunt in the country. The boys never saw Mrs. Gribble's aunt but they felt fond of her because on these afternoons they were allowed to go where they liked and had the privilege of earning their own supper.

They would wander along the waterfront, stopping while Pambo played his fiddle, still asking for Brown's Wharf, where ships from Virginia unloaded their cargoes. There were wharves owned by men named Brown, but the ships came from Venice or Constantinople or Leith near Edinburgh. At first they did not mention the name of Caryl, but as weeks became months they began to feel safe. For a long time Nick had dreamed at night that Sir John Desmond with a bloody sword was chasing him through dark streets, that Sir John and Gilbert caught him and buried him in the tomb next to Sandy. Or that Frederick

Caryl found him under the counter, dragged him away, clamped fetters on his wrists and shut him up in one of the cold towers of Caryl's Mount. But by spring, after people had tossed Pambo some pennies, he would ask openly for the Caryl ships. No one ever knew where they were unloaded. Years later Nick learned that the place they were looking for had been called Marlowe's Stairs ever since Queen Elizabeth's time. It must have had many owners since but none had changed the name.

For a while they talked of finding a ship, any ship, bound for Virginia, stowing away on her, sailing up to Caryl's Maze, telling everyone that its real master was in a tomb in a London garden. They would whisper about it under the counter at night. In the darkness it all seemed easy. Daylight showed difficulties.

Who would, as Pambo said, believe his word against Mistoh Sandy's? Because everyone was going to believe Gilbert was Sandy. Even when you saw both, it was hard to tell which was which. Colored boys got into trouble if they mixed in white folks' business. He'd be sold and digging ditches in some South Carolina swamp first thing he knew. Nick had had fever that night and knew nothing about any of it except what Pambo told him. They'd think both boys were crazy. Maybe they'd both be chained up somewhere. Anyway, Nick was supposed to be dead. They'd say Pambo was lying. And it was true—Pambo *had* told lies to the chaplain about Nick being dead.

"And if you hadn't, maybe I would be dead," Nick would say. "So let's not worry about it. Only someday let's get on a good ship and go to sea. Not one of these little, old ships that creep alongshore. I want to go on a king's ship on some great voyage, to India or Brazil or Madagascar."

"How we going to find a ship like that, Mistoh Nick Young—I mean Nick?" Pambo would ask.

"Some purser will come in to buy orange marmalade for the Captain's cabin and we'll hear," Nick would say. "Something will turn up."

And at last, on the morning when he sat drawing the redbirds in the magnolia tree, something did turn up.

The knocker clanged. He jumped off his stool, knocking his papers to the floor, and ran to the door.

Three gentlemen were standing there—a very tall young man in dark red and silver, a plump one a little older in dove-colored cloth, and one of medium height in dark blue and gold with white waistcoat and breeches. He was the oldest of the three and he had been to sea. Nick was sure about that even before he spoke. His tanned face, the deep lines around his keen blue eyes, his way of standing, his strong, sunburned hands, one of them deeply scarred between the forefinger and the thumb, all made Nick think of sea captains he had known in Portsmouth.

The man had a sea captain's voice too, a voice with a ring in it, even when he spoke quietly as he did now, asking for Mr. Gribble.

He would fetch him at once, Nick said, for he knew these were the kind of customers for whom Mr. Gribble would leave his game of draughts and his cup of coffee.

"Tell him, please, that Lieutenant James Cook is here and that Mr. Joseph Banks and Dr. Solander are with me."

The young man in red smiled, saying, "You mean Captain Cook, sir. You are forgetting your promotion."

"I'll remember at sea, Mr. Banks. Say Lieutenant Cook, my lad, and be off with you."

"Aye, aye, sir!" said Nick.

He tugged at the bell that would bring Pambo into the

shop and ran up the street so fast that he was panting when he reached the coffee shop.

He gasped out to Mr. Gribble, "Important customers, sir! Captain—I mean, Lieutenant Cook, Mr. Banks, Dr.—somebody—I can't remember—queer name—"

"Run back, boy. Quick, now. Say I'll be there immediately."

Nick dashed down the hill again.

Pambo was in the shop, picking up Nick's sketches and handing them to Mr. Banks, who was looking with interest at owls, hawks, passenger pigeons, brigs, frigates, Caryl's Maze, azaleas, redbirds, magnolias.

"Look at that, Dr. Solander!" Nick heard him say, as he handed over a sketch of a titmouse on a branch of apple blossoms. To Nick he said, "This boy here—what are your names?—says you drew these."

"His name's Pambo, sir, and mine's Nick Young. Yes, I drew them."

"Who taught you to draw?"

"Well, no one, I reckon, sir. I wish they had."

"I've seen some that have had lessons do worse—eh, Dr. Solander?"

"Much worse," the little doctor said, smiling. "That titmouse, now, it has spirit. It is very good."

Dr. Solander had a slight foreign accent. Nick found out later that he came from Sweden and was a botanist, a pupil of the great Linnaeus.

The sketches were tucked back into Nick's book when Mr. Gribble bounced into the shop from the back. He had changed to his best bottle-green coat and put on his best wig, Nick noticed. Certainly these were important customers.

Nick and Pambo were kept busy bringing in samples from

the storeroom. Nick learned a good deal about the voyage they were planning, in between trips to get cheese and raisins and marmalade. They would be gone more than a year, perhaps two years, Captain Cook said. From the first, Nick thought of him as the Captain. He might be only a lieutenant on a navy frigate or ship of the line, but on his own ship, the *Endeavor*, he would be the Captain and a good one. Nick felt sure of that.

They were going to the South Seas, to Otaheite. Some people called it Tahiti, Mr. Banks said, and added that the Royal Society was sending them out to observe the transit of Venus. He was interested in astronomy and anxious to learn more, Mr. Banks said, so the Royal Society was kindly letting him go along. Later Nick learned that Mr. Banks had spent ten thousand pounds of his own money to make the expedition possible.

"I have some excellent salt beef, sir, that will keep in splendid condition for a long voyage," said Mr. Gribble, rubbing his fat pink hands.

Mr. Gribble did not know any more than Nick did what the transit of Venus was, but he approved of long voyages, no matter for what purpose.

Captain Cook said, "That will be a matter for the purser, Mr. Gribble. What Mr. Banks and I are chiefly interested in is some form of lemon juice or orange juice that will keep until we can get fresh fruit again."

"To see if we can keep our ship's company free from scurvy, you know. We heard you could supply it," added Mr. Banks.

"And you couldn't do a wiser thing, gentlemen," Mr. Gribble said solemnly. "For scurvy is the great enemy of man at sea. It kills more than pirates do, more than are lost in storms. Of that I am convinced. Nick, get a flask of orange juice and one of lemon and spoons and glasses for the gentlemen."

They were still talking about scurvy when Nick came back. Mr. Gribble would talk about it for hours if anyone would listen to him, as Nick well knew. He was always trying to sell his cooked-down lemon and orange juice to sea captains.

Occasionally one would say, "Sounds like pretty good stuff to put in a rum punch when the lemons get moldy," and would perhaps buy a flask for the cabin. No one had ever thought of giving it to a whole ship's company.

Mr. Gribble almost spilled the lemon juice, he was so excited.

"There's the juice of a whole lemon, Mr. Banks, in a tea-spoonful. We simmer it gently until most of the water is out."

He handed the glass to Mr. Banks, who swallowed the lemon juice and began choking and coughing.

"I should think so! Ought to keep off scurvy for a month. Sourest thing I ever tasted!" he announced when he was able to speak.

Captain Cook and Dr. Solander tried theirs more cautiously. The orange juice was more palatable, they decided. "Yet the lemon juice might be more effective," Captain Cook said.

"How would we get the crew to take it?" Mr. Banks asked.

"It makes a most pleasant beverage with water and a little sugar, sir," Mr. Gribble said.

Mr. Banks laughed.

"Now, Gribble," he said, "you can scarcely expect the Captain to mix drinks for the crew and run around the ship with glasses on a silver tray."

Captain Cook said quietly, with a twinkle in his blue eyes, "That won't be necessary, Mr. Banks. If I know seamen, as soon as they hear it's a special delicacy in the cabin, they'll want it.

In fact, the difficulty will be to store the juice where the men won't get in and steal it. They have a natural craving for fruit. I've noticed it often when I go ashore myself after a long voyage. It was that made me think that a physician, a friend of Dr. Solander's, might be right in thinking the lack of it might cause scurvy. The men eat any kind of fruit they can get and the scurvy certainly improves—the mild cases, anyway—while the ship is in port."

"We should take plenty of both orange and lemon juice, don't you think, Dr. Solander?" Mr. Banks asked, and Dr. Solander nodded and said, "A wise provision, I am certain."

Only, Nick noticed, he said "a vise prowision."

The visitors gave Mr. Gribble the biggest order for his concentrated lemon and orange juice he had ever had. Mr. Banks also ordered a long list of other delicacies for the cabin. They included raisins, currants, citron, spices, and an enormous cheese. It was specially treated to keep for more than a year and improve in flavor all the time, Mr. Gribble said.

Mr. Banks ate some raisins. They were so good that the cook's mates would certainly have to whistle while they were taking out the seeds when there was going to be a plum duff for dinner, he said.

He turned suddenly and said to Nick, "Do you know why?"

"Yes, sir. So the cook will know his mates are not eating the raisins," Nick answered.

Mr. Banks laughed.

"Oh, you've been to sea, have you?" he said.

"Not a great deal," said Nick. "I did act as midshipman on a brig, on a voyage from Jamaica to Whitehaven, sir."

Captain Cook was on the other side of the shop, discussing prices with Mr. Gribble. Dr. Solander had laid some of

Nick's sketches on the counter and was looking at them. Mr. Banks called across the shop, "Captain Cook, I've found something else we need on the voyage—if Mr. Gribble will let us have it."

"At your service, sir," Mr. Gribble said, rubbing his hands. "Here, Pambo! Fetch what the gentleman wants."

Nick felt the blood beating hard in his ears. He did not think Mr. Banks meant more cheese or raisins. He looked across at Pambo. The whites of Pambo's eyes showed the way they did when he was excited.

"Here's a boy I could use, sir. Draws birds and plants, writes a fair hand. Knows his lines, I'll be bound."

"On a bark, mostly," Nick said. "On a brig, some."

"Modest about his accomplishments," Mr. Banks went on, smiling. "Haven't we a place for him, sir?"

Captain Cook turned his keen gaze on Nick and said, after a slight pause, "If you can use him, Mr. Banks, I dare say we could make an acting midshipman of him. Would you like to sail to the South Seas, my lad?"

Nick felt his face getting hot.

"Yes, sir, I would but—"

"The voyage seems too long?"

"No, sir. It's just—I couldn't go without Pambo. We've always been together."

"And what can Pambo do?" Mr. Banks asked good-naturedly.

"Pambo," Nick declared eagerly, "can do anything! He's a better seaman than I am, sir. He's furled sails in a real gale. He isn't afraid of anything. He can powder hair. He can play the fiddle. He's a great fisherman and a wonderful cook."

"Well," Mr. Banks said, "I have a couple of Negro servants already. I suppose I can use another. Will that suit you, Pambo?"

"If Mistoh Nick Young says so, sir. I'm Mistoh Nick Young's boy."

Mr. Banks laughed and said: "You can powder Mr. Nick's hair in your spare time. He'll be the only acting midshipman in the King's Navy that I ever heard of who brought his valet along."

Mr. Gribble had stopped smiling and rubbing his hands.

"It would be not quite convenient to let both boys go, Mr. Banks," he said.

He added that they were unusual boys. He had never, he said, employed boys who were more willing, prompt, and industrious. Nick and Pambo stared at each other. Could Mr. Gribble be talking about them? Or some other boys? Model boys—like Duncan!

"But, of course," Mr. Gribble went on, "to customers such as Captain Cook and Mr. Banks—"

"Naturally I shall make it all right with you, Gribble," Mr. Banks said. "They are not apprentices, I understand. You took them in out of charity, I think you said."

"Out of the kindness of my heart, yes, Mr. Banks."

"And your kindness shall not go unrewarded, Gribble," Mr. Banks said solemnly, but Nick got the impression that it was hard work for him not to smile. "Of course, the ship will not sail for some weeks. They can stay and help you until you get someone else. They'll be glad to, I'm sure, in return for your kindness."

Nick and Pambo exchanged looks of gloom.

Perhaps Mr. Banks saw them, for he added: "You said you could have the fruit juices ready in a week, didn't you? Suppose the boys stay a week and squeeze lemons, eh? The purser can pick up lemon juice, boys, and all and bring them to the *Endeavor*. If Captain Cook approves."

Captain Cook made no objections. He liked Mr. Banks's enthusiasm and thought it was Mr. Banks's own affair who powdered his hair, or drew pictures of plants, or—like Dr. Solander—taught him long Latin names for them. All three men were interested in science—Captain Cook especially in astronomy and geography, Dr. Solander in botany, Mr. Banks in whatever was new and strange on land, on sea or in the air.

Nick found this out that June morning. He also decided that morning to be a great scientist. He told Pambo so under the counter that night. They were both too excited to sleep.

"I thought you were going to be a sea captain," Pambo said.

"So I am, like Captain Cook. Only I'll be an artist, too, of course. I'm going to draw everything we see on the voyage. And write all about it, too."

"Yes, Mistoh Nick Young. I reckon you going to be right busy. Sounds like a mighty long voyage ahead," said Pambo.

CHAPTER 8

TAHITI

IT WAS a long voyage. Nick wrote about it and drew pictures of the things they saw for Mr. Banks. His own book was almost full by the time Nick had described the squeezing and simmering down of hundreds of lemons and oranges, and their weeks before the *Endeavor* sailed. Mr. Banks had had other books of blank paper neatly bound in red leather. He showed them to Nick, saying, "Write what you like, draw what you like, only do it the best you can."

The first thing Nick drew was two pictures of the *Endeavor*, one without sails and one under full sail. He had made pictures of the *Pocahontas* and the brig *John* and would do so—he told Pambo—of every ship they sailed on.

On the next page he began his journal:

July 30th, 1768. We left Deptford and sailed for Plymouth.

August 26th, 1768. We sailed from Plymouth today. Our ship is the *Endeavor*, Captain James Cook. She is a vessel of 300 tons. We are carrying a great many things to trade with the

natives when we see any down under the world. We shall bring
back new plants and seeds, or, anyway, pictures of new plants.

Plymouth is where Drake used to play bowls on the Hoe,
where there is a wonderful green lawn. It is as green in August
as the greenest spring grass in Virginia. This is where Drake
was bowling when they told him the Spanish Armada was
coming. He finished his game and then went out and beat
them. The Pilgrims sailed from here and went to a place in

Massachusetts which they called Plymouth. This was in 1620. Jamestown is older—1607.

We played bowls on the Hoe and explored the town. There is an old stone mill here that was used as a prison for captured seamen, French or Dutch. I am glad there is no one in it now. I am sorry for anyone who is shut away from sunshine and rain and wind and salt spray.

October 25th. We crossed the Equator today. The sailors ducked everyone who had not crossed it before. This was how they did it. A block with a long rope through it was made fast to the main yard. The boy or man who was going to be ducked had three pieces of wood to help him. One was put between his legs and he was tied fast to it. He held another between his hands and there was a third above his head to keep him from being hit by the block. I was the first to be ducked. When the boatswain whistled, they hoisted me up—the water looked about a mile away and then let go. I went *whoosh* down into it. They did this three times. I liked it and so did Pambo and a redheaded midshipman. I don't know his name. He is not in my watch. The ducking went on all day and part of the night. At last the whistling and shouting and splashing stopped. We are all Old Salts now!

The Captain and Mr. Banks and Dr. Solander were let off being ducked but were told they must pay a fine, which they did—in brandy, which most sailors seem to like. I like orange juice better, myself. We have not opened ours yet, having no sign of scurvy. One of the casks holds seven gallons. That would be more than fourteen gallons before it was cooked down. There is also a two-gallon cask of lemon juice, which was more than six gallons when we squeezed the lemons, and a smaller cask holding five quarts. We still have plenty of fresh fruit and will get more in Rio de Janeiro.

Mr. Banks has all kinds of equipment for studying natural history. He has nets for catching butterflies and nets and trawls for fish. There are big bottles with glass stoppers in which he can preserve small animals in spirits. There are special salts in which seeds can be packed and beeswax to seal up the jars. He has wonderful books with drawings of plants and animals which he lets me study.

He has pots and jars and racks for taking care of live plants and presses and paper to mount dried specimens on. There are also reams of fine drawing paper, plenty of colors to paint with, brushes of camel's hair and sable. He already has let me use them to paint things that I remember in Virginia.

I have told him that Pambo and I came from Virginia but nothing about Gilbert and Sandy. Even now I cannot believe what happened that night. At least, I do believe it, but it seems as if it had happened to someone else.

December 8th, 1768. We left Rio de Janeiro today. The mountains around the harbor are so high that it was a long time before I saw the last of them, though I was in the maintop.

January 4th, 1769. We saw a great fog bank so large that at first we thought it was an island.

Jan. 14th. We are anchored in St. Vincent's Bay. I went ashore with Mr. Banks and Dr. Solander. They found one hundred new plants not known to Europeans. The Indians here have broad, flat faces and noses. They are not so tall as our North American Indians. They wear red and brown paint on their faces. The women, like our Indians, carry their children on their backs and do the hard work.

Nick wrote that Mr. Banks found this country—Tierra del Fuego—less barren than he had expected. There were some trees and some of the hills were green though bare at the top. Still the people were outcasts among human beings, having no comforts of any sort, living miserably on shellfish. Yet they seemed content. One thing they did have was plenty of fresh water. Captain Cook had the casks filled. It was reddish in color, but the best they took in during their whole voyage.

It was summer when they rounded Cape Horn. The weather was fair with mild, temperate breezes. Perhaps not even the Captain realized how fortunate they were in the weather. It sometimes took weeks for a ship to double the Cape. More than one captain in years to come would turn back and take the eastward course around the Cape of Good Hope rather than face the gales around Cape Horn or the dangers of the Straits of Magellan.

For a long time after they left South America, they were busy working on the specimens they had found, pressing them, mounting them, drawing pictures of them, making labels for the jars of seeds. After a while there was no more work to do except take care of the live plants and learn the long Latin names that Dr. Solander gave to the new plants they had found. Nick sometimes wished he had studied Latin better with his tutor in Virginia and sometimes—rather oftener—that he had never heard of it.

The Pacific Ocean seemed endless. Mr. Banks told Pambo it was larger than the Atlantic.

Pambo said, "Yes, sir. I see it is," a remark which made Mr. Banks laugh.

April 10th Nick wrote:

At last we have found Otaheite. It is all mountains that rise up in sharp points out of the sea. They were volcanoes long ago, Mr. Banks says. First it looked like a strangely shaped blue cloud. When we got closer we saw that the blue mountains were green all the way to the top. Except where the waterfalls came foaming down it was all as green as Plymouth Hoe. The valleys are filled with palms and breadfruit trees. All around the island there is a reef of coral. The sea foams against it and breaks into white water all the time but inside it there is a wide lagoon of calm water. It is a most wonderful color, clear blue in some lights, green in others.

We were becalmed about two miles from the reef for two days but Mr. Banks let me look through his telescope and I could see where the islanders live. There is some flat land close to the water and their houses are there. They have thatched roofs but no sides. Around them are palms and breadfruit trees. It all looks like a garden.

The island inside the reef is really two islands, with a neck of land in between them. Mr. Banks calls it an isthmus.

The only breeze there was came from the land. It was not enough to fill a sail. It was just, Dr. Solander said, the island breathing. It smelled wonderful—like honey and smoke from Ambrosine's kitchen, when she is cooking spareribs and there's an almond cake baking, and Aunt Dorothy's spiced rose petals and the river at dawn when the canvasbacks fly out of the reeds.

At sunset the dark came so quickly that the stars flashed out like candles suddenly lighted. We could see the Southern Cross. Mr. Banks told me the names of some of the stars. He said they were the brightest he had ever seen, but I told him there were clear, cold, winter nights in Virginia when the Great Bear and Orion shone even brighter.

Mr. Banks laughed and said, "Oh, in Virginia everything's

a little brighter and bigger, I expect. Lemons the size of pumpkins, I'm sure."

The Captain heard us talking and said, "All those lemons and oranges you squeezed are still with us, Mr. Young." He always calls me Mr. Young just as if I were really a midshipman. Of course I do go aloft on lookout duty now and then but mostly I work for Mr. Banks. He will pay Pambo and me our wages, he said. We asked him to save them till we get back to London.

The Captain went on and said he thought the fresh fruit we shipped with us, what we got at Rio and the wild celery we ate that grew near the cape had kept off scurvy so far, but he was glad we still had the cooked-down juice for the voyage home. He sounded very pleased about it.

April 12th. The sea breeze sprang up. The *Endeavor* moved inshore. Natives began to paddle out in their canoes. They brought green branches as a sign of peace. They handed them to us and we put them up in the rigging. The ship looked like a growing tree. They brought us, also, figs, coconuts, breadfruit, bananas. The breadfruit tree is as big as a horse chestnut, with leaves a foot long. The fruit is like a cantaloupe. You eat only the core which is soft like new bread and white as an almond. It has to be roasted before you eat it. There is not much taste to it, I like bananas better.

The native canoes have high, curved prows and sails and outriggers to keep them steady in the water. There are small thatched shelters on them something like their own houses where the chief sits sheltered from sun and wind. An old man came in one of the boats. His name is Owhaw. Mr. Gore—he was here with Captain Wallis who discovered Tahiti—knows him and talked to him in his own language. Owhaw was glad to see him.

The Captain, Mr. Banks, and Dr. Solander went on shore. They took an armed guard of marines. I watched through the spyglass. I saw the natives waving more green branches. The marines picked some and waved them too.

April 13th. Two great chiefs came out to the ship, escorted by many men. They took the Captain and Mr. Banks for their *taios* which means special friend. One tall fine-looking man who came was called Tupia. He had a boy with him called Tayota. He and I took each other for our *taios*. I gave him a present of a penknife and he was very pleased. We seemed to understand each other though neither speaks the other's language. I am going to try to learn Tayota's. Pambo already knows some words.

Today I went ashore. A chief called Tubora Tumaida invited us to a dinner of plantains, breadfruit, and fish.

April 15th, Saturday. Several chiefs, one very fat one, came on board the ship. They brought hogs for a present. In return for some things the Captain gave them, they agreed that we might have a piece of land and build a fort.

April 18th. The carpenters began to build the fort. They made palisades on three sides. The fourth side is the water. Along the water side, casks were used for a breastwork. The natives helped make pickets for the palisades and set them up.

April 27th. The guns are now mounted on the fort and many natives come to visit it. We saw the Queen, who is tall with a very light skin and quite handsome. Her name is Oberea. The Queen liked a child's doll they gave her very much. Tootaha, the chief, was jealous and the Captain gave him one too. They also gave him an iron adze. It had been copied from a stone one that Captain Wallis brought home in the *Dolphin*. The chief was much pleased with it.

May 2nd. The quadrant, which Captain Cook is to use in observing the transit of Venus, was taken ashore. It was in a tent guarded by marines but the Indians—as everyone calls them, though they are not like any Indians I ever saw—stole it right from under the marines' noses. They carried it off in the woods and took it to pieces. Tubora Tumaida got it back. It was not damaged.

May 5th. I went with Mr. Banks and Dr. Solander to Tootaha's house. He had a court nearby and had some of his men show us their skill in wrestling there. I expect the smallest of them could throw me though I have grown lately and am taller than many of them.

May 9th. The blacksmith set up his forge on shore. The Indians came in crowds to visit it and brought axes they had received from Captain Wallis to be reforged.

I am trying to learn to talk with the natives. I know some of the names they have for the English. The Captain is Toote. Mr. Gore is Toura. Tolano is the name for Dr. Solander and Opana for Mr. Banks.

"Opana" is setting up two observatories, one on Tahiti (as we call Otaheite now) and the other on an island not far from here called Eimayo. The place where the observatory on Tahiti is we call Point Venus.

June 3rd. I am on Eimayo with Mr. Banks. Very early this morning, the day of the transit, King Tarrao arrived to visit the observatory. We heard him coming because his fifer was playing some very squeaky music. Mr. Banks now wears a turban of Indian cloth instead of a hat. He spread his turban out on the ground and he and the King sat down on it. The King brought presents of a hog, coconuts, and breadfruit. Mr. Banks gave him an adze, a shirt, and some nails, which delighted the King.

The King watched the transit through the telescope and so did three beautiful young ladies who are his daughters, I think. So did his fifer, who is called Nuna. The King asked my name and I told him Nick Young. He tried to say it but the nearest he could get was Nuna so I reckon that is my name now. My *taio* Tayota is here with us. He is pleased that I now have a name he can say. The natives call Pambo Papo. They want him to play his fiddle all the time. The more it squeaks the better they like it. He played it a great deal during the transit which began at 9:25:4 and lasted till 3:32:10.

While we were watching it, the seamen on the *Endeavor* broke into the storeroom and stole nails so they could trade with the Indians. Another day they stole bows and arrows from some Indians. Captain Cook is not harsh like some captains I have heard of but he had the sailors lashed, especially one who said it was all right to steal from an Indian. The sailors are always talking about what thieves the Indians are. I don't see much difference myself.

June 26th. We have started to sail all around Tahiti. The island across the isthmus has another king. In the houses of one of the chiefs there, we saw a semi-circular board with human teeth and jawbones, teeth and all, arranged around it. Mr. Banks could not find out anything about it.

We saw one of their gods. They call it an *etaua*. It was shaped like a man seven feet tall. It was made of basketwork covered with black and white feathers. We were also shown the *morai*, which is Queen Oberea's burial place. It is a stone pyramid, 270 feet long, 90 feet wide, and 50 feet high. The bottom of it is rocks. Then there are steps of coral and at the top there are pebbles all the same size. In the center of the *morai* were a carved wooden bird and a fish carved of stone.

The only tools they have are stone adzes of different sizes and bone chisels made of a man's forearm. They use coral and coral sand for filing tools and polishing. Dr. Solander says that to build the *morai* without iron tools or mortar took infinite labor and skill.

June 28th. We found out that the inhabitants of Tiarrabon, which was where we saw the board with the teeth, had been at war with Queen Oberea's people. The jawbones were those of men killed in battle. Their weapons are slings, stone-headed pikes, and hardwood clubs, very long and heavy. Pambo thinks they eat their enemies but when he asked them straight out they only said, "Oh! Do the English eat their enemies?" So we do not really know.

July 1st. We got back to Point Venus. It was 100 miles around the island.

July 4th. We planted seeds of watermelons, oranges, lemons, limes, and plants from Rio de Janeiro outside the fort. We are getting ready to leave Tahiti now. We have some good friends here whom we shall miss, especially Tayota's master, Tupia. He was once Queen Oberea's prime minister and head priest. He has sailed to many distant islands and is a fine navigator. He says there are 6000 fighting men on Tahiti.

The chiefs of the island are taller than most Europeans. Their skin is no darker than mine now I am sunburned. Their hair is usually black. They have fine, white teeth, like Pambo's. Their manners are most friendly and courteous.

Both men and women have their skin tattooed. This is pricking the skin with a piece of bone filed into sharp points and then rubbing dark blue or black stuff into the pricks. Some of the patterns are very beautiful. It is first done at twelve years old. I saw a girl being tattooed. She stood the pain for a time but then began to cry and the women scolded her.

The native cloth, out of which their turbans and other clothes are made, is very beautiful. It is made by pounding mulberry bark. Sometimes it is white but it may be dyed brown or black or yellow or red.

The men make strong fishlines out of the bark of a kind of nettle. They are wonderful fishermen and swimmers. They live much of their life in or on the water. I reckon they are the cleanest people in the world. They bathe at least three times a day. One of their sports is to take boards and shoot through the highest waves to a beach. Pambo and I tried it but usually fell off. Small children do better than we did.

They eat a great deal of fish. No grain of any kind grows on the island but there is plenty to eat—breadfruit, coconuts, yams, sugar cane, and other fruits. The only tame animals are hogs and dogs. One of the chiefs gave us fat roasted dog to eat. We didn't know what it was until we had eaten it. We all liked it till we knew. Mr. Banks still says it was better than boiled mutton. Captain Cook is going to leave a bull and a cow here. Also some hens. He brought them on purpose. There are plenty of wild birds, ducks, pigeons, parrots. No snakes. No fierce wild animals. You can go safely anywhere.

Houses are used only when it rains and for sleeping. People eat outdoors in the shade of a tree. Men and women never eat together. Chiefs eat alone unless they have visitors. They use leaves for a tablecloth. On them the servants put coconut shells of fresh and salt water. First the chief washes his hands. Then he dips breadfruit or fish into the salt water and eats it.

They do not talk much at meals but attend to the main business, which is eating. Even brothers do not talk together but have separate baskets and sit with their backs to each other.

July 8th. The fort is being pulled down. The wood is being stowed in the *Endeavor* to be used in the galley for cooking. The cook has salted down pork for the voyage and we are taking all the fresh fruit we can, especially coconuts, which are good to drink as well as to eat. The casks are being filled with fresh water. All our friends are coming to visit us. Tupia came on board today and brought Tayota. We climbed the rigging, chasing each other. Tayota can beat me.

July 9th. Tupia wants to go with us and take Tayota! They want to see King George. Pambo and I saw him walking in Hyde Park. He is a fat, red-faced man and he did not seem so courteous as the great men of Tahiti of whom Tupia is one.

Captain Cook said he had no authority to take any Indians back to England.

"Then with your permission, I will take him as my guest," said Mr. Banks. "I have friends who bring home pet lions and tigers and monkeys from foreign lands. Tupia seems more interesting to me than such pets. If he is not happy in England, he can sail back again when we come for the breadfruit trees."

Mr. Banks was talking about a plan he has for taking young breadfruit trees to the West Indies where they will grow well, he thinks, and be a good source of food. Mr. Banks will get all kinds of plants moved around the world if he has his way. We are taking many seeds and dried plants from Tahiti. I have spent almost every minute painting lately. The flies were very troublesome. They tried to eat the colors off the paper. We had to make tents of mosquito netting and work under them.

July 12th. Tupia is really going with us. He came on board today and brought Tayota. Mr. Banks gave Tupia nails and beads and other ornaments. He went back on shore and gave them to his friends for farewell presents.

July 13th, Thursday. The ship was surrounded by many canoes. Most of the people had come to say goodbye to Tupia. They wept openly. Tupia did too but tried to hide his sorrow.

Mr. Banks said: "Poor fellow, the effort to conceal his tears does him additional honor."

At any time, even after we were under full sail, he could have gone back, for the canoes followed us far out to sea. The great skill and strength of the paddlers drove the canoes forward for some time as fast as the *Endeavor* sailed. Tupia did not change his mind. He said he still wanted to see King Torata—which is what he calls King George. Mr. Banks brought him up to the masthead where Tayota and I were. He stood there waving to the canoes as long as he could see them and brushing the tears out of his eyes but smiling courteously when Mr. Banks spoke to him.

He is a tall fine-looking man of a pale bronze color. He was dressed in brown cloth, patterned in black. The best of the island cloth is delicately perfumed. This cloth of Tupia's is new and smells like the island—sweet and spicy. A skilled carver of figureheads would like him for a model, I think, just as he stood there, looking back at the canoes. After a while they seemed to sink in the sea. Then he looked at the island until it changed from green to blue and faded into a pale blue shadow against the clear blue sky. At last it too sank into the blue water.

Mr. Banks said, "You will see it again, Tupia, when we come for the breadfruit trees," and Tupia said politely, though not smiling, "Thank you, Opana. May it be so."

Then he looked down at me—he is taller than Mr. Banks,

who stands a good six feet in his stockings—and said, "Nuna will not see it again. But he will sail many seas and lie in dark places."

Now unless you are the captain of a ship or an important man like Mr. Banks and sleep in the Great Cabin, it is usual to have your bed in a dark place. My own sleeping place on the *Endeavor* is amidships and not much roomier or lighter than Mr. Gribble's counter. So I would not have thought it strange that Tupia said this except for something in his voice and the way he was staring at the flag above us. The ship had been all trimmed with flags for the departure and he was looking at the Union Jack.

I said, "A dark place on a ship, Tupia?" and he answered, still watching the flag, "Below the water, below the earth that is under it, through hot fire and cold earth and water again, and above into the night. A battle. A dark ship." Then he looked back to where the mountaintops of Tahiti had vanished and said so softly that I could hardly hear him, "Under a new flag—under the stars."

CHAPTER 9

NEW ZEALAND

NICK BEGAN the third volume of his journal on July 14th, 1769, when the *Endeavor* had left Tahiti.

He wrote:

We are sailing south and west. We have been gone from England a year now. The Captain ordered the big Cheshire cheese he bought from Mr. Gribble brought out and the whole ship's company had some. It had a fine, snappy taste. This is something surprising I found out because of the cheese. Lately, since we left Tahiti, the redheaded midshipman, Duncan McTavish, and I have been in the same mess and on watch together in the maintop. He is a great hand aloft, can furl a sail in the windiest weather and is always first up the rigging. He drives the cook wild by stealing things from the galley. While the cook is looking right at him, he'll snatch a chunk of plum duff, a whole coconut, or some of the fried cakes the sailors call doughboys. It's a sort of game between them. The cook never tells and gets him punished because you can't help liking Duncan.

He can mimic anyone. You would think Dr. Solander was talking when Duncan copies him. He'll say, "Now this vlower is werry pretty and I vill name it *Misanthropos ephemeras*." He sings, has a fine clear voice, never forgets a tune he has once learned. He can do card tricks and tell fortunes with cards.

He swims like a shark and climbs like a cat. I never saw him glum or angry. On Tahiti the natives loved him. He ran away once for two days and lived with his *taio*. It was during the transit. None of the officers ever found out. The ones on Eimayo thought he was at Point Venus and vice versa. All the time he was eating roast pig and surfboarding with his *taio*.

It wasn't the first time he had run away, he told me, He ran away from Kircudbright and was on the very ship on which Captain Paul sailed to Jamaica. He says that John Paul joined a group of players in Jamaica. Duncan saw him act in a play. He says Captain Paul was always acting whether he was on the stage or the quarter-deck. He says he does not remember the name of the play. The speeches were very long and he went to sleep. He says Captain Paul was more interesting in his cabin or on the quarter-deck. Still I wish I could see a play. I have never seen one.

Duncan ran away from Jamaica, stowed away on a ship, and worked his passage to London. He tried different kinds of work but did not like any of the people he worked for and ran away from them all. At last he met a cousin of his who knew Captain Cook and got the Captain to take Duncan as a midshipman.

"The McTavishes stick together," he said. "And a lucky day for Captain Cook. It makes me tremble to think where this expedition would be without Duncan McTavish!" Duncan added.

"Where indeed?" I said.

Pambo had been cooking our cheese for us with beer and mustard. We ate it hot on ship's biscuit in my cabin.

I said, "Pambo, if you please, a little more of that Cheshire cheese of Mr. Gribble's."

Duncan's green eyes flashed like a cat's in a dark room when you walk in with a candle.

"Mr. Gribble!" he said and began talking just like him.

He looked surprised when Pambo and I laughed till we rolled on the cabin floor.

"Why," Duncan said, "I did not know I was such a wit."

"Wit!" I gasped. "You're no wit. You're *Duncan the model boy!*" and soon all three of us were rolling around punching each other!

The *Endeavor* was out of sight of land for almost two months. On October 7th, 1769. Nick wrote proudly:

We are anchored near what the Captain has named Nick Young's Head. It is the S.W. point of this bay and of this continent, if it is one, or anyway a very great island. I saw it first from the masthead. I called "Land ho!" so loud that Duncan says he almost fell from the masthead into the sea. At least it was loud enough so the Captain heard me in his cabin and said the point should have my name.

October 15th. The natives here are unfriendly. Some came to trade but while Tupia was talking to them, they seized his boy Tayota, my *taio*. They carried him off in their canoe. I heard him calling me, "Nuna! Nuna!"

Captain Cook has told the whole crew to make friends with the natives, to treat them with kindness, never to use firearms except in case of real trouble. When we heard Tayota call, the Captain ordered one of the marines to fire his musket. He did so, wounding one of the paddlers.

They stopped holding Tayota and he leaped into the sea and swam back to the ship. He had on English clothes Mr. Banks had given him and he was greatly tired by the weight of them. Duncan and I jumped overboard and helped him to the ship. The Captain called the place where this happened Cape Kidnappers.

The next day Tayota caught a large fish and told us he wished to make a thank offering to his *etaua* but how could he do it since the god was far away. We did not know so we asked Tupia who said: "God is everywhere. Cast it into the sea!"

It was still flapping and it swam off very fast. Perhaps for Tahiti, Duncan said.

Later in October they found friendly, courteous natives who traded with them, bringing quails, pigeons, lobsters and mackerel. Some of them wore garments of white flax with a border of red and white. The women smeared their faces all over with red paint, which—as Mr. Banks remarked—"much diminished the little beauty they have." They greeted each other by gently pressing their noses together. The men wore stones as green as emeralds around their necks but Mr. Banks said they were not emeralds.

The natives entertained them with military exercises. They had lances of sharpened hardwood ten feet long and stone axes which they called patoo patoos. An old warrior, handsomely tattooed and dressed in white, set up a stake which he pretended was his enemy. First he pierced it with his lance and then he brought his patoo patoo down on it with force enough to crush a man's skull.

These people [Nick wrote] admitted that they ate the enemies they killed in battle. They sang their war song for us, shouting, gasping, making faces. Duncan can copy them to perfection. We saw one of their canoes, 57 feet long, 6 wide. It was made of the trunks of three trees. The sides were carved with a pattern of whirlpools and circles. It was beautifully done though their only tools are stone adzes and bone chisels. They eat parrots and use the feathers for ornaments. They also eat dogs.

Duncan said, "Have you noticed, Nick, that it shocks our English officers more to learn that these people eat dogs than when they hear that they eat their enemies. Yet I dare say dogs taste better than most of our sailors would."

"Yes," I said, "the English treat dogs better than they do boys. I noticed that. Do you remember how Mr. Gribble's spaniel enjoyed the drumstick of a fat fowl?"

We both remembered.

"In Scotland," Duncan said, "it's the other way. We feed people first and dogs afterwards—if there's any oatmeal left."

For the rest of October, November, and December they sailed along the coast of what afterwards came to be called New Zealand. Much of this part of the world had never been carefully explored by a European ship before. Captain Cook's charts of it were the first accurate ones. By February 27th, 1770, they had sailed around the whole country. They had found it was not the southern continent that Europeans had thought must lie in this part of the world but two very large islands.

The impression Nick had of the northern island was one of fierce, warlike men, many of them cannibals, of women mourning for their dead husbands by gashing themselves with sharp shells, of canoes as strong as New England whaleboats and holding a hundred men. There were great forests of tall trees, hundreds of plants never seen in Europe, birds that sang all night as sweetly as nightingales. He caught new kinds of butterflies, ate new kinds of fish. He saw green valleys with a stream in every one and high, rocky mountains capped with snow.

The southern island was so barren that it was almost uninhabited. Yet it was strangely beautiful, especially at sunset when the snow suddenly turned rose-colored with deep pools of blue shadow in it. In the northern island Mr. Banks said the climate and soil would make the growing of European fruits and grains possible.

Nick wrote of a meeting with the natives:

They were all sitting or lying near the water. When they saw us, their chief stood up and put on a garment of dog's skin.

He had a hole bored in his nose and a feather thrust through the hole. There was also a hole in his ear with a bone chisel stuck through it. He had a string of teeth around his neck. The men all had spears sharpened at both ends, darts, stones, and patoo patoos.

When they found they could not hit us with darts or stones, the chief called out, *"Haromai, haromai, harreuta a patoo patoo oge."* Tupia says this means, "Come to us, come ashore and we will kill you with our patoo patoos!"

Our captain did not accept this courteous invitation. The men began their war dance. They shook their spears, waved their patoo patoos in the air, and sang their war song. This began with a loud shout and ended with a deep sigh. Their faces and bodies were all twisted around. Their tongues hung out of their mouths. They got into their canoes, still singing. They kept such time to the music that 50 paddlers could strike their paddles against the side with one sound. These paddles are six feet long, with an oval blade, widening out from the handle. They steer with the paddles at the stern. The canoes have sails of matting but can sail only before the wind. Yet even against it they send the canoes swiftly forward.

Tupia says that the chiefs told him that their ancestors came to this country in their canoes from far north and east. By their language, he thinks they may have come from Tahiti. He says they are proud of their ancestors and can say over their names for generations back to the ones who first landed. They even know in which canoes their ancestors traveled.

A friend of Sandy's once came to Portsmouth from Massachusetts. He used to talk the same way about the people who sailed on the *Mayflower*. One of his ancestors, called

John Howland, fell overboard but grabbed hold of the end of a rope and was pulled on board.

He said that John Howland had so many descendants that if the rope had not held, practically everyone in Massachusetts would have been someone else. He said too that if it had not been for Pocahontas, a lot of Virginians would have been someone else. I was puzzled by these ideas but Sandy said, "Give him no mind, Nick Young, he learned to talk that way at Harvard College. Now at William and Mary, we have better sense."

I have not thought of Sandy and Gilbert and that night for a long time now. At first, Pambo and I were always making plans for going home and telling everyone that Gilbert was a traitor and a thief. Lately it has all seemed like something I read about in a book long ago. Yet someday—

CHAPTER 10

AUSTRALIA

NICK BEGAN the fourth volume of his journal with a description of their voyage along the coast of what was then called New Holland. Many people thought it was a continent, though it was really the largest island in the world. (Later it became known as Australia.)

On March 27th, 1770, we had sailed around the whole country. [He meant New Zealand.] We had found it was not part of a southern continent, as we had hoped, but two large islands. It was now time to decide what route we should choose for our voyage home. The Captain called us to his cabin to talk it over. Even the midshipmen were invited. Mr. Banks wanted to sail due south because he still thought there might be a continent there. I was the only other one who wanted to sail south. The others all said if there were land, it would be only rocks and ice. I daresay they are right but I would like to see.

Some of the officers wanted to turn back and go by Tahiti and Cape Horn. Others were for making straight for the Cape of Good Hope. Most agreed with the Captain when he suggested that we should sail north, explore the coast of New Holland, and then sail home by way of the East Indies and Africa.

This course was decided on. Afterwards, Mr. Banks said to me, 'Well, Nick, we'll just have to come back another time. Whichever way the wind blows now, everyone smells the roast beef of Old England and feels hungry. How is it you don't smell it, eh?"

I said I supposed I was hungry for Virginia ham.

He said, "Oh, yes, I had forgotten you were a Virginian. You haven't much colonial accent. I'd really never know you weren't English."

English people mean kindly when they say this but I never quite know what answer to make. Duncan says, "Tell them you'd never know they weren't Virginians," but not being a model boy, I didn't say anything to Mr. Banks.

He went on, "Tell me about your home in Virginia, Nick. I hope to visit America someday."

I started to tell him about Caryl's Maze and would have spoken about Sandy but the Captain called us back to the cabin and I thought I would wait until another day.

Captain Cook said, in his kind way, "You are not disappointed in our decision, Mr. Banks? Mr. Young?"

Mr. Banks said, "Not really, sir, our voyage has solid accomplishments. If it were only the discovery of what I expect will always be Cook's Straits, it would be worth while."

He meant the passage between the north and south islands. The natives call the north one Eaheinomawe and the south one Tory Poenammo. We midshipmen just call them Ea and Tory.

Mr. Banks went on, "And though of course I'm disappointed that we haven't found the southern continent, merely the discovery that the islands are islands is important. We have taken possession of a fine country for the King. No, sir, I think you are right. Everyone's homesick except Nick Young.

"By sailing along close to the east coast of New Holland, we'll add to geographic knowledge. We are sure to find new plants and animals. Perhaps it will be more interesting than my continent, which will keep, sir, until another voyage. We should sail home while we are all well—not a case of scurvy, ship still sound, and Mr. Young will like a look at the East Indies, eh Mr. Young?"

I said I would. The Captain smiled and said I might go. I left them looking at charts of New Holland. They are not very good. The Dutch have tried to keep it a secret, Mr. Banks says, in case they need new territory. Their possessions in the East Indies are all they can manage at present so they have never taken formal possession of New Holland or charted it properly. He says that Tasman, who discovered Ea and Tory, never landed because he was afraid of the natives. (I don't blame him!) You have to land to take possession. Otherwise anyone could just wave at an island from twenty miles away and claim it for his country.

Captain Cook set up posts with English flags at Queen Charlotte's Sound and George the Third Bay, so now the islands belong to England.

They sailed from New Zealand on March 31st and on April 19th they saw land again. It was New Holland. They sailed close to the coast, discovering and naming many points and bays. They called one place Ram's Head because it reminded the Captain of a hill near Plymouth.

The natives along this coast [Nick wrote] are dark-skinned

and smaller than those of Ea and Tory. They are hostile and do not trade with us. Their bodies and legs are painted with white streaks. They smear their faces with white, too. One old woman glanced at the *Endeavor*, then turned away and went on with her cooking as if she saw such ships every day. Whenever we landed, the men threw lances at us.

Early in May we explored a beautiful bay. We saw so many new plants that Mr. Banks and the Captain decided to call it Botany Bay. Nearby is Port Jackson, which is as fine a harbor as Rio de Janeiro or Hampton Roads. Duncan laughed at me for saying this and added, "Or Solway Firth." I said, "Yes, Whitehaven was a pleasant little harbor," and he almost knocked me off the masthead.

We displayed English colors every day while we were on shore. When we left we carved the name of the ship and the date—May 6, 1770—on a tree near the watering place. One of the seamen has some skill as an engraver. The Captain often has him engrave a pewter plate with the date and King George's name. We leave it with some chief as a sign we have visited the place.

We have landed in many bays and have seen strange things. There are birds here such as Mr. Banks says he never heard of anywhere in the world. There are ants that make clay nests as big as a bushel basket, high up in trees. Duncan found caterpillars with green hair that stings like nettles. Once I saw a tree covered with butterflies. They were on every twig and branch and in the air all around it. It looked as if the tree would flutter away in a minute.

We have seen tracks of four-footed animals different from any Mr. Banks knows and a small fish with strong fins that can leap as nimbly as a frog on either land or water.

For hundreds of miles the Captain has sailed the *Endeavor* close enough to the shore to make charts. It is a dangerous coast because of the many rocks and hidden reefs and shoals. At all times, night and day, the leadsman must heave the lead and call out the depth of the water. If you are on watch at night or even awake in your bed, you hear his voice calling "Forty fathoms five—twenty fathoms—thirty fathoms to port..."

At last, after avoiding many dangers, we met misfortune at a place well named by the Captain, Cape Tribulation. None of us on the *Endeavor* will ever forget this place. Here, with a fair breeze and a bright moon, the leadsman calling twenty fathoms, there was a terrible, grinding crash. The ship had struck a rock. We lay fixed except for the motion given to the ship by the waves beating against her side.

The Captain ordered the anchor cast out. The whole force of the capstan was applied but it could not move the ship. She beat so violently that we could scarce keep our legs. By the bright moonlight I saw sheathing boards and part of the keel float away from under the ship.

We tried to lighten her by throwing over oil jars and casks and guns but the tide went down so fast that it made no difference. The Captain and all the officers kept calm and cool, giving their orders clearly. There was no confusion. The crew went about their business cheerfully and quietly. There was no grumbling. Not an oath was sworn, though, as Mr. Banks said, in general we have as good a supply of them as any ship in His Majesty's Navy.

They knew the danger they were in. They could all see that the mainland was many miles away. There were no islands near, not enough boats to take the whole crew to the mainland, only the reef and the sea beating against the ship.

Luckily, the next morning the wind died to a dead calm. High water was at eleven but it did not float her though we must have thrown over fifty tons of weight. We kept the pumps going but the water came in as fast as we could pump it out. Our only hope now was the midnight tide. At 9 o'clock the ship righted. We thought she would sink. Only one pump was going. The water was growing deeper in the hold.

We all knew that our chances were bad. Either we would go down with the ship or, if we reached land, find death at the hands of hostile savages or at best a miserable life as castaways. At 10:20 she floated and we kedged her into deep water. There was almost four feet of water in the hold. We all took turns at the pumps. Mr. Banks pumped with the rest of us.

We could only pump a few minutes, then throw ourselves into the stream of water flowing from the pump while the next man took his turn. By 8 in the morning we had gained on the water a little. While I way lying there gasping, Pambo lay down beside me, panting from his turn.

When he could speak, he said that it was like that time on the *Pocahontas*. Only worse.

"But Captain Farrand stopped that leak," he said.

All those long hours I had never once thought of the time the *Pocahontas* struck a rock. I hauled myself off the deck and went aft where the Captain and Mr. Banks were. I told them Pambo and I had once seen a leak, caused like this one, stopped.

Captain Cook listened to me kindly. He never once in all those hours changed from his usual calm, quiet way of speaking and acting. I do not think he had great hopes from the plan but he told me to go ahead and try it. So with the help of the boatswain we got out an old studding sail. We mixed chopped oakum and wool and dung from the sheep pens. We put it in bunches on the canvas five or six inches apart and the sailmaker stitched it between two pieces of the sail. I can still see his tarry hands as he pushed the big needle through the canvas with his leather palm.

I found myself thinking of Caryl's Maze and Cherry with a small gold thimble on her finger, hemming ruffles for my shirt. Two such shirts would not cover me now but I still keep one of them in my sea chest. It has the Golden Horseshoe pinned in the ruffle and the first volume of my journal wrapped up in it.

I felt suddenly that our oakum mattress—as Pambo called it—would work and that I would race through Caryl's Maze again some day. And the mattress did work. We attached it to the yards by ropes. Duncan went up with one end. I took the other. Pambo cast it off at the bow. When it reached the leak, the pressure of the water outside carried it into the hole. Before long we had to use only one pump.

We were still in great danger from shoals and reefs and it was not until the 17th of June that we landed. No one had noticed till then that poor Tupia had on his legs the dark purple, brownish spots like bruises that are the first sign of scurvy. Others of the crew showed the same signs. The Captain had a tent set up on shore for the sick men and gave them lemon juice and fresh fish. Tupia soon recovered and began catching fish for himself and the others.

June 22nd. The ship was brought close inshore and we cleared everything we could out of her. The Captain ordered the smith to set up his forge on shore so he could do the iron-work for the repairs. When the tide left the ship, we examined her keel. The rock had cut through her timbers. The cut was as smooth as if a Tahitian had done it with a stone adze. We were saved by a strange thing. One hole, large enough to have sunk the ship in a short time, was blocked up by a big chunk of coral left sticking in it. The oakum and wool mattress had got around it and had stopped up the rest of the hole. If Pambo had not remembered the *Pocahontas*—well, anyway, he did.

While the smith made bolts and nails and the carpenters began their work, many of the crew went ashore to shoot pigeons for our sick men. I went with them. We saw a mouse-colored animal, extremely swift, as big as one of Mr. Banks's greyhounds. He has two dogs with him. They sleep in his cabin.

July 1st. We have been working on Mr. Banks's plants. We thought they were safe but when the ship was hove down, water got into the plant room. Most of those we had growing were destroyed. So were some of the dried specimens. Others we are trying to save by drying them over again. It is lucky we had also painted pictures of them.

It was a great task drying them in the first place, but to get them dry again and mounted on fresh paper after they had been soaked in sea water is even worse. I had left the Ea and Tory volume of my journal in the plant room and it got soaked too. Fortunately the jars of seeds were so well sealed that they are all right.

Our food is good since we came here. We have shellfish, turtle, other kinds of fish, and plenty of greens to boil with our peas. We have seen the animal like a greyhound again. I was with Mr. Banks and he had his own greyhound, Lady, with him. She chased the animal but could not catch it because it could leap over the high grass and she had to run through it. This animal leaped forward on two legs, not four.

July 14th. Mr. Gore shot one of the mouse-colored animals. It was as big as a sheep. We had it roasted for dinner. Tupia found out from some natives that it is called a *kangaroo*.

August 4th. The ship is now repaired and we are at sea again.

August 13th. We are still among dangerous shoals. The leadsmen take soundings every minute as they have done for 1000 miles. Captain Cook says the *Endeavor* is probably the only ship that ever traveled for three months among shoals, sounding all the time.

August 14th. At last today we were able to leave these dangerous shoals. We got out through an opening in the reef east and north to see if we could find a passage between New Holland and New Guinea.

August 15th. I came on watch just before daylight. As the light came I saw a dreadful sight. Surf of a vast height broke like a white mountain over a great rock two miles away. I called out and the Captain at once sent all our boats ahead to tow our ship away from the rock. Yet we drove on toward it. Within a hundred yards of it, when there was nothing between us but a great valley left by the last wave, a light breeze sprang up and helped the boats tow us away.

Then the breeze dropped. There was an awful moment of calm when it seemed we would lose what ground we had gained and be sucked toward the rock again. Then from the masthead I saw an opening in the reef. The Captain sent Duncan and me in a boat to explore it. We found it was about as wide as the ship was long. The Captain tried to sail the *Endeavor* through it but the tide turned. It ebbed so fast that we were carried a quarter of a mile out to sea in one rush. With the help of the boats we got two miles off shore but the flood tide carried us back toward the rock.

Just as it seemed once more that destruction had seized us, we found another passage in the reef. A puff of wind filled our sails. The Captain took us through. He named the place

Providential Channel. Mr. Banks said no one else could have taken a ship through it and it should be called Cook's Passage. He marked it so on his own chart.

The ship could now be anchored. We were glad enough to get back inside the reef, though for weeks we have longed for the open sea.

August 21st. We have been sailing north, still inside the reef, still sounding every minute. Today we discovered some islands. The Captain named them York Islands. We landed on one of them and went to the top of the hill. From it we could see the most wonderful sight that has met our eyes for months—open water to the west for forty miles or more.

Mr. Banks said, "A strait! A strait!"

The Captain, who is always cautious, said, "The existence of a channel now seems ascertained."

He ordered the English colors displayed and took possession of the whole east coast we had explored, from 38° south latitude to the spot where we were now standing, for King George. If King George had had to sail along this coast for more than three months, taking soundings every minute, I reckon this country would still be called New Holland. Captain Cook named it New South Wales and the island where we were standing Possession Island.

This country of New South Wales is much larger than anyone ever knew before. Mr. Banks says it cannot be considered a continent. He still dreams of a real southern one, I suppose. However, he says it is bigger than Europe. The *Endeavor* has sailed more than 2000 miles, not counting turns and twists in the course. The northern part of New South Wales does not have such rich grass as in the south nor are the trees so high.

I remember one tree on Tory that was 98 feet, we figured, to the first branch.

We have not seen any kangaroos lately but we have seen many birds. Some of them are like European or American birds such as owls, hawks, eagles, herons. There are also parrots and cockatoos and other birds with elegant plumage that are new to us. One is so beautiful that we call it the Bird of Paradise. There is also one that has a crown of feathers on its head and is a sort of silvery blue with eyes like rubies. I expect fashionable ladies in London would like such feathers for their turbans but I hope the birds will keep them.

Men here often wear feathers, but in their noses. They bore a hole in the part between the nostrils and draw a feather through it. Our sailors call this ornament the spritsail yard. The natives make fire by spinning a blunt stick rapidly back and forth on a piece of dry wood. They can make fire as quickly as we can with flint, steel, and tinder. Their weapons are lances tipped with fish bones and barbed with other pieces of bone. They make bad wounds, leaving splinters in the flesh and tearing it badly. The canoes here are hollowed out of tree trunks, probably by fire. They are usually about fourteen feet long and so narrow that they have to be kept from upsetting by outriggers. The men are good paddlers but the canoes are poor things compared to those of Tahiti and of Ea and Tory.

The Indians here cook shellfish—crabs, oysters, lobsters much as our Indians do at home. They heat stones first, put them in a hole they have dug, wrap the fish in seaweed, cover the whole thing, and leave it till the fish is done. They figure the time well, by the sun, I suppose. Our English seamen prefer their fish boiled, as they do most things. I like the native fashion. It tasted like Virginia to me.

When we left New South Wales we sailed west among some islands the Captain called Prince of Wales Islands. We called the straits *Endeavor* Straits.

As we came out of the shoals and islands and sailed toward New Guinea, Mr. Banks said to the helmsman, "The compass seems to work perfectly now."

He spoke in a serious voice but I knew he was joking. Once when the whole ship's company were sighing for roast beef—as he calls their homesickness—we were getting west fast but the compass seemed to show a northern variation.

At the time the helmsman said he thought a current had thrown us off our course. Afterwards, Mr. Banks laughed and said to me, "Their hearts are all pulling west, that's what made the variation. The current is just what navigators always call anything that makes reckonings disagree with the way they want to go."

I said, "Does your private compass still try to point south, sir?" And he answered, "Oh, you know, Nick, I still dream of my continent, even if it is only ice mountains and inhabited by penguins."

For that matter, so do I.

CHAPTER 11

CROCODILE TWIN

O F THE MONTHS spent in the East Indies Nick wrote afterwards:

This is the only part of our voyage I could not bear to repeat. I do not like to think of it even now when we are out in the clean air and headed for the Cape of Good Hope. We were cheated and lied to both by Europeans in laced hats and waistcoats and by rajas in chintz nightgowns. We were bitten by mosquitoes. We lived in houses that leaked when it rained and it rained all the time, sometimes with thunder, sometimes without but enough so that you could run a mill wheel with the water that ran through the house. The frogs croaked ten times as loud as Virginia frogs. Mosquitoes bred in every splash of water. I used to think Portsmouth was hot in summer! It is nothing to Batavia which is on the island of Java.

No one was ill when we came there but soon almost everyone was. Poor Tupia and my *taio* Tayota were the first to have chills and fever. Soon Tayota could hardly breathe. Only a few days before, the poor boy had been dancing about the streets, exclaiming over the houses and the carriages and the canals. He and Tupia were puzzled because of the many different kinds of clothes they saw. Mr. Banks explained to Tupia that in Batavia there were people from many distant lands and that each wore his own kind of clothing. So Tupia took Tayota and went back to the *Endeavor* where they took off the English clothes Mr. Banks had given them and dressed themselves in their own native cloth of yellow glazed with red. With the tattooed pattern on their legs and arms and chests, Tupia's great height and graceful but dignified way of moving and Tayota's happy, dancing steps, they were more noticed than the governor himself.

Their happiness did not last long. Soon they were so wasted away that, except for the tattooing, I would not have known them. Soon Mr. Banks began to have fever every day, but he took care of Dr. Solander who was even sicker. Pambo was ill and also Duncan. I took care of them and did what I could for Tupia and Tayota.

We set up tents on shore for the seamen, the *Endeavor* being hove down for repairs. The Captain hired Malays to nurse our sick. They would run away and leave their patients calling for them and too weak to leave their beds, so I stayed mostly at the tents.

On the 9th of October, Tayota died. Tupia's despair was terrible to see. I had hard work not to cry but did not, for fear of hurting him more. He was always quiet and gentle but now he almost never spoke. He was so thin that he was like a skeleton covered with bronze and the tattoo marks were like engraving on some old sword. He would try to smile when I brought him water. His teeth would just flash white for a second. Then he would stare at the sea to the southeast. His eyes were very large and his nose as sharp as a stone adze.

He kept his dress of sweet-smelling Tahitian cloth with its patterned border beside him where he could touch it. Tayota's was folded with it. It was shining white with a border of yellow and brown. The Tahitian flute on which Tayota used to play was with the cloth.

Two mornings after Tayota died, Tupia gave me the flute.

"It is for you, Nuna," he said. "Take the cloth to Opana (Mr. Banks). I shall not see King Torata so I shall not need it."

Then he smiled at me and said: "You will come safely out of the dark ship, Nuna."

Now the *Endeavor* seemed like a dark ship to me then, but not so dark as the land.

"They are cleaning the ship, Tupia," I said, "and putting in new wood. Some was worn almost as thin as that." I showed him my thumbnail and, indeed, the carpenter had showed me a plank now barely an eighth of an inch thick.

"She will be as good as new, Tupia," I went on. "The Captain said so. He came to see you yesterday but you were sleeping. We'll soon be at sea again, he says. You will get well in the good air and go to London and see the King."

He only smiled that narrow smile and said, "Not the *Endeavor*, Nuna. Another ship. Another flag. Under the stars."

He never said anything more in English but murmured in Tahitian, names mostly, I think. He died that evening. I took the cloth to Mr. Banks. Dr. Solander was so ill that Mr. Banks was desperate. He said the doctors believed in blistering and bleeding but he thought it only made Dr. Solander worse.

He soaked cinchona bark in water himself and drank the water, he said.

"I drink cinchona water, too," I told him. "That or something has kept me well. I make Duncan and Pambo drink it, too. You should see the faces they make!"

Mr. Banks smiled. "I am getting better," he said, but he looked very ill, so thin and yellow. He grieved much for Tupia. "I should never have let him come," he said. "And poor Tayota. I remember his playing the flute on the deck and the sailors dancing."

"Tupia gave me the flute," I said.

Mr. Banks turned and looked out at the canal with the rain swishing down into it. After a while he said in his kind, courteous way: "If you could spare the time, Nick, we might work a little."

I said that Pambo and Duncan were better and that I would be glad to stay. He had some notes he had made about fruits and flowers here. His illness and Dr. Solander's had prevented their doing much work. I wrote down what he told me, things like: "The edible part of the *Durian* tastes like sugared cream flavored with onions and smells like rotten onions," or "The *Jack* smells like apples mixed with garlic. The taste makes up for the smell."

(That's what he thinks! I think it tastes like a Batavian canal.)

The many kinds of flowers, however, as he said, are fragrant. I drew for him a picture of the *Champacka*, which is yellower than a jonquil, with long, narrow petals and smells a little like a jonquil. Also, I drew the *Sambac*, which is a delicately perfumed jasmine. The women here wear wreaths of jasmine in their hair. It made me think of the women of Tahiti with their wreaths of gardenias. That's what Dr. Solander called the kind of jasmine they had there. They were named for a friend of his, a Dr. Garden, also pupil of Linnaeus, he told me. Some of the Batavia women would have been pretty, only they chew betel so their teeth are black.

Mixtures of petals of all sorts of fragrant flowers are strewn among clothes and in the beds. This is a luxury we could never have at home, Mr. Banks said. "They need something to make you forget how the canals smell," I said.

From the table where I was drawing, I could see the canal. There was a dead pig floating in it. Also three dead hens. The natives throw dead animals, scraps of food, anything they don't want into the canals. I saw a crocodile on the muddy bank waddling down to the water. He seemed interested in the pig.

"At least the crocodiles help clean the place up," I said. "I don't see what we'd do without them."

Mr. Banks said that one of the servants, a Malay girl who helps the cook, had told him that men sometimes have a twin brother who is a crocodile. She said her father had a crocodile twin. He used to go to the river to feed him. When her father was dying, he told her to be sure to feed his twin. He told her what part of the river this crocodile lived in. So she went there and called his name, "Raja Ponti!" which means White King. The crocodile came up out of the water close to the bank and ate what she threw down to him.

She said he was handsomer than other crocodiles, finely marked, and with a scarlet nose. He wore earrings and gold bracelets.

Mr. Banks told her that crocodiles couldn't wear earrings because they didn't have ears.

"Ah," she said, "these twins are different from other crocodiles. They have five toes on their hands and feet and large tongues. Their ears are rather small, it is true, so you might not notice them. But they certainly wear bracelets."

I was writing all this down for Mr. Banks.

I stopped and said, "My grandfather had a crocodile twin and so did my brother."

Mr. Banks stared at me. I suppose he thought I was coming down with fever and beginning to wander in my speech, because he said, "Are you all right, Nick?"

"Oh, yes," I said. "I'm all right, Mr. Banks. You mustn't worry about me."

If we had gone on talking perhaps I would have told him about Sandy and Gilbert but Dr. Solander called out to him just then. Mr. Banks went to him. I put my notes aside finished my drawing, and went back to my tents.

One day soon after this we got news of England from the crew of a Dutch East Indiaman that came into the harbor. They said that in London people were tramping the streets crying "Down with King George! Liberty forever!" And that in America the colonists were refusing to pay taxes without representation in the British parliament. They said that the King had sent large forces of both army and navy to the colonies. England might soon be at war with Spain, too, they said, as well as with America.

When I heard that England might fight America I felt strange to be a midshipman, though only an acting one, on a King's ship. I am wearing a uniform belonging to one of the men who died. My own clothes were outgrown long ago. Pambo measured me against the mainmast. Though not fifteen yet, I am 6 feet and ½ inch in my stockings.

The crew of this Dutch ship that brought the news looked fat and healthy and rosy. We stared at each other as if we were people from different worlds. I remembered how, when we first came to Batavia, there was the crew of an English ship, looking as we look now, like yellow-faced ghosts. We gazed at them with pity as these Dutchmen looked at us. I know now that the sick men looked back pityingly at us, pink-faced though we were then. They knew we would soon look thin and yellow, too.

So, as we talked to these plump, healthy Dutchmen, each pitied the other. They were sorry for what had happened to us. We knew what would happen to them and were sorry, too.

All through November and most of December the Endeavor was being repaired and our men lay sick in the tents. Eight died before we left Batavia, and were buried in that muddy ground. At last the work on the ship was done and the Captain told us we should sail on Christmas Day.

Every one of the ship's company except myself and the old sailmaker, seventy years old or more, had been ill at some time during our stay. Forty men were still sick when we left. The rest were only shadows of the men who had come there. Still everyone gave what strength he had to setting the sails and getting up the anchor. We could not leave the place too quickly.

We all thought that when we got to sea, our troubles would be over but they came with us. Like the mosquitoes, sickness followed us to sea. We could not see how mosquitoes could be on the ship in such swarms but Dr. Solander showed us how they were breeding in the water casks. Duncan and I skimmed them out and dumped them into the sea. At last we were free of them, but not of sickness. Twenty of our company died on the passage from Batavia to Cape of Good Hope. At one time in January there were only eight of us who could keep the deck.

Dr. Solander was very ill all during the voyage. He no longer looked like the plump, cheerful man who came into Mr. Gribble's shop. Mr. Banks had several bad attacks of fever but suddenly recovered. He said he did not know any reason either for the illness or the cure. Fortunately the Captain had only a mild attack of fever in Batavia and none during the voyage. We were lucky, too, in having fair winds and no bad storms.

Still, it took us many long weeks to round the Cape of Good Hope and sail into Table Bay on the Atlantic side of the Cape. We saw fires burning on a mountain called the Lion's Rump and on the top of Table Mountain. Wind came up strong in the night. We could not land for two days.

There were French ships in the harbor. Mr. Banks learned that the French claim that they discovered Tahiti, though we know that Captain Wallis was there in the *Dolphin* before any other European. Mr. Banks said we must get to England as soon as possible and publish our discoveries.

Capetown is a great place for news. It is probably visited by more Europeans than any distant place on the globe because of the many ships that stop here on the way to and from India. News of our discoveries, most of it incorrect, had come here ahead of us, we do not know just how.

We heard here that King George has had to give in to the proposals of the American colonists. All the importation taxes except the one on tea have been taken off. Mr. Banks said he thought the colonists would now be satisfied. I told him that I was afraid they would not like the tax on the tea.

"I'll be glad if there is no war," I said.

"Why, so will I," Mr. Banks said. "There are better things for men to do in this world than fighting each other. I'm glad you see that, Nick."

"It isn't just that, sir," I said. "I meant that if there were a war I couldn't fight against Virginia. And here I am in a King's ship, wearing his uniform, though not properly commissioned."

"Well," he said, "it looks as if we were not going to fight anyone at present. They say here the Spaniards have made peace with us. Perhaps you and I can go on collecting plants for a while."

"I hope so, sir," I said.

I do not see much of him now. He and Dr. Solander, who is still quite ill, live on shore. I live on the ship. I am writing this in the cabin. It has a red cloth on the floor. A seaman washes it with salt water every morning. When it is dry—it dries quickly in the windy weather here—I get to work on my book. It is a catalogue of our dried plants and of those that were ruined by water in New South Wales. I did a great many small sketches of flowers everywhere we went, besides the large pictures I made in Tahiti. I am doing the smaller one over larger for my book. It is a present for Mr. Banks and is a secret. Pambo is the only one who knows.

Because Dr. Solander still needed so much care, we have not explored the country or found any new plants. The vegetables here are mostly from seeds brought from Europe, such as broccoli and asparagus. Apples, pears, and peaches are grown here, too. At the end of one of the main streets is a menagerie with ostriches, antelopes, and zebras. There are also some rare birds. I do not much care to see things in cages.

The natives here are called Hottentots. The men are about as tall as I am, dark-skinned, with thickly curled hair. They dress in skins of sheep or lions or zebras, with belts and necklaces of beads and copper. They are armed with lances, which they poison with cobra venom. They throw stones well. I saw one man strike a dollar at a hundred paces. They are said to train bulls to protect their villages and they can make them fight by certain words and the tone of their voices. This I did not see, but I saw how they managed their ox teams. These oxen have vast, spreading horns. Most traveling to other settlements is done by oxcart and the oxen obey their masters' commands well. There are also other natives called Kaffirs, fine-looking men. I have learned to speak a little with both tribes. Pambo, as usual, can chatter easily in both tongues.

April 14th, 1771. Today we sailed for England.

April 28th. We crossed the zero meridian, so, since London is on it, we have now been all the way around the globe. It does not seem as remarkable as I thought it would. As Pambo said, "Water looks about as wet one side of the line as the other."

I finished the book for Mr. Banks yesterday and gave it to him. He was very pleased. He and Dr. Solander, who is much better now, spent a long time looking at it.

June 5th. I am fifteen today and 6'1 tall. We saw three New England fishing schooners. They were hunting whales. Captain Cook sent me in charge of a boat to buy fish from one of them. They had had no meat but whale meat for a long time. We gave them some beef and they gave us fish. I asked one of the sailors what the news was from America.

"Your king's behaved very ill, but we've brought him to terms, Admiral," he said.

"He's your king as much as mine, I'm from Virginia," I said and asked him if he'd ever been to Portsmouth.

He said yes, but it turned out he meant Portsmouth, New Hampshire. He came from Boston, he said.

The trumpet sounded just then for the boat to go back to the *Endeavor*.

The New Englander said, "Better shed that pretty coat, Admiral, and sail back to Boston with us."

I wished I could but I shoved off and went back to the ship with the four big albacores he let us have.

He said, "See you in Boston someday, Admiral," and I said what John Paul said at Whitehaven: "Where there are ports, men meet. See you in Hampton Roads—or Capetown."

July 4th. Mr. Banks's greyhound, Lady, died last night on the stool in his cabin on which she was sleeping. He sleeps in the great cabin nearby. He and the others who sleep there heard her cry out in the night, but as she was then quiet, no one thought anything of it. Poor Lady, she loved to run about on land. We all felt sad to bury her at sea, for land must be close now.

July 8th. Dead calm. The ship hardly moved. I went out in a boat, fishing. I did not catch anything.

July 9th. I told the Captain I could smell land. He laughed and said I had better go up in the maintop and keep us from running into it.

He said, "We need a red Indian who can see twice as far as a sea eagle up there."

Pambo had told the cook, who told the Captain's servant, who told the Captain, that Pocahontas was my grandmother. Of course, she died, homesick in England, before my grandmother was ever born but I reckon I am sunburned enough now so if I had a tomahawk and a wampum belt, I might pass for an Indian.

I have grown a little tired of jokes about my height and being an Indian. The sailors ask "How is it up there?" or "Is it raining up aloft, sir?" or ask me to lend them my bow and arrow or to smoke a peace pipe with them. There are no very good answers to these remarks.

However, the Captain laughs so seldom that I was glad to hear him. He took such pains to keep us from scurvy, and succeeded, but he had no weapons against those Batavian fevers. He thinks there was more than one kind, but knows no more than I do what caused them.

It was chilly at the masthead. The night was short but seemed long. The ship crept slowly through mist that lay close to the water. From the masthead I could see the Great Bear and Vega shining blue, and Altair with his two companions. When dawn came the fog thickened and I could see nothing. Then a puff of wind blew the fog away. Where it had been there was a darker shadow.

I called, "Land! Land ho!"

I can still hear the feet thudding on the deck and the seaman with me grumbling that I had roused up the ship for a fog bank.

His fog bank was the tip of Cornwall called The Lizard and we had not seen it for almost three years.

CHAPTER 12

SAILING MASTER

THEY LANDED at Deal on July 12th, 1771.

During the two days it took to sail from The Lizard to Deal, Nick tried to decide what he ought to do when they landed. One thing was clear in his mind: when he took off his borrowed uniform with the anchor buttons, it would be for good. It was only through the kindness of Mr. Banks that he had ever worn it. It was because of Mr. Banks that Captain Cook had made him an acting midshipman and it was Mr. Banks who would pay Nick and Pambo when the voyage was over, as he did for so many of the expenses of the expedition.

Nick would always be grateful, he thought, to Mr. Banks for taking him and Pambo away from Mr. Gribble's shop and giving them a chance to see the world. Mr. Banks had spoken of Nick's staying in England and working for him.

But England is not my country, Nick thought.

Every time he had heard talk of war with the colonies, he had felt like a traitor to be wearing a British uniform. The New Englander on the whaling ship had made him feel this more sharply than ever before.

Yet, as the end of the voyage came closer, going back to Virginia seemed more and more difficult. He had never written. He had tried to more than once, but had always dropped the pen before he began. What could he say? That the man they knew as Sandy was really Gilbert—the crocodile twin as, since Batavia, Nick always called him? If it were Gilbert, he would find ways to make Nick, not himself, look like a liar, a thief, a false claimant to the Caryl estate with a ridiculous story. If it really were Sandy, suspicion would be unjustly aroused against him. And Nick had never been quite sure that Pambo had been right about the events of that strange night.

Yet there were things that made him think the story must be true. Would Sandy, he kept asking himself, the Sandy he knew in Virginia, have left his brother sick of a fever, to die perhaps in a strange country, and taken ship for Virginia?

No—Nick thought sadly, as he always did when he came to this part of the puzzle—no, the Sandy he knew would not have done it. But had Sandy changed? Or was he, in spite of his satin and lace, his quizzing glass, his elegant snuffbox, his fashionable chatter, still the kind brother who used to carry Nick on his back through the maze?

As the *Endeavor* entered the harbor at Deal, Nick made his decision. He must know the truth and to know it he must go to Virginia. If it was Gilbert at Caryl's Maze, the estate was rightfully Nick's. He would not leave the crocodile twin to ruin it by neglect or gamble it away—if he had not already done so. If the real Sandy was there, perhaps the influence of the old place, of his uncle and aunt, of McFarland the overseer, of Mrs. Ashton and Cherry might have brought him back to his old self. Then Nick would be glad.

He would have his fortune to seek, but that had always

been so. He would find it at sea, which was kinder than the land. Like many sailors, Nick had learned to dread land, not water. A ship in the open sea had a chance even in the worst storms. The greatest dangers were from hidden rocks, from being driven on a lee shore, from the people who lived on the shore. The worst things that had happened to Nick had not happened at sea.

I'm big enough and strong enough to face Gilbert, he thought, looking down at his brown wrists. The sleeves of the borrowed coat were already too short. He must buy some new clothes as soon as Mr. Banks paid him, he thought.

Once more he thought of telling his story to Mr. Banks but once more he decided to keep silent. Except for Pambo's word, there was no evidence that the story was true. Mr. Banks liked Pambo, who had learned to shave him beautifully even when the sea was rough. He had never even nicked him, Mr. Banks said. Pambo kept Mr. Banks's wavy hair well brushed and with just the right touch of powder. He smoothed his bushy eyebrows and made a neat job of shaving what Mr. Banks called "this confounded cleft in my chin." Still, a steady hand with a razor was not evidence of the truth of anything.

No, Nick decided, he would not tell this story of disgrace and treachery and murder to Mr. Banks. He would feel sure of the truth first and the truth was in Virginia. If it is really Sandy at Caryl's Maze, he thought, I'll come back to England and go on another voyage with Mr. Banks. No navy uniform this time. Perhaps we'll find our continent and new animals as strange as kangaroos, he thought. I'll be his secretary and help take care of the plants. Pambo can be his valet.

Pambo, Nick thought, had better stay in England. If Gilbert were at Caryl's Maze, Pambo would be in worse danger than

Nick would. Gilbert might prove Nick to be a liar and a cheat but he could hardly sell him as a slave, but poor Pambo—

Mr. Banks came along the deck just then. Nick told him that he had decided to take the first ship he could get for Virginia.

"But I'll leave Pambo, sir. You need him, I know."

Mr. Banks laughed. He was fresh from Pambo's hands, his queue neatly tied with a new ribbon, his rosy cheeks smoothly shaven.

He said: "Oh, I can't do without Pambo. I need you too, Nick, but I expect you're hungry for Virginia ham. Come back as soon as you can. We might go to Iceland. And Dr. Solander wants to see Sweden again. There are plenty of plants we haven't found yet."

"Thank you, sir," Nick said. "I'd like to go on another voyage with you."

He tried to thank Mr. Banks for all his kindness but Mr. Banks only said, "Nonsense. Let's not speak of it. You did just as much for me." He started to walk on, then turned back, saying, "You'll go right ashore, I suppose? Feet itching for the land? Well, I feel a little that way myself. I've even begun to think of roast beef!"

"I'm going to buy some clothes big enough for me," Nick said. "I can just about move in these."

Mr. Banks laughed and said, "You'll need money, then. Here, take this. It's all I have now. I'll give you the rest when we get ashore. Come back and show me your new suit."

"Yes, sir, I'll do that, and thank you," Nick said, taking the gold pieces Mr. Banks put in his hand.

But Mr. Banks never saw Nick in his new dark blue coat and buff waistcoat and breeches.

Duncan had found the shop. It was a secondhand clothing shop. They could not go to a tailor's where it would take several days to make a suit. One of the other midshipmen had told them about the shop. They found the clothes clean and in good condition. Nick bought clothes for him and Pambo and Duncan. Mr. Banks had not paid Pambo yet and Duncan had only a ticket from the purser. It would have to be presented to the paymaster at the Navy Yard. Nick and Duncan bought sensible dark clothes with room to grow in them. Pambo, however, could not decide between a tight coat of an especially violent shade of purple and one of sky-blue with scarlet facings.

Nick left him making up his mind.

"Take my old clothes back to the ship, Pambo. Mr. McTavish and I will walk around and see the town. I'll see you later," Nick said, not guessing how much later it would be.

The four years that followed were not years Nick cared to remember in detail.

The press gang came into the inn where he and Duncan were eating roast beef and Yorkshire pudding. It always annoyed Nick that he had not finished his beef. There was still a fine, juicy slice on his plate.

The head of the press gang began by stating that they were two hearty young men who looked as if they'd like to see the world. Duncan jumped up, scowling, and said that they'd seen it.

In the fight that followed, Nick was knocked on the head. Three days later he woke up in a dark, stifling place that proved to be the forecastle of a British Indiaman. He was not treated with special cruelty on the ship. Having decided he would not wear a British uniform, he did not claim to have been an acting midshipman on the *Endeavor*. He signed the ship's articles by which he promised to obey the officers. He was soon recognized by the boatswain as a good foremast hand. He obeyed

orders without grumbling. He was never flogged, never put on short rations.

Yet life on the *Princess Anne* was very different from being on the *Endeavor*. She carried a large crew. Her officers, whose handsomely furnished cabins Nick heard described but never even saw, walked the decks like another race of human beings. If they knew the crew were human, too, they gave no sign of it. Unlike Captain Cook, they took no interest in whether the men had scurvy or not. The rations were the regulation salt beef, salt fish, and ship's biscuit with rancid cheese and worse butter. The purser, who supplied the provisions, must have made plenty of money out of the contract.

The *Princess Anne* was a much bigger ship than the *Endeavor*. With her high poop and forecastle she was like pictures of ships of Queen Elizabeth's time. Sir Francis Drake might have sailed in her. If he had, he would doubtless have found ways to improve her. She was a slow, clumsy, lumbering ship to sail. She seemed tired of the sea. Probably she was. Nick never knew whether she ever reached India. He was blown overboard one night when the foremast cracked and fell into the sea in a gale off the east coast of Africa.

It was a long swim, but, with the aid of a broken spar, he reached land safely. Some of the kindest people he ever met, Nick wrote, were those cannibals on the east coast of Africa.

"I suppose," Nick used to say, "they thought I was too tough and stringy to eat. They ate only their enemies. After they had squeezed the salt water out of me and fed me, they felt I was their friend. They shared their food with me, fish, yams, birds shot with bows and arrows, on great occasions roast pig."

During the year and a half he spent with the cannibals, Nick became a good shot with a bow and a not very good spearer of fish. The skill with which the Africans judged through shifting water the place where a fish would be the next minute was always a marvel to him. Luckily, he had something that was a wonder to them—a folding two-bladed pocketknife. His very first day on shore he spent carving a top out of a piece of driftwood. He made it for the chief's oldest son, a small, fuzzy-headed, bronze-skinned little boy who reminded him of Pambo.

Nick was sorry he had lost the new blue and buff clothes he had worn only two hours but he knew he was lucky that he was washed overboard in clothes from the *Princess Anne's* slop chest. The striped jersey was comfortable. The flapping trousers had useful things in the pockets. There were bits of string, a small pocket compass, a bright red handkerchief, two nails, the hull of a tiny ship with scraps of cloth to make sails for it.

He had been carving it out of a piece of bone the day the storm had broken over the *Princess Anne*. He gave one of the nails to the chief and the handkerchief to his wife. He finished the ship for the chief's daughter. He rather enjoyed working on it in a circle of dark faces, with eyeballs and white teeth flashing, as his new friends admired his skill. The other nail he concealed between his fingers and made the compass needle move with it. This was evidently considered magic. No one offered to touch the compass, though exhibitions of his power over it were often requested. He had learned a little of the Kaffir language in Capetown. This tribe spoke in a way not very different. He could soon understand them and be understood. He liked them.

They kept me [Nick wrote later] as a sort of pet, much as they might have kept a lion cub or a pet monkey. They boasted to visitors of my cleverness. I was always shown off at my carving or making the compass needle spin or drawing portraits in the sand. I would draw the chief with his beads and lion skin, his sharply filed teeth and the tattoo marks on his face. Gainsborough never painted anything so popular, I'm sure. I never heard that any of Gainsborough's patrons ever rolled on the ground or turned somersaults or stood on their heads. My sitters did and were so pleased that I had put in their tattooed dots and crosses correctly that I was often given an extra piece of roast pig. Sometimes when I had drawn an especially fine likeness, the chief's son and I would make a frame for it out of shells. When wind or rain or footprints spoiled the picture I could always make a new one and find the materials for the frame again. We used to give the ladies in our pictures shell necklaces and shells in their lips. This was a fashion among the upper classes of that tribe.

Nick was—he wrote—almost sorry when he woke up one morning after a fierce gale and saw a ship anchored in the bay and a boat with water casks coming toward the shore.

His African friends saw the guns with which the sailors were armed and fled into the jungle. Evidently they had seen white men before. These men were Dutch but spoke some English. They told Nick he was on the coast of Mozambique. To Nick's disappointment they were bound not for Holland but for India. Still a ship, any ship, would start him on his way to Virginia. He found the chief and gave him the compass as a sign of gratitude. He helped the Dutch seamen fill the water casks. In an hour he was signed as a foremasthand on the ship *Amsterdam* and learning the Dutch names for sails and rigging. He cruised in the *Amsterdam* more than two years without finding a chance to take ship either for England or America. They arrived at the Texel in Holland with a cargo of spices, chintz, silks, and porcelain dishes on April 19th, 1775.

What Nick heard in *Amsterdam* made him more anxious than ever to get back to Virginia. King George and his American colonists were still at odds. British soldiers had killed people in the streets of Boston. That was in 1770 but it had not quieted the people of that rebellious city. Only last December, men dressed like Indians had gone aboard East India Company ships and dumped the tea—on which there was a British tax— into Boston Harbor. They called this riot the Boston Tea Party.

"There'll be war if there's not war already. Might be fighting now for all I know," Nick heard a man say in the clean little Dutch inn where he was eating his first meal ashore.

The speaker, a long, lank man with salt-water stains on his blue jacket, had never learned to speak English in England, Nick knew.

"Are you from Boston, sir?" he asked.

"John Hicks, brig *Sea Otter*, Portsmouth, New Hampshire," the man said.

"I'm Nick Young, Portsmouth, Virginia. Just off the *Amsterdam*."

"Shake hands, neighbor. Long at sea?" Mr. Hicks asked.

"Quite a while," Nick said.

"Noticed the floor was still going up and down under your feet. Guess you know your lines, son?"

"Yes, sir."

"Know anything about navigation?"

"A little, sir."

"Ready to sail for Portsmouth when I get my cheese aboard?"

"Yes, sir."

"Finished your dinner?"

"Yes, sir."

"Well, what are we waiting for?" inquired Captain Hicks.

The *Sea Otter* was a smart, freshly painted, briskly moving ship. Her sailing master had died of a lung fever on the voyage to Holland, Captain Hicks said. His mate became the master and Nick the master's mate.

The first part of the voyage went quickly. Off the Grand Banks the wind dropped and for two days they barely moved. One calm May evening a fishing schooner hailed them and her captain came aboard. He brought some fresh cod with him. His name was Thomas Poole, he said.

Captain Hicks gave him some Edam cheese and some sticks of cinnamon and asked if there were any news.

"Guess we licked the British at Lexington, Concord, too," Captain Poole said. "Heard their tongues was hanging out of their mouths all the way to Boston."

"We fighting the British?" Captain Hicks inquired calmly.

"Eyah. Guess so. Some."

"Guessed we would sooner or later. Needed to. Seems as though."

"Eyah. Guess the price of fish will go up. Cheese too," Captain Poole remarked.

"Liable to," said Captain Hicks.

"Trim little craft you have. Make a real neat privateer," Captain Poole suggested. "Few more guns. Just occurred to me."

"Occurred to me, too," Captain Hicks said.

"You headed for Boston?"

"Portsmouth," Captain Hicks stated.

"Might get into Portsmouth all right. Boston's kind of congested. Frigates. Bluecoats. Gold lace. Redcoats ashore. Thought I'd mention it."

"Much obliged."

They got safely into Portsmouth, New Hampshire. This was no time for his private affairs, Nick realized. When the *Sea Otter*, fitted with extra guns, went to sea, he went with her. Captain Hicks needed him, for his sailing master had left to become captain of a privateer of his own.

"Guess you're the master now," Captain Hicks said to Nick.

The *Sea Otter* sailed July 1st, 1775, with probably the proudest sailing master on the coast of America at her helm.

It was late August and they were off the coast of Nova Scotia when they heard of the Declaration of Independence. The news came to them from the captain of one of their prizes, a British ship carrying lumber, bound for Liverpool.

"Not that this sort of thing is going to last long," the British captain told them. "His Majesty can't allow it, you know. Really."

Neither Nick nor Captain Hicks made any reply to this remark. Later, when they were captured in their turn, they were glad they had had practice in holding their tongues. It was in September of 1776 that they lost their ship.

CHAPTER 13

SLOOPS AND FRIGATES

NIGHTS WERE already growing cold in those northern waters. They tried to give the enemy the slip but they were within range of her guns on a lee shore. They fought as long as they could in an afternoon that grew always darker and stormier. They were no match for the British frigate and their guns were soon silenced. She was called the *Milford*, a name Nick was always to remember.

Of their defeat he wrote:

The black storm that seemed at first our enemy proved after all to be our friend. We already knew we were beaten but perhaps we might still have escaped in the darkness if our mainmast had not been shot down. The wind, by this time grown into a howling gale from the east, was carrying us rapidly toward a rocky shore. Probably the *Milford* liked the look of it no better than we did for she did not come alongside to take possession of us but shortened sail and tacked out to sea.

Her captain, I suppose, knew that we must soon be wrecked and did not choose to run the chance of being driven on the rocks himself. So at least we were not taken prisoners. We were tossed along, spun first one way, then another, by waves that boiled up white out of the darkness. It seemed sure that we would be dashed to pieces on the rocks but Captain Hicks succeeded in beaching her—though we could feel rocks grind along her sides—in a small cove between two high, rocky points like fortresses.

Luckily, the tide soon started to ebb and we did not break up that night. Morning showed us a sparkling, heaving blue sea, breaking white on the jagged ledges we had driven between. We were afloat, though low in the water. The rocks we had scraped over in the darkness had started some leaks. Worse than that, we had received several shots close to the water line. Any wave a little bigger than the others splashed in through these, though we kept the pumps going to give the carpenter a chance to mend them. The beach, what there was of it, was only a steep wall of pebbles ground smooth by the great tides of that coast. There was no safe space to heave the ship down.

The carpenter did the best he could but still the water in the hold grew deeper. The wind, a light breeze now from the southwest, would have helped us if we had dared to tow her out of the cove but she leaked too badly for that.

"Guess we'll unload cargo, stow it in there," Captain Hicks said, nodding toward a cave in the rocks above high water. He went below to take another look at the leaks.

It was just then that I saw the sloop. She was running along briskly before the wind. Our gunner, Buxton Pratt, had a spyglass in his hand. As I called out "Ship ahoy!" he turned the glass on her.

Buxton had served on the *Alfred* in our navy when she

captured powder at Nassau and later when she fought the British ship *Glasgow*.

He called out excitedly: "She's the *Providence*. I vum. Captain Paul Jones!"

Now I had heard him talk a great deal of this Captain Jones. Buxton had served under him on the *Alfred*. She was the flagship of a fleet that included the *Columbus*, the *Cabot*, the *Andrew Doria*, and the *Providence*. Commander Hopkins, the highest officer in the Navy, was in command of the *Alfred* and of the fleet but, to hear Buxton tell it, the only good fighting was done by the *Alfred's* lower main battery under command of Lieutenant Jones, as he then was. Of course, he was helped by Buxton Pratt.

During the battle with the *Glasgow*, Jones did not direct his shots at her hull, as was the British custom, but at her masts and rigging. He soon made her almost unmanageable.

"You saw what that did to us last night," Buxton said, passing me the spyglass, "though I'll always say they were aiming for the hull, not the mast. A lucky shot, that's what I'll always say. (He always did.) Now, when Paul Jones hits something, he's *aimed* at it. That I'll swear to. Better call the Captain, Nick, for here's our chance to get out of this nest of rocks. I swear yon's the *Providence!*"

The sloop of war was flying British colors and Captain Hicks, when he came on deck, was of a mind to let her pass without attracting her attention, but Buxton was so insistent that at last the Captain sent him and me up to the top of one of the cliffs with our American jack to wave. The flag was like the British union jack, only striped red and white instead of plain red.

Buxton talked all the time as I stood waving it. He told how the battle with the *Glasgow* ended.

"Away she went," he said, "under all the sail she could set, yelping from the mouths of her cannon like a broken-legged dog, as a signal of being badly wounded. She got away from all five of us and safe into Newport. Our squadron had to haul wind and get our prizes into New London. There was an inquiry and Lieutenant Jones was one of the few officers whose conduct got praise, not blame. That's how he came to be Captain of the *Providence* and I bet a pile of Rhode Island jonnycake against a dead sea urchin that we're looking at her... There, see! She's hauling up her American jack. And do you know who first hauled up that flag on an American ship?"

I did, but I let him tell me again.

"It was Paul Jones on the *Alfred* first put the striped jack in the air. A stripe for each of the thirteen colonies. The flag of freedom. That was in December '75. I was there on the deck of the *Alfred*. Next month we had Commodore Hopkins' own flag. Yellow it was, with a coiled rattlesnake and the words 'Don't tread on me!' Though if all rattlers did as little damage as Hopkins is like to do to the British, I'd dance a hornpipe with one for my partner... See, Nick, she's hove to... She's sending a boat... You'll see Captain Jones..."

I had folded the flag by this time [Nick wrote] and I was looking not at the ship but at the boat crossing the water between ship and shore. She would climb over the top of one big, silky blue wave and then slide down into the hollow as smoothly as Sandy's horse, Barbary, would leap a five-barred gate at Caryl's Maze. When the stern of the boat was at the crest of the wave, I could see the officer at the tiller. Something about the way his cocked hat was shoved back on his head and to the side, showing red hair, made my pulse beat fast.

Buxton had the glass at his eye. As the boat climbed the top of the biggest wave yet, he screeched: "Suffering cats and tinker mackerel—it's him!"

"Captain Jones?" I asked, not daring to say what I was hoping.

"Lobsters and porcupines, no! Though he's on the ship, no fear. Yon's McTavish—one of Satan's own imps. Oh, I've tales to tell of that one on the *Alfred*, all right! It was he stole gunpowder and..."

But he had no chance to finish, for I had the speaking trumpet to my mouth and was yelling, "Duncan ahoy! The model boy!"

I climbed so fast down that fortress cliff, hanging by my fingernails, that I was on the beach when the keel of the boat grated on the pebbles. Duncan did not bother about wet feet but dashed through the water, calling, "Nick—Nick Young!"

I hugged him, swinging him off his feet, and he gasped out: "Stop breaking my ribs, you old man Kangaroo!"

I put him down and he stared up at me, stared up quite a distance, for he was under six feet tall and I maybe half a foot higher.

"Nick—Nick Young!" he said again. "Where have you been? But we'll talk later. I must do my errand."

His errand was to see how badly the *Sea Otter* was damaged and to report to Captain Jones what help her captain needed. The poor *Sea Otter* was well down in the water by then and sinking deeper.

"Could be mended if she could be hove down. Only beach slopes too steep, tide runs in and out too strong. Guess we'd better put our cargo aboard the *Providence* and figure we're lucky, I vum!" Captain Hicks said.

This is a New England way of saying "I vow" and is as near as the Captain ever came to swearing. Sometimes he also said

"I snum," which means, I think, that he is surprised and not much pleased. He said it when the *Milford* sent a cannon ball into our port side and tore a hole the size of a hornet's nest in it. "Hit us to port, I snum," he said, I remember.

We spent the rest of the morning shipping our cargo out to the *Providence.* My work was to see that everything was got out of the *Sea Otter* and loaded into the boats. There is a tide of fourteen feet or more on that coast. It runs out so fast that the *Sea Otter* was already aground again when we left her, canted to port among the rocks with the water running out of the holes in her side.

Poor Captain Hicks was alongside us in his own boat. It's a melancholy thing for a man to lose his ship, especially if he is convinced it is not necessary.

"I believe we could still save her, Nick," he had said mournfully two or three times that morning, "but that Captain Jones is such a cayenne-pepper and horse-radish sort of man, I snum!"

"I'm curious to see your captain," I said to Duncan, who had come to take me on the last trip. I had loaded in my sea chest last of all. I had to leave behind the silks I had bought in India for Aunt Dorothy and Mrs. Ashton and Cherry.

"Why, you know him," Duncan said. "Don't you know who he is? Did I not tell you? Why, it's just our John Paul from Kircudbright!"

"John Paul!" I said. "Of the brig *John*? But why does he call himself Jones?"

"Ah, if you knew that, you'd know the answer to a mystery," Duncan said. "Some say a tale of murder and piracy lies behind the change. Others say he changed his name when he changed his country out of compliment to an American benefactor named Jones. All I know is I'm not brave enough to ask him."

"I wonder if he'll know me?" I said.

Duncan snapped his fingers.

"I'll wager five shillings he does. He knew me though I was only a small boy climbing about the wharves of Kircudbright when he left there. He forgets no one and nothing. He'll know your face, your name, and where you came from. You'll see."

"I doubt if he will," I said. "It's too long ago."

But it was not too long for John Paul Jones. He was moving about on the deck, directing the placing of the guns. It had been necessary during the gale to clear the decks of all movable equipment. Now it was being replaced. The Captain's active, slightly round-shouldered figure had changed very little since I saw him walk off into the fog at Whitehaven that November morning. Perhaps his face looked a little more weather-beaten, perhaps the heavy line between his eyebrows had deepened slightly, but I would have known him anywhere.

He looked up at me for the time it takes to open an oyster. Then—"Good morning, Mr. Caryl," he said courteously in that deep, grave voice of his. "I am happy to welcome you to the *Providence*. You must sup with me tonight in my cabin and tell me where you have been since you set out in that Scotch mist for Caryl's Mount."

Then he smiled suddenly and reeled off a string of numbers, at which I smiled too, and said, "Oceans are wide but in all their ports men meet."

He looked pleased.

"Even in harbors as small as this one," he said.

Then Captain Hicks came aboard and Captain Jones began giving orders to get the *Providence* under way.

"For," he remarked to Captain Hicks, "unless we want your friend the *Milford* to come back and shoot us like a sitting duck, we had best be on our way." Some of his crew were out in a boat, fishing. They were called back and just as they came alongside, a man in the maintop called down that there was a sail to windward.

"I think it's the *Milford*, sir," he said.

It was the *Milford*, her sails shining in the morning sun. We were moving under full sail before she saw us. When she did, she came straight for us.

"Most good-natured of her captain," said Captain Jones. "Saves me the trouble of chasing her. We'll just try her speed."

When the *Milford* came within cannon shot, it was soon clear that the trim little *Providence*, though no match in guns, was much the faster sailer. When he was sure of this, John Paul Jones shortened sail, keeping just out of range but close enough so that he tempted the *Milford* to waste powder and shot.

We led her on a fine wild-goose chase. She fired many times, often at twice the proper distance. It was a sort of mock engagement which went on from before noon until darkness. The crew were all laughing and joking as they worked the sails to keep the *Providence* always out of danger but near enough to the frigate to seem like a possible target.

Early in this play-battle she rounded and sent a whole broadside toward us, the shot all splashing into the sea as harmless as dolphins. Captain Jones shoved a loaded musket into my hands and ordered me to reply with a single shot.

This went on—our crew roaring with laughter, puffs of smoke from the *Milford*, cannon balls splashing, the musket sounding like a popgun—until John Paul tired of the sport and vanished into the night under full sail.

What an evening that was in John Paul's cabin over our supper of fresh-caught fish and Rhode Island jonnycake! The

Captain said little but made Duncan and me tell our adventures. He laughed over my drawing portraits of cannibals in the sand and said I must do one of him someday. I have tried many times to take his likeness but nothing without motion gives an idea of him. From Duncan I heard how, when we were both caught by the press gang, he had the good fortune to be taken on board a ship bound for America.

He landed at Boston, a town of hills and crooked streets curved around a great harbor full of islands, with a green pasture for cows in the middle of the town. He ran away from the ship and to be safe from being dragged back to her again, trudged out to the country town of Brookline. There he became a serving man at the Punch Bowl Tavern. For a wonder he did not run away from it for years.

"There was no need," he said. "To go either north or west of Boston you had to pass the Punch Bowl. The world passed our door—and stopped at it, too. Our sign was a great blue and white punch bowl under a lemon tree. There were few who could resist stopping for a glass of our famous punch. I stayed till a man named Dawes rode past one April night and told us the British were marching out to Lexington and that, while most had crossed the river, some would come our way."

"Did you see the lobster-backs go by?" Captain Hicks asked.

"No," Duncan said. "I was waiting for them behind a tree in Concord."

"Hit any?"

"Guess not. Might have made some of 'em walk a little faster. Never was much of a shot. Got a little homesick for the sea that day. Hot day, dusty. Thought I'd better join the Navy. So as soon as there was a Navy I did. And here we all are. Happy days!" Duncan said.

And those were happy days indeed for me. To be with John Paul again, to be with Duncan and hear his tales of the Boston Tea Party, the Concord fight, and of the Battle of Bunker Hill made the years since I had seen them both melt away to nothing. They were busy days, too. Later that week we burned an English schooner, sank another, and made a prize of a third in Canso Bay. Then our captain headed for the Island of Madame where he frightened more than three hundred fishermen into giving up their ships. Although they so greatly outnumbered us that with leadership they could easily have chased us away, he persuaded them to rig and fit out the ships he wanted as prizes. He had pity on them and left them enough ships and provisions to get home. In less than seven weeks he manned and sent in eight prizes, burned and sank at least as many, and destroyed the fisheries at Canso and Madame. He would have brought in more prizes if it had not been for fierce gales and bitter cold.

There was no loss of life in all this cruise.

"I am glad it is so," he said to me. "And it will serve, I hope, to show the British they are not the only ones who can burn towns, though they seldom do so without killing someone."

He had been speaking of Lord Dunmore, of how he had burned not only ships but also houses and plantations in Virginia. Many a night I woke, dreaming I had seen flames glaring from the windows of Caryl's Maze and a face that might be Sandy's with the firelight red on it.

"I wish I were where I could fight them," I said.

He gave me one of those long, piercing looks of his that seemed to understand not only the words I spoke but the thoughts behind them as well.

"Stay with us, Mr. Caryl," he said. "I promise you that we

shall not always run away, not always answer broadsides with a single musket."

I believed him. I stayed and became one of his midshipmen.

John Paul Jones was soon to keep his promise to me.

We were back in the port of Providence, Rhode Island, on October 7th, 1776. When we set out again it was in the *Alfred*. By the 12th of November we had taken the *Mellish*, the most valuable prize captured by any American ship up to that time.

The *Mellish* was a large vessel, fully armed and carrying military supplies, among them ten thousand complete uniforms for the armies of General Burgoyne and General Carleton. She had marines and soldiers on board yet she surrendered to the *Alfred* after a short engagement.

I used to copy letters for Captain Jones and I remember one he wrote to John Hancock in which he said, "The loss of the *Mellish* will distress the enemy more than can be easily imagined as the clothing on board of her is the last intended to be sent out to Canada this season. The situation of Burgoyne's army will soon become insupportable. I will not lose sight of a prize of such importance but will sink her rather than suffer her to fall into their hands."

We next raided the coast of Nova Scotia, burning oil warehouses belonging to the fisheries and another well-loaded transport ship close to shore. In a thick fog we captured four ships of a convoy and a sixteen-gun British privateer. Icebound harbors kept us from what our captain most wished to do. There were at least a hundred American prisoners in the coal mines of Cape Breton and he had planned to rescue them. He had great sympathy for prisoners and he was grieved that it was too late to carry out his plan.

He said, looking fiercely grim, "Nevertheless, I shall empty British prisons before I have done."

When he spoke in that way, I never doubted that he would do as he promised.

By this time our food and water were running low. We had reduced the crew of the *Alfred* to man out our prizes and had taken many prisoners from the prizes aboard our ship. Winter was at hand, the days were short, the nights dark and stormy. It was time to get the prizes, especially the *Mellish*, into port.

We were slipping along under a fresh breeze off George's Bank late one afternoon when, from the maintop, I saw a sail in the distance. I thought it was our old friend the *Milford*, and so it was. With our crew so divided among the prizes and our ship crowded with prisoners, we were in no trim to fight her. Most captains would merely have crammed on sail and escaped in the gathering darkness but John Paul Jones was determined to protect his prizes, especially the *Mellish*.

"She'll not come up with us before tonight," he said. "We'll trick her."

He summoned Lieutenant Saunders, whom he had put in command of the captured sixteen-gun ship, to a conference and told him his plan.

"I'll lead the *Milford* away from the convoy," he said. "I shall hang out lanterns which will appear like signals for you and the convoy to follow me. You will pay no attention. Keep to windward of the convoy on your present course. Crowd on all sail and see that the prizes do the same. If you do not see me in the morning, make the best of your way to Boston. Guard the *Mellish*. Sink her rather than let her be captured."

In the thickening darkness the *Milford* slowly came up with us. At midnight she was nearly within range of our guns.

We tacked, having first hung out a top light, apparently as a signal to the convoy to follow us. Actually it was a decoy for the *Milford*. The poor old tub set every sail and lumbered after us as fast as she could. When morning came she was not far away from us but the convoy had all vanished over the horizon.

Squally weather, followed by a storm, made it possible for Captain Jones to vanish from almost under the *Milford*'s guns. She did not fire on us this time but her gun ports were open and we could see her batteries ready for action and lighted up. Our captain would have liked to fight it out with her—I could see that—but his first duty was to see that the *Mellish* got safely to port. We turned south and headed for Boston.

We arrived in mid-December. We had barely enough food for two days left. The convoy, including the *Mellish*, had all reached port safely. The news that there would soon be ten thousand uniforms and other supplies for his troops instead of for the British reached General Washington just before he crossed the Delaware.

John Paul Jones had accomplished more against the British with the *Providence* and the *Alfred* than the Commodore of the Navy and most of the other captains put together. It was planned to give him a better ship but it was not until June of 1777 that he was put in command of the American sloop of war *Ranger*. The *Ranger* was not yet finished. She was being built at Portsmouth, New Hampshire, and was designed to sail fast and to carry eighteen six-pounders. By a coincidence that Jones always remembered, Congress appointed him captain of the *Ranger* on the same day, June 14th, that it resolved: That the flag of the United States be thirteen stripes, alternate red and white; that the union be thirteen stars, white on a blue field.

He had raised the first American flag ever flown to the masthead of the *Alfred*. Now the new flag would fly above him as he sailed the *Ranger*. He was not, however, the first to display it, for it took months before she was ready for sea.

One of the difficulties ahead of him was recruiting a crew. There were so many American privateers at sea that it was hard to find sailors for Navy ships. There was more chance for prize money in privateers than in the Navy, and less danger. Not all Americans were as patriotic as the Scottish-born captain of the *Ranger*.

During the months while the *Ranger* was being made ready for sea, Captain Jones often sent Nick and Duncan out on recruiting expeditions. They were supplied with posters which they would nail up in roadside taverns.

Once they went to Boston.

GREAT ENCOURAGEMENT FOR SEAMEN, the poster said in fine, large letters. There were pictures of ships and of sailors armed with cutlasses. It announced that all gentlemen seamen who had a mind to distinguish themselves in a glorious cause and make their fortunes might find such an opportunity on the ship *Ranger*, twenty-one guns, commanded by CAPTAIN JOHN PAUL JONES, ESQ. They would find the ship in Portsmouth, New Hampshire.

The announcement promised that any gentlemen volunteers who had a mind for an agreeable voyage in this pleasant season of the year would meet with civility and each would be rewarded according to his merit. All reasonable traveling expenses would be paid, it said, and advance money paid to seamen to be deducted from their future prize money. The bill was dated in Congress, March 29th, 1777, and signed by John Hancock.

The *Ranger* [Nick wrote] missed sailing in the pleasant season of the year. There were delays about her sails and guns. The gentlemen volunteers hung around Portsmouth until November 1st. Captain Jones advanced money for their expenses out of his own pocket. When we left we carried dispatches to Dr. Franklin about Burgoyne's surrender.

When we got back, bringing several volunteers with us, she was almost ready to sail. She was a fine-looking ship. I said, "She looks as if she would sail fast, Captain Jones."

He smiled and said, "Yes, Mr. Caryl, she'll sail fast, which is fortunate, for *I intend to go in harm's way.*"

CHAPTER 14

THE "*RANGER*" TAKES A CRUISE

IN BOSTON Nick bought a new book in which to keep his journal. On October 31st, 1777, he wrote:

We hope to sail tomorrow. I am doing writing for J.P.J. almost every day. I have just copied a letter of his to the marine committee. In it he said, "With all my industry I could not get a single set of sails completed until October 20th. Since that time, the winds and weather have laid me under the necessity of continuing in port. At this time it blows hard from the N.E. The ship with difficulty rides it out, with yards and topmast struck, and whole cables ahead. When it clears up, I expect wind from the N.W. and shall not fail to embrace it, although I have not now a spare sail, nor materials to make one. Some of those I have are made of Hessings (a thin, coarse stuff)."

November 1st. We slipped our moorings this morning, crowded on all sail and set out across the Atlantic.

November 15th. We are lucky in our weather—fair winds, blue skies, blue and white water.

December 2nd. We reached Nantes on the Loire in France

today. We saw few ships. Captain Jones trained us in loading and pointing our guns. We went through the exercise many times, sometimes at night, doing everything except lighting our matches and putting them to the touchhole. Buxton Pratt is on my crew and I have learned from him how to give all eleven commands in what he says is Real Navy Style. I work in the tops also at times and prefer it. I hate being between decks. It feels like a prison.

Lieutenant Simpson, a sullen oaf of a man, grumbled at being called from his cabin for gun practice. Nothing J.P.J. does is right in his eyes. All S. is interested in is prize money. He says he should have gone on a privateer, where all the money from prizes is divided among the officers and crew. On a Navy ship the government gets half the prize money. Besides, it is more dangerous to fight British frigates than to take helpless merchant ships. Simpson sees no sense in running into danger.

He cannot understand a man like the Captain. As I have written letters for him and talked with him many times, I know that Captain Jones would like prize money, too. So would I. So would we all. But he cares most for honor and glory, to be known, to do great things. He wants liberty, not just for himself—for people everywhere, especially for prisoners rotting in coal mines, on British ships, in the Black Holes of Forton Prison in Portsmouth, England and of Mill Prison in Plymouth. He hates the very thought of men shut away from air and sunshine, as I do. Also he loves the sea and his ship, loves to handle her with the great skill he has.

I think his proudest moment was at Quiberon Bay.

When we saw the French ships of war lying at anchor in the bay, Captain Jones said, "I'll see that I get a salute from the Admiral."

"What's the use of that?" said Lieutenant Simpson.

"The use of it, Mr. Simpson," the Captain said, keeping his temper, "is that if an admiral of France salutes our flag, it will show the world that France recognizes our government as independent."

So the Captain sent his boat—Duncan was in charge of it—with a letter to Admiral LaMotte Piquet. The letter announced that the *Ranger* was anxious to salute the Admiral and asked if he would return gun for gun. The Admiral replied that he would return to Captain Jones, as senior American officer in French waters, the same salute he was ordered to give to the Admiral of Holland or any other republic. This would be four less guns than the number given.

Captain Jones was disappointed not to have gun for gun but he decided to be content with what he could get. There was a stiff breeze blowing out of the bay. Before the *Ranger* could work herself near enough to salute the Admiral, it was after sunset.

We fired thirteen guns. The smoke and the twilight almost hid LaMotte Piquet's ship. There was a moment of quiet when we were not sure if she would answer, but then we saw the first flash through the smoke. She fired nine guns.

"America will get gun for gun some day, republic or no," Captain Jones said the next day.

He was sitting writing in his cabin, stooped over his table. I made several copies of what he was writing that afternoon. The letter was to the maritime commission in America. It said that he had plans for several enterprises of importance.

"When an enemy thinks that a design is improbable," he wrote, "he can always be surprised and attacked with advantage. It is true I must run great risks, but no gallant action was ever performed without risk. Therefore, though I cannot insure success, I will endeavor to deserve it."

So we put to sea from Brest on the 10th of April, 1778, to go *in harm's way.*

We sailed north between Ireland and Scotland, taking some prizes. The Captain manned one and sent her back to Brest, but usually he burned the ships, taking any goods of value and the crews as prisoners. It was Benjamin Franklin's order that he should take all the prisoners possible so that they could be exchanged for those in British dungeons.

Lieutenant Simpson, who did America more harm than any British frigate, and the crew grumbled a good deal because there would be little prize money.

April 21st, 1778. We discovered a British warship, the *Drake*, lying in Belfast Lough. The Captain made a bold plan for taking her in a hand-to-hand fight. This could not be done, partly because there was delay in carrying out his orders, partly because the wind suddenly blew up a gale. We had to beat our way out of the Lough.

April 22nd. Luckily, this was at night and in the darkness the *Ranger* passed for a merchant ship. We were almost driven on the lighthouse rocks by the gale. It kept on blowing. This morning we saw something most strange for this country and time of year. Hills in all three kingdoms—Ireland, Scotland, and England—were covered deep in snow!

It melted as quickly as it had fallen. The hills were in their spring green again as the *Ranger* made her way toward Whitehaven.

I started to tell Duncan how Whitehaven lies.

"I know," Duncan said, "on the English side of Solway Firth, looking north to the Scottish shore. I know it well for I used to stay with my Grandfather McTavish at Kircudbright across the firth."

April 23rd. When we reached Whitehaven last night we found the port was crowded with ships. Forts guarded its entrance. Our men were afraid to attack it. Most of the night was spent by the Captain in trying to get volunteers to join him in his scheme.

Thirty of us volunteered. We set off in two boats. I was in the Captain's boat, bound for the southern side of the harbor. Lieutenant Wallingford commanded the other boat. He was to go to the north side and fire the shipping there. We were to fire it on the south side. We had tar and oakum with us. We each had a lantern with a lighted candle in it.

Captain Jones sent Wallingford ahead. He told him he would take care of the forts himself.

"Won't there be soldiers there?" asked Wallingford.

"Yes," Captain Jones said. "British soldiers. They will have drunk too much beer and they will be snoring."

So Wallingford rowed off to the north. We went to the south side and left a party there. They were to start fires as soon as they saw fire on Wallingford's side of the harbor.

We took care of the forts easily. It was just as Captain Jones said. The soldiers were snoring good, hearty British snores. We tied them up and carried them into the boats. The Captain showed me how to spike the guns but he was so quick that he did most of the work himself. We took care of the south fort and then went on and did the same at the north one. Captain Jones got in as he had at the south fort, through a gun embra-sure. He was too short to reach it so he stood on my shoulders. When he was in, he pounded spikes into the guns with arms as strong as blacksmith's while we were tying up the sentries.

By this time Wallingford and the others were supposed to
have ships on fire, but no flicker of flame showed on either side.
We went back to the crew we had left on the south side. While
they were waiting for Wallingford's signal fire, their candle
had burned out—or so they said.

It was now almost dawn. The Captain was angry but he
mastered his temper and went to a house outside the town.
There he asked most politely for light for his lantern, saying
his had gone out. When he came back, he kindled a fire in the
hold of a ship with his own hands and added tar to the blaze.
She was stranded on the beach and there were plenty of others around her. If the fire had been started at night, all would
have burned.

It was broad daylight when we got the fire going and we had to leave. The ship was burning well by then. Fire was running up the masts and rigging.

We went back to the north fort to pick up a party we had left guarding it. Wallingford had joined them. His candle had burned out, he said. He added that the idea of setting the fire "was a rash thing and nothing could be got by burning poor folks' property."

I thought the Captain would explode with rage but he swallowed it down. His face is usually colorless but he turned a sort of gray purple. He sent Wallingford and his crew back to the *Ranger* and told the rest of us to get into our own boat. There were hundreds of people on the pier by then. The Captain stood between them and the boats with a pistol in his hand. When they moved toward him, he ordered them to retire.

You should have seen them run when they heard his voice! Our boats were overloaded so he had us return all but three of the sentinels to the pier. He took the three back to the *Ranger*—"for samples," he said. There were people on every hill around the harbor with their mouths hanging open, watching us. They didn't dare move, not even to put out the fire on the burning ship.

At last the Captain turned, walked quietly down to the boat and got in. The English then started running for the forts and tried to fire the guns at us. Of course they couldn't since we had spiked them. At last they dragged some guns off a ship and got them firing. We were on the *Ranger* by then. The shot splashed into the water far short of us.

Some members of our crew answered the shot with their pistols. I'm afraid the English thought this was uncivil behavior. They roared and bellowed at every shot. They were full of valor by then. So were Lieutenant Simpson and others who had stayed on the ship. Some of them wanted the Captain to turn our guns on the crowd.

He answered that we had perhaps shown the English that not all the burning of property would be done on the coast of Virginia. That this was not the Boston Massacre and that he would not fire on unarmed people. "Let them send out an armed ship to attack us," he added, "and we'll use our guns."

But they gave us no chance.

It was a beautiful morning as we sailed out of Whitehaven Harbor into the Firth.

The crew thought we were bound back for France but our cruise was not over. Indeed, our day had only just begun.

Captain Jones was angry and disappointed over the failure of his Whitehaven scheme. He said, and I think rightly, that except for the delay in getting volunteers to go ashore and Wallingford's hesitation, they would have fired all the ships on the beaches. However, he did not waste time in regrets when there was something else to be done. He shrugged his round shoulders and said that after all we had done enough to show the English that their boasted navy could not protect their own coast while they were burning and killing in America.

He was glad, he said, that if he had taught them any part of such a lesson, it had been done without a single injury either to the enemy or to his own crew. With that he dismissed the subject. He already had another scheme.

To carry it out, we laid our course for St. Mary's Isle. The Earl of Selkirk had an estate there, Captain Jones said. His plan was to land without firing a gun, go quietly to the house, take the Earl prisoner, take him to France, and hold him as a hostage until the English agreed to an exchange of prisoners.

The breeze was fair. The Captain seemed to know every foot of the Solway, every rock, every current, even trees and houses. We were soon close to the landing place at the island, as it is called. Actually it is a wooded peninsula that pushes out into the river Dee.

It was beautiful that morning with the fans on the horse chestnut trees opening, and the sun shining on the new leaves of the great oaks. There were daffodils in bloom everywhere and great drifts of fruit blossoms in the orchard. The grass was like a fine carpet of velvet. Peach trees were trained in patterns against sunny walls. Yews were clipped into shapes like peacocks and swans. There were great masses of tulips, flame red, every shade of pink and yellow, some almost black.

I said to the Captain that the Earl must have a wonderful gardener and he smiled and said, "Aye, laddie, at least he had. One of the best."

I did not know then that the former gardener was his uncle.

He sounded very Scotch, as he did at times, though at others he was quite English and grand and at still others as colonial as jonnycake. He had snatches of French and Spanish, too, and the fine manners to go with them.

He used his clipped English tongue on a man we met near the house in asking him for the Earl of Selkirk. The Earl was away on a journey, the man said.

Here was another disappointment. The Captain quietly ordered us back to the boats but Lieutenant Simpson protested we should have something to show for our morning's work. Simpson, that stupid brute, was always in a state close to mutiny and he had a party on the *Ranger* that sided with him. Their one idea was prize money and they wanted to get it without risking their skins. They could never see that there was any difference between a Navy ship and a privateer.

As the boat I was in shoved off, I heard Simpson arguing with the Captain. After I got back to the *Ranger* I saw Simpson and Wallingford and some sailors going back toward the house. The Captain stayed walking up and down under the great chestnuts near the shore.

When they came back to the ship, Simpson and Wallingford were in great spirits. They had the Selkirks' silver with them—forks, spoons, urns, pitchers, cream pails, ladles, fish slices, gravy boats. There was a teapot with the tea leaves in it, just as it came from the breakfast table. Simpson spread the silver all out on the cabin table and Wallingford, who held a pen as if it were a pitchfork, began making a list of it, stopping at every second word to ask Simpson how to spell it. He was so slow that Simpson at last grabbed the pen. When he finished the list—a schoolboy in the poorest school in Scotland would have been ashamed of it, the Captain said later—he started to dump the tea leaves out of the teapot.

The Captain had just come into the cabin and was standing there, scowling. He said in a quiet voice but one that went through you like a flying splinter of wood in a battle, "Lieutenant Simpson, leave that teapot alone, if you please." Simpson jumped and almost dropped it. Even he knew enough not to cross Captain Jones in certain moods.

"This silver," the Captain went on grimly, "is not your personal property though it has plenty of your finger marks on it, I perceive. It is a prize of the ship *Ranger* and will be dealt with as property of the United States of America. The Selkirk family may wish to ransom it. If so, it is my duty to return it intact and that, sir, I shall do. And you may go on deck and ask the master from me to set a course for Belfast Lough. I have a letter to write and I wish the cabin to myself."

Simpson and Wallingford stumbled out as if they had been kicked. I was following them but the Captain said, speaking kindly, "Come back in an hour, Mr. Caryl. I may have some copying for you to do."

It took him more than an hour but later he gave it to me to copy. It was a letter to the Countess of Selkirk, written, I do believe, in a style elegant enough for any earl or duke. He told her he was sorry for any annoyance his men might have caused her and stated that it was his intention to purchase the silver from the prize court and return it to her. The Captain was proud of the letter, as well he might be—a poor Scottish lad, a gardener's son, her gardener's nephew, with little schooling, at sea since he was twelve. He showed me the small white cottage near the shore where he was born. He looked longingly at it, I thought, but we did not stay. We went back to Ireland and attacked the *Drake* again...

April 25th. His Majesty's ship *Drake* had more guns than the *Ranger*. She belonged to what was rightly considered the finest navy in the world. Her crew was almost twice as large as the *Ranger's*. Her Captain was warned of what the *Ranger* had done at Whitehaven and at St. Mary's Isle. She was in familiar waters. She had every advantage—except John Paul Jones.

Many of the *Ranger's* crew objected to fighting a ship of the British Navy. Under Simpson's leadership they were planning to seize Jones, throw him into the sea, and use the *Ranger* as a privateer, attacking only ships that could not fight back.

The *Drake* was in the harbor of Carrickfergus in Belfast Lough. England and Scotland had just learned that the American Navy existed. The inhabitants of Whitehaven were carrying their jewels and silver inland to hide them from the American pirates. The people of Kircudbright had dragged an old gun down to the beach of St. Mary's Isle. They fired it all night, we heard afterwards, at a large rock thought to be the rebel ship. Now it was Ireland's turn.

It was yesterday morning, April 24th, when Captain Jones, who was looking for the *Drake*, was pleased to see her coming out of the harbor into the Lough. The *Drake's* commander, Captain Burton, saw the *Ranger* in the distance. He sent a boat to her, asking for information about the American raider. Captain Jones kept the *Ranger's* stern toward the boat to conceal her appearance as much as possible. This worked so well that the English officer was on the *Ranger's* quarter-deck and taken prisoner before he knew where he was.

He told J.P.J., perhaps with the idea of frightening him, that the smoke rising from both sides of the channel was from signal fires. They showed that the *Ranger* was in the neighborhood. The *Drake* was pursuing her, he said. The *Drake*, he added, had a hundred and sixty men on board, including a number of volunteers who had come to take part in the battle.

Duncan and I were put in charge of the seamen who had been taken prisoner with the officer. Most of them were grumpily silent but there was one talkative one. He told us a great deal of the *Drake*, including the fact that she had a hogshead of rum on her deck. They were going to celebrate their victory with it, he said.

The tide was against the *Drake* and the wind was so light that it took her a long time to work out of the Lough. By this time Captain Burton must have known that the ship he was approaching was the *Ranger*. In fact, everyone knew it. Five small vessels full of people escorted the *Drake*.

"What are those boats?" Duncan asked our talkative prisoner.

"Oh, just folks that have come out to see the battle. The Irish love a fight. Happen when the *Drake* sinks you, they'll pick us out of the water. Maybe I'll get a taste of the rum after all."

Duncan said politely that he understood rum was good for anyone who had been in cold water.

Now the *Drake* was near enough so that the sun shone on her beautifully carved figurehead of Sir Francis Drake in the very clothes he may have worn that day on Plymouth Hoe when the sails of the Armada were first seen in the distance. Captain Jones ordered his courses hauled up. The *Ranger* lay to with main topsail close against her mast, the Stars and Stripes fluttering above it.

A hail came from the *Drake*.

"What ship is that?"

We saw John Paul Jones say something to the sailing master and then heard the master's voice say through the speaking trumpet:

"This is the American Continental ship *Ranger*. We wait for you and desire you to come on. The sun is now a little more than an hour from setting. It is time to begin."

Though his letter to the Countess of Selkirk was so grandly written, I liked this message even better.

The *Drake* was now astern of the *Ranger*. Captain Jones ordered his helm put up and the first broadside fired. The *Drake* soon replied.

At the end of an hour the *Drake* was much damaged. Her yards hung down from her masts. Her jib and her red ensign were both trailing in the water. Her sails were cut to ribbons, spars shot to splinters, hull shattered. Then her captain was hit by a musket ball. At the end of one hundred and four minutes, the crew asked for quarter.

They buried the captain, the lieutenant, and forty-two British seamen killed in the battle with full honors of war. The *Ranger* lost three men killed. One of them was Lieutenant Wallingford. Five men were wounded.

No one drank the rum. One of our cannon balls hit the cask. The deck was well washed with it.

May, 1778. The sea was calm that night, I remember. By the next day both ships were sufficiently repaired so that they could make sail again. Captain Jones spent some time rewriting his letter to Lady Selkirk. He made it even more elegant and poetical than the first draft and included an account of the victory over the *Drake*. While the repairs were being made to the ships, I made several copies of the letter.

I was sent with Lieutenant Simpson and others to take charge of the *Drake*. We sailed north around Ireland, then west and south along her west coast. Simpson was ordered to proceed to Brest but took the first opportunity he found and sailed away from Captain Jones. While the *Drake* was separated from the *Ranger*, we chased some prizes and took one.

Simpson put me in command of it and ordered me to take it to Dunkirk. Before I could come anywhere near Dunkirk, we were stopped by a British frigate. So I lost my first command. It's just possible that I'm not the material out of which a great commander is made. Of course, I felt like one when I was with Captain Jones.

We were allowed to take our sea chests on board the frigate but the chests were promptly emptied by the British sailors.

As soon as the Americans were below decks out of sight of the officers, the sailors began snatching clothes from what they called the Bostonians. According to their ideas Boston seemed to be the whole of America. Even I was a Bostonian.

A sailor yanked open my chest, saying, "Now here's a fine, tall red Indian lad from Boston! And he has two fine shirts. Now, my lad, you don't need two shirts. It's hot in the hold where you're going. Do you think he needs two shirts, Bill? This one would fit you within a yard or so. And the other one would fit me. Do you think he needs any shirts, Bill?"

Bill, a strong, silent Britisher, merely pulled the shirt over his head and rolled up the sleeves.

His friend went on, "And this gentleman from Boston has a neat blue jacket with brass buttons. And blue breeches. And white ones! He won't need *those* in that good warm hold, will he Bill?"

This went on until the chest was empty, or appeared to be. Actually, it had a false bottom beneath which I kept things I cared far more about than I did about shirts and jackets. My supply of paper was there. A slab of dried India ink, my penknife, a netted purse of green silk with a few shillings in it. The purse had been in my pocket when I was washed off the *Princess Anne*. It was much faded and stained with salt water. It was my only link now with Caryl's Maze; that and the ring with the Caryl arms cut on it. The ring had grown too small for me long ago and I kept it in the purse. The purse was now wrapped in a scarf of green cashmere. I had bought it in India for Cherry. There had been silks for Aunt Dorothy and Mrs. Ashton but they were on the *Sea Otter*, which was, I felt sure, broken to pieces by those fierce tides in the Nova Scotia cove.

It was hot and stifling in the hold of the frigate. The hatches were shut tightly above us and opened only to give us our rations. We were given half a pint of water a day and a little bread and salt beef. The crew of the frigate already had scurvy. Many of them died on the voyage to England but we "Bostonians" were still healthy at the end of it.

The storeroom for the officers' mess was just above our prison. Using my knife and other pocketknives, we succeeded in cutting out a piece of plank big enough so that a small boy could squirm through the opening into the storeroom above. There were ox tongues, raisins, hams, and beef in casks, biscuits and sugar in kegs, lemons in nets. These good things and others were carefully used and fairly portioned out among the prisoners.

"Guess we'd better act starved when they bring that old salt horse," I told them, so we continued to snatch at our rations like hungry wolves. No one ever found out we were getting enough to eat.

When the frigate at last reached the coast of England, we were brought before the Captain, a plump, purple-faced gentleman who addressed us as follows:

"What! Are none of you confounded Yankees sick? Did none of you die—not even one? Why, curse you, I believe nothing but lightning will kill you!"

His lieutenant said, "You're right, sir. They're savages, sir. Really savages. They don't even speak English."

The frigate was coming into a harbor through green water, surrounded by green hills. There was a broad level stretch, greener still, close to the water's edge.

"Wish I knew where we were," Buxton Pratt said.

"You are looking at Plymouth Hoe," I told him.

"You've been here before, then?"

"Oh, yes," I said. "I've been here before. And I can guess where they are going to put us. Those old stone buildings with the spiked wall around them are what they call Mill Prison."

"Well," Buxton drawled, "when we escape and want to steal a boat, guess there'll be plenty handy."

CHAPTER 15

BLACK HOLE

WHILE HE WAS in Mill Prison Nick made mostly short entries in his journal, many of them in the code he had learned long before from Captain Paul. His supply of paper was small. Prisoners were not supposed to have paper and ink. A prisoner who had them might communicate with someone outside and have a place to go when he escaped. The Americans escaped constantly but were usually brought back. Still, though some English people brought them back and collected the reward for returning them, there were others who helped them on their way.

Writing, even on a piece of wood, was regarded with suspicion by the red-coated guards. Nick kept his paper either in his boots or in the false bottom of his chest. He wrote at night, usually by the light of a marrowbone. A good marrowbone would burn almost as long as a candle. They were not allowed candles. They were not allowed to burn marrowbones either, for that matter.

As commander of the captured prize, Nick was placed in the officers' prison. There was another building for the com-

mon seamen. The British officers, who examined the prisoners, when they arrived, were neither cruel nor harsh in their manners. They spoke politely as they told each American that he was imprisoned as a rebel, pirate, and traitor, that if the King and minister so decided, he would be hanged. The prisoners were given a chance to repent of their crimes and join the British Navy. No one did so at first. Nick learned later that a few of the younger sailors had exchanged their prison on land for one at sea. That was what most of them would no doubt find life on a British warship to be. However, there was always a chance of escape on a ship as well as a chance of being killed, drowned, or dying of scurvy. They had, of course, an excellent chance of getting scurvy in prison, too.

On June 1st, 1778, Nick wrote:

Our daily allowance of food is ¼ lb. salt beef and the water it was cooked in, 1 lb. bread, 1 lb. greens. We do not always get the greens. If the cook throws cabbage stalks into the mud of the yard, we snatch them up and eat them raw.

June 5th. I am twenty-three today.

June 10th. We are allowed to make woodenware and sell it at the market outside the gate. I used my few shillings to buy some wood and a small chisel. I keep them in my chest. I am making a punch ladle. I hope I can earn money to buy extra food.

June 12th. Made a carved box. Sold it—1 shilling. Bought milk, bread.

Sunday. People are allowed to look at us. The guards make them pay. I heard one woman say: "Why look, Kitty, these be white folk like us, not savages at all. They talk as good as you and me. Except I don't know if this tall one be a red Indian. Speak English?... See, Kitty, he's no savage. Now isn't it a shame to hang such nice-looking lads? Here's something for you, my lad." She gave me sixpence and she said, "See, Kitty, he talks plain enough." Kitty bought a bowl from me for a shilling.

We had put up a box and I wrote "Contributions" above it. I had carved on the board "Health and Prosperity to the Donors." There were several shillings in it, mostly in pence. We bought milk with it.

June 15th. Two escaped prisoners, Capt. & Lieut. of Virginia pilot boat, were brought in. They know Richard Dale! They say he was in this prison—that he escaped when they did. I then asked other prisoners about him. They said he was brought back before I came and is now in the Black Hole and will be up tomorrow!

June 16th. They let Richard up out of the Black Hole today. He looked very thin and white but I knew him. He did not know me at first and even after I told him who I was, he just stared up at me. He was sure I died long ago. We talked all night. He believes I am myself now. Says "Sandy" is considered a Tory. Many plantations near Portsmouth burned. Caryl's Maze spared. Will not write what more he says of Sandy. Sure now it is really Gilbert. Richard says Cherry has grown up very beautiful and is the toast of the town. This I can scarce believe. My uncle almost blind now, very deaf, much impoverished by war. Aunt Dorothy and Mrs. Ashton having a hard time running the plantation. Luckily, McFarland still there and Dickson, the butler. "Sandy" no help, of course.

Richard was on the *Lexington*. She fought a British ship four hours. Her stays and braces shot away. All shot used. Six killed. Others wounded. Prisoners allowed to keep clothes. Captain's money taken from him. He gets it back a shilling at a time. Richard had only a few shillings. Gave most of them to sailors of the *Lexington*.

June 17th. Joined with Richard and others and bought a bag of potatoes for 3 shillings, which is cheaper than by the peck.

June 18th. New prisoners brought in. Say Dr. Franklin has proposed to the British ambassador in France to exchange prisoners.

June 20th. New hammocks, one foot shorter than old ones. I was about doubled up in the old one. I am 6'6 now. Taller than Richard. He is very handsome—straight nose, curly hair. Has his bright color back now. Sailors say he is a fine, clever officer, fair, courteous, patient, firm, knows his business. I reckon *so!* Prison not so bad since Richard came.

July 1st. A new company of Grenadier Guards is on duty at the prison now. Frederick—yes, I mean it—my cousin, Frederick Caryl, is their captain!

July 3rd. Decided to have a celebration because tomorrow is three years since the Declaration of Independence. Several of us are making cockades. We draw them on paper cut in the form of a half-moon. Then we paint the 13 stripes and the union of 13 stars. On the top is printed INDEPENDENCE and below, LIBERTY OR DEATH.

July 4th, 1778. This morning we all hoisted the American flag upon our hats. My cousin Frederick looked at one of the cockades (it seems he can read though this is hard to believe) and thought we were going to riot. He ordered double safety at the gate!

At one o'clock we drew up in thirteen divisions, all with the greatest regularity, and each gave three cheers. We kept our colors hoisted till sunset and then took them down.

July 15th. For the two months past have received 10 shillings for woodenware. All spent on food. Should have saved it for journey.

July 16th. Tunnel almost finished.

Sunday. There are two ministers who come to visit us. We call them our "fathers," for a smile from them is like a smile from a father. One of them gave me a book on geography.

July 20th. Hear from our fathers that a donation of £800 has been raised in London by private gentlemen for the relief of prisoners. It is like something Mr. Banks would do except I suppose he is voyaging somewhere! Pambo, too, probably.

July 21st. We received from the donation bread, cheese, blankets, shirts (checked shirts for seamen, white for officers) and other clothing. We washed ourselves with soap and our clothes are now clean for the first time in months.

July 30th. Our plans are made. We drew lots to see who should go out through the tunnel tomorrow. Captain Boardman, Richard and I are to go. We have sworn never to tell the names of the friends outside who help us. We know where to go. We call the route the Underground Road...

Nick never did tell who helped them after they crawled out through the tunnel on the night of the 31st of July. They got safely into open fields but there was a heavy mist and they wandered around in it for hours. Richard Dale had a compass but they could not see to read it.

When morning came, they were only two miles from the prison. They spent the day hiding behind hedges, shivering in the cold rain. The only food they had was prison bread, the kind with straw in it, and rancid cheese.

However, straw—as Nick remarked—is a good thing in the right place. They slept in stacks of it many times on their journey to London. More than one kind English family gave them clothes, fed and sheltered them while they were being hunted. They kept their promise and never told the names of those whose houses were on the Underground Road. While they were in London, waiting for a chance to get on a ship for France, they saw newspapers several times. They learned that Dr. Franklin kept writing letters about exchanging prisoners. Since Burgoyne's defeat it was more likely that the exchange might be made. The King of France had recognized the independence of America. Many of the best men in England hated the war and talked against it in Parliament. The common people talked against it on the streets.

At last their friends found a chance for them to cross the channel to France. They got to Dover safely and were actually on a ship bound for Dunkirk when the press gang found them. Since they would not fight against America, they told who they were and were sent back to Mill Prison.

Perhaps England seemed especially green and fresh, as they rode in a coach back to Plymouth, because they knew they would soon be shut away from air and sunshine in the Black Hole. The journey that had taken so many weeks was all too short now.

It was the tenth of September when they reached Mill Prison. Men they knew were playing ball and quoits in the prison yard. Balls and quoits fell to the ground, hollow eyes stared out of white faces as the red-coated grenadiers in their bearskin hats marched the prisoners across the yard.

Nick had often stood, knowing he was a dirty, ragged scarecrow, and watched well-fed, clean prisoners brought in. He would think of Batavia where the sick sailors had looked at a healthy crew and each had pitied the other. It was the same now. He knew that the hungry, half-naked men were sorry for him as he was for them. They knew that after he reached the Black Hole, he would not be clean and sunburned long.

The Black Hole looked black indeed as he went down into it. Yet it was not completely black to those who lived in it. There was a small grating in the stone floor. Through this, at certain times of day, something that was not quite darkness came. If a man stood directly under the grating, a prisoner whose eyes were used to the dark could see him. That is, he could see if the newcomer was tall and black-haired or short and blond.

They stopped under the grating. They could hear men moving in the darkness but no one spoke until they heard the iron lid above them clang shut, the key turn in the lock, and the footsteps of the grenadiers marching off.

Someone in the darkness asked, "Who's come?"

Captain Boardman said, "Boardman here. Richard Dale, Nick Young. Back from Dover. Pleasant journey. Do we know anyone here?"

Voices they knew greeted them from the shadows. Yet the voices seemed shadowy too, as if they belonged to people without flesh and bones.

His eyes grew used to the darkness. Faces he knew came into the little circle that was almost gray twilight. At least, Nick thought, they have bones enough.

He was always thin for his great height and he was soon little more than skin and bones himself.

They were on half-rations, of course. Whole rations had never been enough. Men outside risked their comparative freedom to get the lid open—there was a locksmith among them—and lower down packets of bread and salt beef to them. They divided these provisions among the eleven men who were in the Black Hole the first week. Their visitors would tell them what day it was.

One night, when they had been there about two weeks, there came the three taps on the grating that meant food would be lowered. Nick was nearest to the grating. He climbed up the iron ladder to undo the precious piece of string from around the package so the string could be pulled up and used again.

This time, however, the man who had brought the package did not wait to pull up the string but hurried away, leaving it still tied to the grating.

"Guards coming," Nick thought.

He fumbled at the knot with cold, clumsy fingers, trying desperately to get it undone and hide the string. Before he could do so the key turned in the lock, the lid was yanked open, and he was seized by the shoulders and dragged partway out of the hole. Light from a lantern flashed in his eyes.

A drawling, peevish, high voice said, "Filthy Yankee rebel. His name, Sergeant?"

"Name's Young, I think, Captain Caryl."

The candlelight showed Nick a plump, pink face, a curled white wig, scarlet and gold lace, a gorget of gold.

And I know your name, you clean British tyrant, Nick thought. It's Frederick and you are getting to look more like your grandfather.

"Ask him if he knows who brought the food, Sergeant," Frederick Caryl said.

He looked contemptuously over Nick's head as if his cousin were a worm crawling out of the ground.

"I don't know," Nick said, "and I wouldn't tell if I did."

"Says he doesn't know, sir," the sergeant reported.

"Shove him back, Sergeant, till he finds out. Take the food. What is it? Oh, bread and beef wrapped in cabbage leaves—how unappetizing!"

It took three of them to shove him back. It was stupid to resist, Nick knew, but his cousin's face, sneering in the candlelight, drove him beyond sense and reason. He was still in the Black Hole when Captain Boardman and Richard Dale were released.

At last the days in the Black Hole came to an end for Nick, too. It was a fine, fresh October morning when he came out and saw blue sky over his head. Clouds like frigates sailed across it. Real frigates like clouds sailed over the blue of the harbor.

Things had changed while he had been shut away from the world. They were allowed pens, ink, and paper now. Food was a little better than it was when he went down. They could go to the kitchen, have their own beef weighed out, and cook it themselves. The guards did not knock them around so roughly as they did before. The talk was all that they would be exchanged soon.

Newspapers were allowed now. An old one that had been read almost to pieces told about the Whitehaven Raid. It said that the vile pirate, John Paul Jones, had been chased out of the harbor by the brave inhabitants. Then he had attacked the defenseless people of St. Mary's Isle, had stolen £5000 worth of the Selkirks' family silver, and had driven off the Selkirk cattle.

Next the pirate had attacked H.M.S. *Drake*. She was not ready for battle. Her crew was new and untrained. The gunners did not have her matches burning. The rebels killed her captain and the crew had to surrender to these pirates. The writer seemed to think that the fact that the crew of a Navy ship was not ready for battle was somehow the pirates' fault. He also seemed annoyed because it had become necessary to organize militia companies to protect towns on the coast from such foul attacks. The citizens, he said, were aroused. They were carrying their silver to banks farther inland.

The writer was shocked to learn that the pirate, Jones, was really John Paul, son of the gardener of Mr. Craik of Arbigland, nephew of Lord Selkirk's gardener. He had received much kindness from the Selkirk family, the paper said. However, now that the citizens were aroused—the writer seemed to take a good deal of comfort from this fact—it would not be long before the fiendish pirate would be dangling from a British gallows.

"Somehow, I wish he had not attacked the place where he grew up," Nick said, handing back the paper to Richard Dale. "How do you feel about it, Richard?"

"I regret it, too," Richard Dale said. "Yet war is war, Nick Young. We did not begin it. We did not fire on unarmed people in Boston. We did not fire the first shot at *Lexington*. We had the words said there written up in the cabin of our ship, the *Lexington*. Do you know them?"

"No," Nick said, and Richard Dale repeated them: "Hold your ground. Don't fire unless fired upon. But if they want a war, let it begin here!"

"Well," he added, "they fired. It began there. Where it will end no one knows. But I do know this. We have few enough weapons to fight with. Paul Jones's special knowledge of rocks and currents in Solway Firth is just as much a weapon as a cannon or a sword. Perhaps more. For look what this raid has done. Here are people calling for British frigates to defend their harbors, dressing up in scarlet and gold and dragging guns to protect their own shores instead of sending them against ours. Perhaps they will stop burning Virginia plantations now they know it can happen here, too. But that's enough preaching. Shall we go to the market?"

"I have no money," Nick said, "and I've had no time to make any ladles yet."

"I have money—two whole shillings! Come, I'll treat you to a loaf of bread," Richard Dale said.

The market was just outside the prison yard. Before going out of the prison itself the prisoners were counted by the prison guards.

"Eighty-one, eighty-two, eighty-three—I make it eighty-three, sir."

"Very well, Corporal Miller. Be sure you get eighty-three of the brutes back. Too cursed many escapes, you know, lately," drawled Frederick Caryl's voice.

Nick could have picked Frederick up and broken him into several pieces, but—he thought—looking over the top of his cousin's bearskin hat, he had better not.

"That's a cousin of mine back there," he said to Richard as they left the prison yard, were counted again at the outer gate, and went out into market.

"You know the strangest people," Richard Dale said.

"Well, luckily he doesn't know me," Nick said. "Odd he should turn up here."

Richard Dale said it was a small world. Plymouth was a sort of crossroads. If you stayed there long enough, just about everyone you knew would go by.

"Sometimes," he added with a sigh, "I think I've been here long enough."

"Oh, Richard—you're not planning to go out again!"

"No. Not just yet. But did you notice, Nick Young, that your cousin is going to be perfectly content if the right *number* of us goes back into the prison. Some skinny little runt who can get into the yard by wriggling through the window bars will do just as well as a fine, tall, upstanding Indian like yourself, who can barely get through the door."

"Well—what of it?"

"You've no head for arithmetic, Nick Young. I vow you're as stupid as your cousin. Say two boys get into the yard without being counted. You and I go through the door and out into the market. So long as the boys take our places and are counted when the bell rings, we need never come back."

"We'll still need money," Nick said.

"Yes, we'd better make some more punch ladles."

"The English will have to swim in punch for us to earn enough," Nick said, "but I suppose we might as well try."

It was hard to save the few shillings they earned. Starved as they were from the Black Hole, they could not help spending money on food.

On November 18th, 1778, Nick wrote:

There are four men still in the Black Hole. We get food to them in the usual way. Things are better lately, for our "fathers" come often to see us. We always ask them about being exchanged. They say the exchange will come but we must have patience. We cannot gather much patience in this yard. What grows here mostly is nettles.

November 20th. Mr. Walsh of the *Lexington* escaped. A small boy went out a window into the yard and back through the door so he was counted and the number was right. The boy did this every time we went into the yard for exercise so it was more than thirty hours before the escape was found out. So Richard was right—this scheme works.

November 21st. Some prisoners were caught digging out and are sent to the Black Hole. It is foolish to try to escape. We all know it, but it is so melancholy and hard to content our minds within these walls.

November 22nd. We hear from our "fathers" that there are 250 English prisoners, mostly taken by John Paul Jones, who will be exchanged for us. We have been disappointed so many times that we lose hope and scarce believe it. Still, since John Paul took so many prisoners things are better here. The guards are told not to strike us or thrust bayonets at us.

November 23rd. Many men have escaped lately by the scheme Richard thought of. (Boys going out windows.) All who escape have now been brought back and are in the Black Hole.

November 24th. I am taking lessons in French from one of the prisoners. I have also bought a book on navigation. Cost 2 shillings. Richard and I are studying it.

November 25th. Today Buxton Pratt took a mason's coat, put a basket on his head, and walked out of prison, past the guards. Unluckily, he met the owner of the coat, who recognized it. He was brought back but is not in the Black Hole. It's already full. He is on ½ rations but we share ours with him. While he was out he heard that forty-five men escaped from Forton Prison in Portsmouth but that Captain Cunningham, our great American raider, is kept in irons there. He used to come to Caryl's Maze and I remember him well.

November 27th. Thirty-three Americans signed up to join King George's Navy and are to get a free pardon. They made so much noise we could not sleep, so in return we had an Indian powwow. Solid as this old prison is, we made its walls shake.

December 24th. We have bought for pudding: 5 lbs. flour, 1 lb. suet, 1 lb. raisins, ½ lb. sugar, 1 oz. spice, and milk.

December 25th. Our bakers sent us today white bread instead of brown, fresh mutton instead of salt beef, turnips instead of cabbage, oatmeal to thicken our broth. Our pudding was good so we had a fine Christmas dinner. Perhaps next year Richard and I will eat it at Caryl's Maze.

January 8th. Hunger rages in prison. Today a fat dog strayed into the yard. I remembered Tahiti and told Richard about Mr. Banks's eating roast dog. We caught the dog, killed, dressed it, roasted it in the dripping pan. I bought potatoes to roast with it. It was as good as the roast dog we used to eat in the South Seas, tasted a bit like venison. Some of us had to be content with rats.

January 10th. Our "fathers" tell us there is a cartel made that says 100 prisoners will be exchanged and go to Nantes in France.

January 22nd. The names of the first 100 to be exchanged have been read to us. My name was the 91st. It would have been earlier since I have been here so long but for my having escaped. I felt sick waiting to hear it read and when I heard it, my ears rang so loud I thought I would fall. I listened for Richard's, too, but it was not read.

January 31st. Every day we hear the cartel ship is coming but the next morning finds us still in Mill Prison. Three of us have died since we heard of the cartel. Eight since I came to prison. Today in the yard Richard spoke to me. He told me he would go tomorrow.

He said, "I cannot take you, Nick Young, for I have promised never to let anyone know how I go. Anyway, since your name is on the list, it is better you should wait."

I said, "Oh, Richard, wait too! You will only be taken again and be in the Black Hole."

He said, "No, I will not be taken this time. Have no fear for me. Bring my chest if you can when you come. I am going to find your friend Paul Jones. We'll meet again."

February 1st. Richard escaped, no one knows how. I could guess but will not try.

February 10th. Yesterday we were told by our "father," Mr. Heath, that His Majesty had been graciously pleased to pardon 100 of us whose names had been read. He said the transport, *Milford*, waiting for a fair wind at Dartmouth, will take us to France. The *Milford*! Our old friend!

February 24th. We hear that the *Milford* is still detained by contrary winds.

February 25th. The news of our having eaten a dog was in the London papers. The English are much shocked. They cannot believe we are really hungry. They say it is evidently an American custom to eat dogs and it is only to be expected of savages. Still, I have seen Mr. Banks, one of the finest Englishmen that ever walked, eating roast dog and liking it.

February 26th. Mr. Heath came again today. We flock around him like children when he comes. He asked us whether we ate the dog from actual necessity. I told him we did and he asked me to write out the facts for him. So I did. I told how I had been with Captain Cook in the South Sea Islands, how we had learned roast dog was good to eat and that we preferred it to boiled nettles and moldy cabbage stalks and rats, on which many of us live in Mill Prison.

March 3rd. Something strange has happened as a result of our eating the dog. When I went into the market with two boxes and a sugar scoop to sell, I saw a tall man, not much shorter than I am, with his back to me. He was buying a carved bowl from a prisoner. He was dressed in black velvet. There was something about the way he stood that reminded me of someone. He turned. It was Mr. Banks! And beyond him, very grand in a green livery with silver buttons, was Pambo. I rushed over, saying, "Mr. Banks! Pambo!" but they both looked as if they had never seen me before and walked on past me.

I stood there, staring. I could not believe they would be so cruel. I wondered if I could have changed so much that Pambo would not know me. Mr. Banks, perhaps, but not Pambo. Of course, I am now taller than Mr. Banks and I have a beard, but Pambo would know me still, I thought. I felt worse than I have any time since Sandy died. I walked back toward the gate. I was alone, the prisoners all having gone to the market place.

I heard footsteps and Pambo's voice saying, "Don't feel so bad, Mistoh Nick Young. Here—take this."

He had tears running down over his fat cheeks. He put something into my hand and said, "You'll understand when you read it. Give me one of the boxes. So I'll look as if I'm buying it. I mustn't be seen talking long with you."

I handed him both boxes and the sugar scoop and stood there, holding the packet he had given me and looking at him, not able to speak. He wiped the tears off with one of his fine ruffles and said, "Goodbye, Mistoh Nick Young. Good luck."

Then he turned and went back to Mr. Banks, who had

never looked my way at all. They bought some more things from prisoners and then got into a handsome claret-colored carriage that was waiting. Pambo got up on the box beside the coachman and Mr. Banks inside.

I heard the horses' feet clatter on the paving stones. The carriage swung around a curve into the road and they were gone. I went back into the prison. I was all alone in the big room. All the prisoners were in the market or playing games in the yard. I opened my packet. There was a purse of gold, a small box, and a letter in Mr. Banks's handwriting.

Nick welcomed the chance of reading Mr. Banks's letter in private. It said:

My dear Nick,

When I read in the paper about prisoners at Mill Prison in Plymouth eating roast dog I was less shocked than my fellow Britons, since I have done the same myself. Still, it was a shock, but of a different kind. I realized for the first time that we have been starving our American prisoners. Then came the explanation in the paper saying that a prisoner had been with Captain Cook and had eaten roast dog. It did not give your name but I thought it must be you, since it said that the prisoner had been in my employ, though I had heard that you had been lost from the *Princess Anne* on the coast of Mozambique. I had traced you to the *Princess* after I learned from the owner of the tavern where you ate your roast beef that you had been seized by the press gang.

Before I could get to Plymouth came the news that a cartel had been agreed on and that prisoners would soon be exchanged. If you are really in Mill Prison, I want to get money to you before you sail. After all, I still owe you most of your wages. Pambo says that if you go back to Virginia, you will also need what is in the box.

If I can find you, I must give you this package without anyone's seeing that I know you. If it should be known that you had actually worn His Majesty's uniform, it might go hard with you. That your pardon would be revoked and that you would be left in Mill Prison would be the least bad thing that would happen. You must not feel badly if I do not speak to you. I shall like it no better than you will.

I am keeping your journals for you, my dear Nick. You shall have them after this unjust war is over. Say nothing to anyone about this letter. When we heard you had been lost at sea, Pambo told me your whole story. Sir George Caryl and his son Lawrence have died. Osborne is Sir Osborne now and a member of Parliament. He is a Tory, of course. No doubt you have seen Frederick, that noble grenadier. I went to school with him and say nothing worse about him than that I understand a bearskin hat two feet high has not changed him. If he should find out who you are, Nick, you will never get on that cartel ship. He and Osborne will see to that. So take care—call no attention to yourself. Eat no more dogs. *It's not English.*

Captain Cook made a second voyage and found our continent but he was right. It was only ice. I did not go, having had a slight difference of opinion with the Admiralty. Now our good captain has sailed once more, first to the west coast of America to look for the Northwest Passage. Then, I believe, to the South Seas again. I wish I were with him. There is no place so beautiful, no people so good. I still miss Tupia, still grieve for him and Tayota.

On his next voyage I hope Captain Cook will carry out my

scheme of taking young breadfruit trees to the West Indies. I am sure it is practical and will be of great benefit to humanity. Some day I must see America.

Farewell, my dear Nick. Come safe home!

Always faithfully your friend

JOSEPH BANKS

P.S. When you are come to your own in Virginia at last, please send me specimens, dried as you know how, and seeds of anything unusual. You shall have in exchange one perfect valet in good condition.

J.B.

Nick read the letter three times before he opened the small package. He knew Pambo's deft fingers had tied those neat square knots. He heard the guards counting off prisoners at the door. He had just time to get off the wrappings and look in the box. Yes, it was what he hoped. Pinned into a piece of crimson velvet and shining against it, was the Golden Horseshoe.

He had time for only one look at the garnet nailheads shining against the gold. He had hidden box and letter in the false bottom of his chest and was standing, looking out the window, when the prisoners returned.

They were full of excitement. Buxton Pratt was shouting: "Nick, Nick! The wind has hauled around. It blows northeast! The cartel will come soon!"

The cartel ship did actually arrive on March 5th and it was the *Milford*. There were more delays. To Nick, with the fear of being recognized by Frederick Caryl, the days seemed longer than to anyone else in the prison. On the 6th, they heard that orders must come from London before they embarked. On the 10th the *Milford* sailed up Stonehouse Creek. They could see her from their prison. If she had been plated with gold she could not have looked more beautiful. Five days more dragged by. At last, on March 15th, 1779, Nick wrote:

It is more than ten months since I have been a prisoner, first on a British frigate and afterwards in this place, except for my two escapes. This morning at eleven o'clock, ninety-seven of us were guarded down to the creek by forty red-coated grenadiers and embarked on the *Milford*. I never thought when I fired a musket in return for her cannon balls that she would look to me like a ship straight out of Paradise.

March 16th. We are now aboard the *Milford*, waiting only for a fair wind to sail. We are allowed the liberty of the deck by day and night. We have tolerable good accommodations. We lodge in cabins: the sick in single rooms. Those of us who have no beds of our own—of whom I am one—have King's bedding. That means a mattress as thick as the sole of your boot and a blanket like a board. I try to find the soft side of a plank to lay my mattress on. We have salt beef for dinner, and pudding, which is a great treat to us. Frederick is in command of our guards and will exchange us at Nantes. I keep out of his way all I can.

April 12th. Our voyage is over. We are at Nantes. We have our board paid until we are exchanged and have nothing to do but walk around the town. Business is very poor here because of war with Britain. More than forty merchantmen are hauled up and idle. Duncan was here to meet us. He is on leave from the *Bon Homme Richard*. This is J.P.J.'s new ship. She is not ready to sail yet.

April 16th. They told us here that Dr. Franklin likes to receive visits from American sailors, so since I am now exchanged and I have plenty of money from Mr. Banks, I decided to visit Paris and take Duncan with me. I intend to enlist for another cruise with John Paul Jones, but since his ship is not ready to sail, we will make the journey before we go to L'Orient where he is. About forty of our people have already gone there to enlist. It is about seventy-five miles from here. I thought I might get news of Richard here but no one has heard of him. I fear he is in the Black Hole at Mill Prison again.

April 21st. We got to Paris at 9 A.M. We bought new clothes and went to Passy, four miles off, where Dr. Franklin stays. He was most kind to us and looked at us shrewdly through his spectacles, which are different from most, being larger. He wears his own hair rather long and is a short, plump little man, no higher than my shoulder. The morning being chilly and wet, he wore an old fur cap such as a woodsman might wear out hunting deer. Altogether he has an odd look but is still a man of wisdom and dignity.

He ordered his servants to give us breakfast, only this was more like a dinner than any meal I have eaten since I was a boy in Virginia.

Dr. Franklin had his footman find lodgings for us nearby. His house is a small one, lent to our country by a great nobleman who lives next door. He is called Monsieur Le Ray de Chaumont and is a good friend to America.

April 22nd. We went into Paris, saw the King and Queen and many other curious objects. The King and Queen were in a coach. I saw them quite close.

We went again to see Dr. Franklin, who asked us much about our life in prison. He laughed when we told him about the dog. We also saw Mr. John Adams who comes from Boston or nearby and whom I did not much like because of the way he spoke of John Paul Jones. He did not, I suppose, know we intended to enlist with Captain Jones. He came bustling into Dr. Franklin's library where the doctor was talking to us. Mr. Adams had a letter in his hand and kept striking it angrily as he spoke. He paid no attention to us.

It seems Captain Jones needed more money to repair his ship. The letter was to Dr. Franklin. Mr. Adams said he had read it and if they tried to do what Captain Jones asked it would ruin them.

"This fellow would not be content if we gave him the whole French Navy and our own, too," he said. "So the *Bon Homme Richard* isn't good enough for him! He wants more guns—new guns. Can I make guns? Can you? He wants a whole squadron at his command. I tell you, sir, this is vanity—the fellow's full of vanity. He's a braggart, sir. He pretends he's only interested in the cause of Liberty. He wants prize money as much as anyone."

Dr. Franklin started to speak but Mr. Adams went right on.

"He wants to make a show. It's his way of getting up in the world. Look how he talks." Here Mr. Adams slapped the paper again. "Our American officers are not gentlemen; they can barely read and write, he says, and are fit only to be boatswains! Landais of the *Alliance* is not a gentleman and is mad besides, he thinks. Jones says officers should be gentlemen such as he would not be ashamed to sit down at the table with! Are you and I, sir, I a farm boy, you a printer, good enough to sit down with this—this *gentleman?* Though I understand he's the son of a Scottish gardener!"

Dr. Franklin said mildly, "These young men here plan to serve under Captain Jones, Mr. Adams. One of them was released from prison because he was exchanged for an Eng-lishman Jones captured."

Mr. Adams growled that he wished us luck, threw the paper on the table and went out.

Dr. Franklin said, "We have many perplexities here, gentle-men. You must not be surprised if we sometimes show we are vexed by them."

He didn't show he was vexed by anything, even by Mr. Adams, but smiled and added that he felt sure we would find Captain Jones a most able commander.

Duncan was grinding his teeth over Mr. Adams's remarks and was not likely to say anything very polite, so I said, "McTav-ish knows it already, sir. We were on the *Ranger* at Whitehaven and again when the *Drake* was taken and he has been with Captain Jones ever since."

I thought Dr. Franklin would never let us go after that. We had to run in and out of Whitehaven, visit St. Mary's Isle, and capture the *Drake* all over again.

Dr. Franklin sat with his thumb on his chin, nodding now and then.

At last he said, "If we had a dozen like him, this war would be over already."

I asked him, "Sir, you think it was right then, that he should attack the home of his boyhood?"

Dr. Franklin said, "Mr. Young, I am a man of peace. Noth-ing about war is either right or reasonable in my eyes. Men should use their reason to make the world a decent place to live in, not powder and shot to kill each other. Yet neither is it right that a small group of selfish men should oppress a whole nation. The colonists were loyal subjects of King George. They wanted simple justice. Only tyranny could have made them rise against him. When the first shot was fired—and we did not fire it—the second was bound to follow. I do not know when this war will end, but I can tell you this: it will never end with a British victory."

He was silent a moment and then went on, "As a man of peace I wish to see it over as soon as possible. To that end I will use John Paul Jones and his special knowledge of Scottish firths and Irish loughs and only wish there were more like him. Let him brag a little and kick a few lieutenants down ladders to their cabins, and strut around in fine clothes ashore. Since talking with you, I see more clearly than ever what he is like where he belongs—on the quarterdeck. And now, sirs, since you start your journey early tomorrow, I think you said, I wish you good fortune and a fair breeze."

We thanked him and went back to our lodgings. He is a great man, next to George Washington the best I know.

April 23rd. We started early for Paris today. In a printshop I saw an engraved portrait of Dr. Franklin, wearing his fur cap and spectacles. I went in to buy a copy of it, for the French make such things well and sell them cheap. In the portfolio with it was one of General Washington.

Then what should Duncan find but a picture of John Paul Jones! He was in battle on the *Ranger*. Clouds of smoke billowed behind him. He had a cocked hat, pistols at his belt, a sword in his hand. It did not look much like him, but we bought it anyway.

The last thing Captain Jones does in a battle is to stand still as if he were posing for his picture. To show him truly you would need pictures that would show him all over the ship. We bought a portfolio to keep the pictures in. Then it was time to start for L'Orient, which is more than 300 miles from Paris. It was fair weather all the way.

We traveled day and night. All the first night I kept dreaming I was back in Mill Prison.

By day Duncan and I often talked of Tahiti and of hunting kangaroos in New South Wales. I used to tell him about Virginia and what it would be like when he and Richard Dale and I sailed into Hampton Roads.

Yet at night I never dreamed of these things but only of Mill Prison.

Chapter 16

"BON HOMME RICHARD"

ON THE QUAY at L'Orient two men were walking up and down. One was elegantly dressed in a fine laced coat and waistcoat, spotless white breeches and stockings, shining shoes with shining buckles. He wore his cocked hat tipped just a little to one side. The man with him had no hat. Nick recognized him as one of the prisoners from the cartel *Milford*.

Nick recognized Captain Jones, too, of course. In the months since they had met, the line between the Captain's eyes had deepened. The muscles of his face seemed harder but he still looked at the world through eyes that could be mysterious and melancholy one minute, shrewd and humorous the next, then suddenly gay and friendly or coldly stern.

Of course there were other people on the quay besides Captain Jones and this ragged sailor, but the Scotch gardener's son had a way of making any place his own and of becoming the central figure in it. The big quay, the great harbor with masts everywhere stabbing the blue sky, the gulls veering and soaring, all seemed like a painted background for his small figure.

"He's at his old tricks again," Duncan said. "I've seen him walk up and down like this for hours to get a single seaman to sign the articles. I think he has this one under his spell now. The poor fellow sees himself sailing into Boston with money running out of his pockets. That neat little desk of leather and mahogany under the Captain's arm has the ship's articles in it... He'll find something to rest it on. Yes—there's a handy post. Now he gets out the ink and the pen and tests it on his thumbnail. It's all right—our sailor friend will make his mark... No, better still—he writes his name! Why, he's a scholar, fit to be an admiral, as I've heard the Captain say."

Captain Jones gave the man money and dismissed him with a friendly smile. The sailor bowed and pulled his forelock. The Captain courteously returned the salute, touching his hand to his cockaded hat. Then he tucked the desk back under his arm and started strolling across the quay toward where Duncan and Nick were standing.

"Now he'll begin on us," Duncan murmured. "He saw us out of the tail of his eye five minutes ago. He misses nothing, I can tell you."

Captain Jones's deep voice was already saying, "Mr. McTavish, I'm vastly pleased to see you, sir. And you, too, Mr. Caryl. I am glad the old *Milford* brought you back safely. Lucky you did not sink her with that musket, eh? And now, gentlemen, I must put you in the way of fame and fortune. You signed only for the *Ranger's* cruise but I still need midshipmen. I see two excellent ones, soon to grow into lieutenants and captains, springing up out of the planks under my feet! This seems a fortunate day for me and my ships. I have two under my command, hope to have others. There they lie," he added, with a wave of his hand. "That's the *Bon Homme Richard*, formerly the

Duc de Duras. I named her in honor of Dr. Franklin. Would you like to hear why?"

"Yes, indeed, sir."

"The *Ranger* sailed back to America. I was ordered to remain here and told I would receive command of a much better ship. There was one disappointment after another, too many to speak of. I wrote letter after letter to Paris and waited in vain for answers. One day I picked up an old copy of *Poor Richard's Almanack*—written, as you know, by Dr. Franklin.

"My eye fell on this sentence: 'If you wish your business done, go; if not, send.' I went to Paris! Soon I was given command of the *Duc de Duras*, with permission to change her name to the *Bon Homme Richard*, which is the French way of saying Poor Richard.

"That neat, trim vessel lying beyond the Richard is the *Alliance*," he went on. "She is the best frigate built in America so far. I need you on her, Mr. McTavish. Mr. Caryl and those eagle eyes of his are needed in the maintop of the *Bon Homme Richard*. I knew I need not spend an hour persuading you, gentlemen. I see love of liberty, hope of glory written on both your faces. A few scratches of the pen and you'll be members of my squadron. I have authority to issue commissions directly. It will be a pleasure to write your name on one, Mr. McTavish, and Mr. Caryl's on another."

The commissions were written in the cabin of the *Richard*, as the Americans of her crew called her. There were not yet many of them. There were English, Scotch, and Irish, who had been taken captive at sea. They preferred life even on an enemy ship to prison ashore. At sea, if they lost a battle, they had a chance of being rescued by a British ship. If they won the fight, they might get prize money. There were also sailors from France, Sweden, Spain and Portugal. There were some from the island of Malta and even Malays from the East Indies.

The crew of the *Alliance* was a similar mixture but with rather more Americans. Her captain, Pierre Landais, called himself an American but was really French. He had been an officer in the French Navy from which he had been dishonorably discharged. The American Congress, in a burst of enthusiasm over the French alliance, had given the command of their fine new frigate to Landais without inquiring about his record in the French Navy.

He was a man capable of making himself rapidly disliked and he did not waste time with Duncan. The ink was hardly dry on Duncan's new commission before he began to wish that he could be on the *Richard*, clumsy and old-fashioned as she looked with her high poop and forecastle, instead of on the trim, swift frigate.

Captain Landais, who spoke English with an accent as French as a ragout, claimed that he was the only American officer in the fleet. The others, he said, were a lot of Scotch traitors. He drank a great deal of wine and brandy. He mocked Captain Jones for drinking sweetened lemon and lime juice with his dinner and a single glass of wine afterwards. He boasted of his courage, offered to fight everyone in the cabin, brandished his pistols, and finally went to sleep with his head on the table.

Captain Jones remained calm during this scene but Nick noticed a vein throbbing in his temple and wondered how long his patience would last. It was Duncan's duty, with the help of another midshipman from the *Alliance*, to get Captain Landais back to his ship.

"I wish I'd dropped him in the harbor," he said to Nick the next morning.

Before he saw the last of Captain Pierre Landais, Nick wished so, too.

Of the Americans who came from Mill Prison, all but five enlisted with Captain Jones. Many of them took those long walks on the quay before signing the articles and being assigned either to the *Alliance* or the *Richard*. In this way both ships got American gunners, carpenters, boatswains and their mates. The *Alliance* needed only a complete crew to be ready for sea. The *Richard* had to be made over from an old merchantman—she reminded Nick of the *Princess Anne*—into a ship of war.

She was not only old-fashioned looking, with her poop more like an Elizabethan ship than a modern frigate, but her timbers were so rotten that it was difficult to make repairs. However, Captain Jones pushed the work ahead enthusiastically.

New guns could not be found for the *Richard*. Old ones had to serve. There were twelve-pounders on her gun deck, smaller guns on her quarter-deck and forecastle. A gun room was made aft. Six old-fashioned eighteen-pounders were placed there. Gun ports were cut for them so that all could be fired at once from either side. Altogether the *Richard* mounted forty-two guns and could throw three hundred pounds of metal.

Dr. Franklin took great interest in the ship that was his namesake. He wrote often to Captain Jones, who said that the letters "would make a coward brave."

Nick, who was again acting as the Captain's secretary, making copies of his letters, remembered especially one in which Benjamin Franklin wrote: "You are to try to bring to France all the Englishmen you may happen to take prisoners, in order to complete the good work you have made such progress in, of delivering by an exchange the rest of our countrymen now languishing in the jails of Great Britain. As many of your officers and crew have lately escaped from English prisons, you are to be particularly attentive to their conduct toward the prisoners whom fortunes of war may throw into your hands, lest resentment of the more than barbarous usage by the English toward the Americans should occasion a retaliation, and an imitation of what ought to be rather detested and avoided for the sake of humanity and the honor of our country."

The letter went on to order Jones not to burn defenseless towns as had been done by the British in America. He should first demand a reasonable ransom. If ransom were refused, he might be obliged to burn the place but he must give warning so that old or sick people, women and children could be removed to safety.

"And George III wants to hang this good man as a pirate," Nick said.

"Well," said Duncan, "there are plenty of English who don't want to hang Americans."

"That's true," Nick said. "I often think of the kind people who bought our punch ladles and who sent us money and of Mr. Heath who brought it to us."

"Yes," Duncan said, "and you said Mr. Banks came and gave you money, but why was he so secret about it?"

Nick told him the whole long story.

After he had heard it, Duncan said, "Then your name is really Caryl, not Young."

"Nicholas Young Caryl. Yes."

"Then you owe me five shillings."

"How is that?"

"I bet you five shillings when you came aboard the Providence that the Captain would know you. When he called you Caryl, I thought he had your name wrong and that you were too polite to offend his vanity by telling him he was mistaken. He's always boasting he never forgets a face or a name."

"And he doesn't," Nick said, handing over the five shillings.

"And that mincing, sneering grenadier captain who came across on the *Milford* was your cousin! Wouldn't he look fine stuffed? And they kill good kind American bears to make hats for such warriors!"

"Oh, Frederick isn't so bad. You ought to have seen his grandfather and his brothers. Really, I liked Frederick the best of my English relatives."

Duncan simply stared in silence and shook his head at this remark.

"Besides," Nick added, "if it had not been for their kindness, I might never have met you. Truly, Mr. McTavish, formerly Duncan, the model boy, I ought to be grateful to my cousins. Think what a chance they gave me to see the world."

"Yes, including the Black Hole at Mill Prison. I wonder if your friend Richard Dale is still in it."

"I keep hoping he will come before we sail," Nick said.

Richard Dale did not appear on the quay at L'Orient before the *Bon Homme Richard* and the *Alliance* set out on their first cruise together. Captain Jones had daring plans for destroying ships in British ports. To his disappointment he was ordered to drive British ships from the Bay of Biscay and to convoy French and American merchantmen from one French port to another.

They sailed from L'Orient on this service on the 17th of June. The cruise lasted only until the night of June 20th.

On this night the *Richard* and the *Alliance* collided with each other. Both ships were damaged and had to return to port for repairs. Officers on both ships—the lieutenant who was on watch on the *Richard*, Captain Landais on the *Alliance*—seem to have been at fault.

Landais lost his head completely. Instead of giving orders to prevent the collision or to get the ships clear after it, he rushed below and loaded his pistols, shouting that he would challenge Captain Jones to a duel. In the meantime Jones came on deck and gave the orders necessary to separate the two ships.

"Landais acted like a madman," Duncan told Nick when they were back in port. "He was trembling with fear when the ships struck. I believe he had no idea what to do and began bellowing challenges to cover up his cowardice. What will he do in battle is a sore thing to think of."

This accident seemed like a misfortune at the time. Yet it resulted in a piece of good luck for John Paul Jones and for everyone on the *Richard*. This was the arrival of the *Milford* again with more American sailors from English prisons, a hundred and nineteen this time. A few days later, strolling on to the quay, as casually as if he did it every day, came Richard Dale.

Richard had promised never to tell how he got the British uniform in which he sauntered out of Mill Prison, nor how he was sheltered and helped on his journey, nor how he got across the Channel. He kept his promise. Perhaps, as some people believed, a mysterious British lady of title helped him. Perhaps it was some farmer's daughter who had seen him at the market and had fallen in love with his handsome face and figure. Quite possibly there was no romance at all. Richard may have simply followed the Underground Road. The secrecy may have been to protect the British clergymen and other generous English people who sheltered American prisoners and gave them money. Whatever the mystery was, it remained a mystery. Even Nick never knew how Richard got to L'Orient.

Whoever helped Richard Dale gave John Paul Jones his best officer. Lieutenant Dale was an intelligent, hard-working man, liked by the crew as well as by the other officers for his courteous manners, his courage, his loyalty.

One of the English prisoners who had signed as a seaman on the *Richard* said to Nick, "Mr. Dale is a good-natured, clever sea officer. He has none of the haughty way with him that English officers show to us poor tars."

Some of those poor tars, Nick thought, are running a good chance of turning into Americans because of Richard Dale.

The men who came on this second trip of the cartel *Milford* were from Forton Prison at Portsmouth, England, and from other British jails and prison ships. Several men who became officers on the *Richard* were among them—Nathaniel Fanning and Samuel Stacey from Massachusetts, Henry Gardner from New Hampshire and John Mayrant from South Carolina. Fanning, a midshipman, was put in command of the maintop. Gardner became a gunner, Stacey the sailing master. Henry and Cutting Lunt had come on the *Milford*'s first trip. They became the *Richard*'s second and third lieutenants. It was Cutting Lunt who had been sent to Nantes to recruit as many men from the *Milford*'s second trip as possible. He had come back with one hundred and fourteen men out of the one hundred and nineteen prisoners.

Of these men, Nick liked Nathaniel Fanning especially. Fanning was about his own age. They had gone through much the same kind of prison experience. The station for both on the *Richard* was the maintop. The *Richard*'s tops were broad, the main one being like a room, almost twenty feet across. Their watch was the same and they spent many hours telling each other stories. Nick liked to hear Fanning tell about the pranks the Americans had played in Forton Prison.

They slept at Forton in the guardroom right over the British officers. They would make so much noise at night, playing fiddles and drums, dancing, singing, playing leapfrog, that the guard would be turned out several times to arrest them. Each time when the soldiers arrived, lights would be out and the Americans would be innocently sleeping in their hammocks.

"We were better drilled than the soldiers," Fanning said. "I learned to stop in the middle of 'Yankee Doodle,' swing my hammock and go to sleep before you could say Paul Revere."

"Who?" Nick asked, and Fanning told him how Revere made the handsomest silver teapots in Boston and engraved a picture of the Boston Massacre and rode to Lexington on the night of the 18th of April to warn people that the British were coming.

Unlike most naval captains of his day, Captain Jones spent much time training his crews for battle duty. He had done this ever since he was a young lieutenant on the *Alfred*. The *Richard* did not have enough supplies to carry out real target practice with the big guns, but in the tops there was small arms practice with powder and shot. The men in charge of the cannon went through all the manoeuvers but did not actually fire the guns.

A midshipman was in charge of a number of guns. His duty before the exercise was to see that each of his guns was supplied with sponge and rammer, powderhorn, powder, crow (an iron bar), hand spike, and ropes for hauling the gun into place.

One of the greatest dangers of a battle was an explosion in the gun room. The man who took care of the powder stayed in the opposite side of the deck from the guns. He was never to give a cartridge for any gun except to the powder monkey who served that gun. That was what the boys were called who carried the filled cartridges to the gunners. No lanterns were allowed on the gun deck at night until the midshipmen ordered them brought.

In these training exercises, except for the matches not being lighted, all the motions were made as they would be in battle. In the tops, Nick and Fanning and the others were trained in the use of mortars called cohorns. These were supposed to lob cannon balls into the enemy's tops or onto his deck. The best marksmen were stationed in the tops. They had small arms of various sorts including muskets and grenades. Firing small arms was one place in which the Americans had a real advantage over the British.

Duncan was visiting the *Richard* one day and joined in the target practice. After missing a gull by a wide margin, he said, "You American lads who got right out of your cradles and went duck shooting make the rest of us look foolish. It was a pity I did not start young as a poacher in England. Then if I had managed to trap a rabbit, I would have been arrested and sent to New Hampshire or Virginia for seven years. There I could have hunted deer and bears and passenger pigeons. After a while I might have been able to hit a gull. Of course," he added, "Captain Landais doesn't have shooting practice. He says the French marines are supposed to do the shooting."

"Captain Jones says the marines on the *Richard* are supposed to keep the crew from killing the officers," Nathaniel Fanning said.

It was now the middle of August. Captain Jones's little squadron was almost ready to sail. It consisted of seven ships. The *Bon Homme Richard* had twenty-eight nine- and twelve-pounders on the gun deck, six eighteen-pounders in the gun room, eight small guns on the quarter-deck and forecastle, making forty-two in all. The *Alliance* had thirty-six guns. The *Pallas*, a former French merchantman, commanded by Captain Cottineau, had thirty twelve-pounders. The *Vengeance*, a brig, Captain Ricot commanding, had twelve three pounders. There was also the *Cerf*, a well-equipped cutter from the French Marine, commanded by Captain Varage. Two privateers, the *Monsieur* and the *Granville*, also joined them.

One hot afternoon Nick was called from his target practice to go to the Captain's cabin. The young midshipman who brought the message had been kicked across the cabin by Captain Jones. He was still limping.

"I only misspelled a few words of his old concordat," he said, "and made a few blots. He almost pulled my ears off before he kicked me."

He was a very pink young midshipman. He was still wiping tears off his pink cheeks. His ears were certainly red.

"He's never angry long." Nick said. "He'll ask you to dinner in the cabin tomorrow, as likely as not. There'll be pigeon pie. Wear a clean shirt. He wouldn't like those spots!"

It was true that Captain Jones would hit a midshipman over the head with a speaking trumpet one morning and that afternoon invite him to dinner, expecting him to be dressed in his best.

The high tide of the Captain's anger with the pink midshipman had ebbed by the time Nick reached the cabin but his face was still darkened by a grim frown. He was pacing the cabin with the light step that always made Nick think of a red fox on the prowl. He had a paper in his hand. The torn and crumpled pieces of the ink-blotted copy were still on the floor.

"Good afternoon, Mr. Caryl," Captain Jones said, with his

formal courtesy but with no lightening of his deeply lined face. "I require six copies of this"—he paused and swallowed—"precious document, which will do more to damage my squadron than if a ship of the line chased us onto a lee shore."

He laid the paper on the table, smoothing it out with exaggerated care, still scowling. Then he smiled suddenly, and added, "Fair copies. I do not expect to pull your ears, especially as it would be difficult for me to reach them. That is, unless you will favor me by sitting down, sir."

Nick sat down at the table and began to trim a quill with his penknife. This was the first time Nick's great height had been mentioned by the Captain. Nick was more than six feet six of bone and muscle now. He had grown tired of jokes about it.

Yet John Paul's voice and smile made Nick smile in return. You couldn't, he thought, slanting his pen just as he liked it, help admiring this small hot-tempered man, so valiant, such a brilliant seaman, so intent on doing great work, and with such poor tools to use. The Captain would drive his half-mutinous crew and his rickety old ship hard, Nick knew, but he would always drive himself harder still. What, he wondered, was this new difficulty that had been put in his way?

The Captain was already beginning to tell him.

"Since you are to copy this—concordat," Captain Jones said, making the word a term of reproach, "I will explain it to you. You know perhaps that Monsieur LeRay de Chaumont is supplying the money for this expedition. He is a man who has the best heart in the world. He loves liberty and has been most generous to America in her struggle for it. Unluckily, his head is not of the same quality as his heart. Someone, foolishly eager that France should not take second place with America, has made him think that our expedition will work best if the commanders of the ships follow their plans without interference. He told me in Paris last June that I was the commander but must not ask any service from the other captains that would interfere with their plans for their own ships."

"You mean, sir, that though you command the squadron, you cannot give orders?"

"You express it very well, Mr. Caryl. As senior American officer, I am in command of the squadron. All the ships are under American commission and will fight under the Stars and Stripes. But they do so only because the other captains, Landais, Cottineau, Varage, and Ricot, signed this agreement, the concordat, as they call it. I must consult them about their plans and get them to agree to mine! The finest fleet that ever sailed could not succeed under such rules. However, we will do what we can. The British shall know the name of Paul Jones yet."

"They know it already, sir. Their newspapers often mention it."

"Favorably?"

"Well—" Nick began.

"Never mind, Mr. Caryl," Paul Jones said, smiling. "I've read them. Like Dr. Franklin, General Washington, and yourself, sir, I am a traitor and a rebel. If I am hanged, it will be in good company. Six copies, please. I know they will be well written."

CHAPTER 17

A PRAYER FOR WIND

THE BAD EFFECTS of the concordat soon became evident. It was important, as Captain Jones knew, that all the captains should feel they were fighting for the interests of America and under command of the American Congress. Yet the French officers, though they were to fight—or run away—under the American flag, did not consider themselves part of the American Navy.

They wanted to take prizes and become rich. Monsieur LeRay de Chaumont, though he had been generous in equipping the expedition, wanted prizes taken so he could get his money back. Landais, who constantly told people that he was the only American officer in the squadron and ought to be in command of it, was interested in prize money, not in fighting British frigates. Captain Jones was not indifferent to prize money. It was the system of the time. No crew would have enlisted without promise of a share in valuable captures.

Prize money was important to the Captain, but he cared far more for bringing the war to an end by his courage and daring than he did for becoming rich. If he had wanted money, he

could easily have become captain of a privateer. He had been offered such commands more than once and had refused them. He often advanced money to seamen out of his own share of prize money. He never received from the American Congress any pay for his services.

The squadron sailed on August 14th, 1779. Early in the cruise they saw a large ship in the distance. Captain Jones ordered Landais to go and see what she was. Landais sailed toward her but soon returned, having found out nothing. Jones called him a coward, a true but unfortunate remark. There had never been a liking between them. Now there was hatred.

On the 18th the squadron recaptured a large Dutch ship from an English privateer. The *Monsieur's* captain took goods from the prize and manned her out for port without consulting Captain Jones. He countermanded the orders and had her sent to L'Orient according to Monsieur LeRay de Chaumont's instructions. This action offended the captain of the *Monsieur.* She sailed off and never joined the squadron again.

The rest of the fleet reached Cape Clear, the southernmost part of Ireland, on the 23rd of August. They had taken several prizes. English prisoners were being crowded into the darkness of the *Richard's* hold. The evening was calm. Jones sent his ships inshore to capture a brigantine. The tide carried the *Richard* toward some dangerous rocks and the Captain ordered his barge out to tow her away from them.

As darkness came on, some Englishmen of the barge's crew cut the towline and rowed the barge ashore. Lieutenant Cutting Lunt tried to follow the barge and capture it. Fog came up. He went too close to shore and was captured himself with several of the *Richard's* best American seamen.

The next morning Captain Landais came on board the *Richard* apparently to insult her captain. He reproached Jones for the loss of his boats and said that, as the only American in the squadron, he would from here on, use his own judgment about when to chase ships. He added that Jones was endangering the whole fleet by staying so close to Ireland and that they would soon all be prisoners.

Jones controlled his temper. He consulted Captain Cottineau and Captain Varage of the *Cerf* about what to do. With their advice, Varage went in search of Cutting Lunt and the barge. He was threatened by a British ship and sailed back to France. Later the *Granville* took a prize and returned to France with it.

The squadron now consisted of the *Richard*, the *Alliance*, the *Pallas* and the *Vengeance*.

On the night of the 26th of August, it began to blow hard from the southwest. Jones ordered the squadron to run north along the coast of Ireland. They obeyed except that Landais sailed on a course of his own choosing and disappeared. However, the *Alliance* joined the squadron again on the 31st. She had with her a valuable prize, a West Indiaman.

When the *Alliance* appeared, Captain Jones had just captured a twenty-two gun ship, the *Union*, bound for Canada with naval stores. Landais sent an insolent message asking if he should man his own prize for France, in which case no men from the *Richard* were to come on board her. For the sake of peace Jones agreed to this demand. Landais put a crew on board his prize but sent the prisoners from her to the *Richard*.

The same day Landais disobeyed a signal from Jones to chase a ship. He also sent two prizes to Bergen in Norway instead of to L'Orient as Jones had ordered. This resulted in the British getting back the prizes, a loss of thousands of pounds in prize money. On the evening of the 4th of September, Jones ordered all the captains to come on board the *Richard*. This Landais refused to do. To Captain Cottineau of the *Pallas*, who tried to persuade him to go, he said that he would see Captain Jones on shore where one of them would kill the other.

By the 14th of September they had rounded the north of Scotland and were running down the east coast near the Firth of Forth. Jones captured several vessels from Leith and learned that this rich town, up the Firth above Edinburgh, was defended only by a twenty-gun ship and three or four cutters.

Nick was summoned to the cabin that evening to act as secretary at a meeting. John Paul Jones had made one of his brilliant and daring plans. He needed the help of the rest of the squadron. Only Cottineau and Ricot appeared in the *Richard's* cabin. Duncan brought a message from Landais to say that he was unable to attend.

"I think he's insane," Duncan said to Nick before he returned to the *Alliance.*

The other captains, however, seemed to consider that it was Captain Jones who was mad—or at least that his scheme was. He intended first to capture the warships in the harbor of Leith, then to land his marines and threaten the town with burning unless Leith paid ransom.

"We will teach the British not to burn American towns," he said.

He scowled in his determined way. His eyes flashed as they always did when he spoke of British oppression.

"They shall learn," he went on, "that none of their harbors is safe from attack. The French fleet is soon to attack the south of England. An attack by us in the north will make the British send ships here. That will help the French to a victory in the south. Come, gentlemen, the wind is fair, honor and humanity are on our side. Mr. Caryl will read you the letter I have written to the magistrates."

Nick picked the letter up from the table and read it.

The Honorable J. Paul Jones, Commander-in-chief of the American Squadron now in Europe, to the worshipful Provost of Leith, or in his absence, to the Chief Magistrate now actually present and in authority:

Sir:
The British marine force that has been stationed here for

the protection of your city and commerce, being now taken by the American arms under my command, I have the honor to send you my summons by my officer, Lieutenant Colonel de Chamillard, who commands the vanguard of my troops. I do not wish to distress the poor inhabitants; my intention is only to demand your contribution toward the reimbursement which Britain owes to the much injured citizens of the United States; for savages would blush at the unmannerly violation and rapacity that have marked the tracks of British tyranny in America.

Leith and its port now lie at our mercy; and did not humanity stay the hand of just retaliation, I should, without advertisement, lay it in ashes. Before I proceed to that stern duty as an officer, my duty as a man induces me to propose to you, by means of a reasonable ransom, to prevent such a scene of horror and distress. For this reason, I have authorized Lieutenant Colonel de Chamillard to conclude and agree with you on terms of ransom, allowing you exactly half an hour's reflection before you finally accept or reject the terms which he shall propose. If you accept the terms offered within the time limited, you may rest assured that no further debarkation of troops will be made, but the re-embarkation of the vanguard will immediately follow, and the property of the citizens shall remain unmolested.

"Now, gentlemen," Captain Jones said, as Nick finished reading, "your advice will be welcome. Mr. Dale?"

Richard Dale said: "We have already spent too much time in talk, sir. The wind is fair. Let us go!"

"You do not consider the plan imprudent or unlikely of accomplishment, Mr. Dale?"

"Not if the wind holds," Richard Dale said.

The French captains still hung back. At last Ricot inquired what amount of ransom would be asked.

"Two hundred thousand pounds," Jones said.

The French officers' faces brightened. After asking about cannon at Leith and hearing that there were none, they gave their consent to the plan. So much time had been wasted in argument that they soon lost their fair wind. However, the squadron continued to beat its way up the Firth.

On the 16th the owner of a large estate saw the squadron coming up the Firth. As the ships were flying British flags he thought they were ships of the British Navy, sent to protect the coast from the pirate, Paul Jones. A boat was sent out to the *Richard*, asking for powder and shot to load a cannon to fire at the pirate. Jones sent the owner of the cannon a barrel of powder and a polite message, regretting that he had no suitable shot.

Richard Dale was right. The success of the plan depended on the wind. If they had started sooner things might have been different. As it was, a fierce gale sprang up and blew them away from Leith.

One night later that week, Nick and another midshipman, who had spent much time in England and who had lost most of his American accent, went ashore. They had made several of these visits. Nick told Duncan that they frightened him more than gales at sea, scurvy, cannibals or British warships. However, Captain Jones considered them important. They were a way of getting news about British shipping and about what was being done to capture the pirate, Paul Jones.

They visited taverns, read any newspapers they found, listened to the conversations that went on over boiled haggis and cabbage or smoked haddock. This was not the ideal way to enjoy Scotch cooking. Nick never really learned to like haggis. He had already eaten enough cabbage in Mill Prison. However, he liked haddock and kippers and oatcake. He also enjoyed what an Edinburgh newspaper said about their trip to Leith.

If the paper was correct, the foul pirate, Paul Jones, had been chased away from Leith by the prayers of a Scottish clergyman. On the afternoon of September 16th, the paper said, the American ships were seen from Edinburgh Castle. People suspected it was Jones's squadron. There was terror all along the Firth. When the *Bon Homme Richard* tacked close to Kircaldy on the north shore of the Firth, the minister of the place, the Reverend Mr. Shirra, knelt with his people on the shore. He was well known for his unusual prayers. The one he made at this time was given in the paper. With Duncan's help, Nick wrote it down in something less hard to understand than the original Scottish:

Now, dear Lord, do you not think it a shame to send this vile pirate to rob our poor folk of Kircaldy? For you know they're poor enough already, and have nothing to spare. The way the wind blows, he'll be here in a jiffy and who knows what he may do? He's not too good for anything! Much is the mischief he has done already. He'll burn their houses, take their clothes, and who knows but the bloody villain may take their lives? The poor women are frightened out of their wits and children sobbing after them. I cannot put up with it—I cannot put up with it! I have long been a faithful servant to you, Lord, but if you do not turn the wind about and blow the scoundrel away, I'll not stir a foot but will just sit here till the tide comes. So take your will of it!

Just then the gale began. A prize Jones had taken was blown ashore and—as Nick well knew—the American squadron was literally blown away from Leith.

When asked if he felt he had saved Kircaldy, Mr. Shirra replied modestly, "I prayed but the Lord sent the wind."

Captain Jones was naturally disappointed that his plan had failed but he at once invented equally bold ones for attacking the English towns of Hull and Newcastle. The French captains had no appetite for more such adventures. They refused to help him. Indeed, they threatened to leave him if he even remained near the coast.

The concordat was doing the work that the British could not do.

Since he could not carry out his scheme—and Dr. Franklin's—of putting British towns under ransom, Jones now turned his mind back to destroying shipping. In one of the papers Nick had read in a Scottish tavern was the news that the Baltic Fleet—British merchantmen trading with Baltic ports—would be convoyed by a fine new frigate, H.M.S. *Serapis*, forty-four guns, and by a smaller warship, the *Countess of Scarborough*, twenty guns.

The paper said the *Serapis* was of improved construction. Her commander was Captain Pearson, a brave and experienced captain. She had a crew of more than three hundred well-trained British seamen. The *Countess of Scarborough*, though smaller, was also a good ship. The Baltic Fleet was well protected, the paper said.

If Captain Pearson had learned as much about the pirate Paul Jones, he must have heard that the *Bon Homme Richard* was a rotting, lumbering old merchant ship that did not always answer well to her helm. He would know that her guns were old, many of her crew ready for mutiny, her officers inexperienced, her hold full of British prisoners who in a battle might fight their way out and seize the ship.

She was commanded by a pirate who had—it was true—done some damage to merchant shipping and who stole silver from women. Two small French ships were with him. Captain Pearson did not think much of French seamanship. The swift new American frigate had deserted the squadron. It was the only enemy ship that worried the captain of the *Serapis* at all. He did not realize that Captain Landais was much more dangerous as a friend than as an enemy.

Unfortunately for the American squadron, the *Alliance* rejoined it on September 23rd. Captain Jones had been cruising along the coast of Yorkshire. He had destroyed several colliers bound for London. Interfering with the coal trade was one of his many schemes for making the English realize that the United States had a navy. The squadron now consisted of the *Richard*, the *Alliance*, the *Pallas*, and the *Vengeance*.

At noon that day, a fair day with a gentle breeze from the south-southwest, Nick saw from the maintop Lieutenant Henry Lunt, with fifteen of the *Richard's* best seamen, leave the side of the *Richard* in one of her boats. He heard Captain Jones, in his deep, ringing voice, order Henry Lunt to go and take possession of a brigantine which they had chased close to the shore.

Something about those deep tones of the Captain's voice reminded Nick of the night before they sailed from L'Orient.

Captain Jones had given a dinner at an inn called L'Epée Royale. All the officers of the squadron were present. John Adams, who had come to see the squadron before it sailed, was there. Nick heard him say to Captain Jones as he said good night that the dinner had been a most elegant affair and the conversation agreeable and instructive.

Nick was proud of his captain, who had been agreeable, too, as a host. Even Captain Landais had been less arrogant than usual. After the guests had left, Nick was summoned to the cabin to copy some letters. In one to the head of the French Marine, Captain Jones had written, "Our little squadron appears harmonious and if good understanding continues, we shall be able to perform essential services."

In writing to Madame de Chaumont, Captain Jones thanked her politely for her kindness to him while he was in Paris and said, "I hope to write my name with honor on the page of history."

As he read these words Nick had a feeling that the page of history was already being written. The feeling came to him again on the morning of the 23rd of September as he heard the Captain give Henry Lunt his orders.

CHAPTER 18

H.M.S. "SERAPIS"

FLAMBOROUGH HEAD is a triangular headland that thrusts itself far out from the east coast of northern England. Vessels cruising along that coast are forced to sail far out from land to avoid the Head. This, as John Paul Jones knew, put them in a position where they could easily be attacked. North of the Head is the port of Scarborough. Southwest of it is Bridlington Bay. Thirty miles south of Flamborough Head another headland, called Spurn Head, juts out near the mouth of the river Humber. It was a good hunting ground for merchant ships. The squadron had cruised in the region for some days, taking several prizes.

Captain Jones knew the ins and outs of the coast as he made it his business to know every coast where his ships sailed. He had spent his leisure moments in studying every detail of charts of the region. If the Baltic Fleet rounded Flamborough Head, he would know what to do.

In the handsome new cabin of the *Serapis*, that fine forty-four-gun British frigate, Captain Pearson was talking with the captain of the *Countess of Scarborough*. They were convoying the Baltic Fleet. Information had been received about John Paul Jones. The English sailors who deserted on the Irish coast had told all they knew about the American squadron. The news had had time to reach English ports. From Edinburgh, too, news had reached the *Serapis*. By now the appearance of the *Richard*, her old-fashioned poop and forecastle, her black-painted sides, the number and position of her gun ports, was well known. She was said to be a dull, slow ship to sail. The French ships with her, the *Pallas* and the *Vengeance*, were small and could do little.

"The only ship that might give us trouble," Captain Pearson said, "is this American frigate, the *Alliance*. If she is with them, that is. She is said to have left them. Captain Jones is not able to maintain discipline, I understand."

He spoke contemptuously.

Captain Pearson was proud of the *Serapis*, of her well-drilled crew, of her clean new sails and fresh paint. She was black with broad yellow streaks along her sides. Gun ports were dark squares against the yellow, giving an effect of checked yellow and black. The masts and spars were bright with new varnish. The mahogany table at which the Captain was sitting, every coil of line on her well-scrubbed deck, her guns, her lanterns were all new and of the best British quality. Everything that should be polished—the decanter of wine, the silver coaster that held it, the youngest midshipman's buttons—shone brightly.

They were running north-northeast to round Flamborough Head. There were thirty-nine ships in the convoy besides the *Serapis* and the *Countess of Scarborough*. Captain Pearson had just learned that morning that the American squadron had been sailing south the day before. He was not much worried about their overtaking the convoy but he told the captain of the *Countess* that they would both get to windward, between the convoy and the enemy. As the wind was blowing from the southwest the convoy could easily sail northeast and round the Head.

The captain of the *Countess* went back to his ship. Captain Pearson went on deck. The sea around him was covered with white sails shining in the noon sunlight as the ships of the convoy kept their course. Captain Pearson had no doubt that he could protect them. The *Serapis* was classed as a forty-four-gun ship. Actually, she had fifty guns. She had two covered gun decks with twenty eighteen-pounders on the lower deck, twenty nine-pounders on the main deck, and ten six-pounders on the uncovered spar deck above. She could throw three hundred pounds of metal at one time. She had no reason to be afraid of American pirates.

In the maintop of the *Bon Homme Richard* two midshipmen, Nicholas Young Caryl and Nathaniel Fanning, were enjoying the soft September sunshine and the light breeze from the southwest. It came over the land and hardly disturbed the sea at all. The *Richard*, leading the American squadron, was moving slowly before the wind with every sail set. Her course would take her to the east of Flamborough Head.

The two midshipmen were pleasantly employed in figuring their prize money. There were a good many ifs in their calculations. *If* the prizes all reached port... *if* the goods and ships brought fair prices... *if* the agent cheated neither Monsieur LeRay de Chaumont nor the Americans... *if* all went well, then Mr. Fanning and Mr. Caryl were going to have plenty of gold jingling in their pockets.

"What will you do with yours?" Nick asked.

"Buy a fast ship, commission her as a privateer. Take more

prizes. Make my fortune. What will you do, Nick?" But Nick was never to tell his plans. His keen eyes had seen something to the northeast. White sails were pricking up all over the pale water between them and Flamborough Head.

Nick's shout, "Sail ho! Twenty-thirty-forty sail. Nor'-nor'east," rang out all over the ship. It reached the cabin where John Paul Jones sat writing one of his elegant letters full of fine long words.

He jumped up and came on deck. The letter was never finished.

Nick called down, "I think it's the Baltic Fleet, sir. And they have seen us. They are tacking, heading for Scarborough. They are letting fly their topgallant sheets. They're firing signal guns—there goes the first puff of powder!"

The sounds of the guns followed the smoke across the sea as Nick added, "There's a frigate with them, sir. I can see the hull now. Looks like a forty-four. She's black, checked with yellow. I think it's the *Serapis*. She's heading southeast now, sir, to get between us and the convoy. There's a smaller ship with her, closer to the convoy—ship of war, I think. Might carry twenty guns. Only one deck."

Captain Jones gave his orders as calmly as if this were training practice. He first ordered the squadron to form a line of battle. The *Pallas* was to engage the British sloop. The *Alliance* was ordered to help the *Richard* with the frigate. They would try to board her. The *Pallas* and the *Vengeance* obeyed and formed a line. Captain Landais, as usual, disobeyed. He sailed to windward, close to the land, where he could safely see what went on.

"Poor Duncan," Nick said to Fanning, "how he must be grinding his teeth over such cowardice!"

Captain Jones did not let the behavior of Landais disturb him, but went on giving orders to get the *Richard* ready for battle. Soon her decks were cleared. Officers and crew were at their stations. On the towering poop were de Chamillard and twenty French marines. Captain Jones, with three midshipmen to carry his messages, was on the quarter-deck. With him, in charge of the guns, was Mr. Mease, the purser. There were also sailors and marines. Henry Lunt, the sailing master, did not return to the *Richard*. His place was taken by Samuel Stacey, who moved wherever he was needed: quarter-deck, poop, gangway, or forecastle. His mate had charge of the six eighteen-pounders in the gun room on the lower deck. There were ten men to fight each gun.

Since both the Lunts were missing—Cutting a prisoner of the British, Henry chasing a ship in Bridlington Bay—Richard Dale was the only lieutenant left. He was in command of the men on the gun deck. The gunner acted as his lieutenant. The boatswain commanded the men and guns on the forecastle. The carpenter and his mates had no special stations but were told to do their duty wherever they were needed. Down in the cockpit, the ship's doctor was laying out his knives and saws and bandages. He had brandy to give a man if he had to cut his leg or arm off. Deep in the hold the British prisoners, more than a hundred of them, guessing by the hurrying feet and shouted orders that a battle was coming, groaned and cursed and beat their fists on the planks above their heads.

Nathaniel Fanning had command of the maintop with Nick as his mate. Other midshipmen, marines, and sailors were in all the tops. The men there were armed with muskets and blunderbusses. They had cohorns (which Nat Fanning called cowhorns), hand grenades, cartridges, powder, flint and steel, and slow matches. Last of all, a double allowance of grog for the men was hauled up to the tops.

When Fanning, Nick, and the other midshipmen went down to the quarter-deck to receive the Captain's orders, they met Richard Dale, just leaving. Richard looked very handsome with his curling hair, bronzed cheeks, and pleasant smile. He was dressed in his best blue and white with buttons shining like gold. Nick thought of how they had looked after forty days in the Black Hole and smiled at him. Richard smiled back, reached up and patted Nick on the shoulder. Richard was a great man on the ship now, next to the Captain in importance. Nick was far below him in rank but their friendship had lasted too long to be changed by circumstances. Neither spoke. Even without speech each knew what the other was thinking.

John Paul Jones had to look up at most of his tall midshipmen but none thought of him as small that day.

He's as big as the ship—he is the ship, Nick thought.

The Captain gave his orders quietly and precisely. The men in the tops were to use their best marksmanship and make every shot count. He said that the cannon of the British frigate were undoubtedly better than the *Richard's*, so a great deal depended on the small arms fire from the tops. He said he would get alongside the frigate and fight yardarm to yardarm and hand to hand. As soon as the ships were yardarm to yardarm, the men must go across and take possession of the enemy's tops. Then they would be in a good position to clear her decks.

He made it all sound as easy as an evening stroll along the quay at L'Orient. He dismissed them with one of his surprisingly gay smiles, saying, "I know I can count on you, gentlemen. We'll take her, never fear!"

The minutes had seemed to race by as they cleared for action.

Now, while they were at their stations waiting for the battle to begin, time moved as slowly as a great turtle Nick had once seen on a beach in New South Wales. He said so to Fanning, who, surprisingly, said nothing. Fanning was pulling his watch out of his fob. He was proud of his watch, a fine French repeater. He had bought it in a pawnshop in L'Orient with his first month's pay after he came to the *Richard* from Forton Prison.

"It's six o'clock," he said.

It was so quiet on the *Richard* that Nick could hear the watch chime six silvery strokes.

All the afternoon the squadron—except for the *Alliance*—had been moving slowly north-northeast with the light breeze from the shore. The British convoy was north of them and closer inshore. From one of the English seamen of the *Richard's* crew, they had learned that the black and yellow frigate was indeed the *Serapis* and that the sloop of war was the *Countess of Scarborough*. She was named for the very harbor for which the convoy, disobeying orders from the *Serapis*, had sailed in such confusion. The *Countess* was closer inshore than the convoy but was now moving away from it toward the *Serapis*, which was hove to, waiting for her.

Just as Fanning's watch stopped striking, the two British warships went about, steering west. Captain Jones could see from the quarter-deck that they meant to get to windward of him. He gave orders that spun the *Richard* sharply around and in turn gained the weather gage. He was now well placed between the British ships and the shore. Yet the *Richard* sailed so slowly in the lightly stirring air that even with the help of the tide they did not come within hail of the *Serapis* until after Fanning's watch had chimed seven.

As slowly as the *Richard* moved that calm evening, the

twilight faded over the green shores of England. Dim blue shadows began to rise from land and sea. On the walls of Scarborough Fort, on the heights of Flamborough Head, Nick could see hundreds of pinkish spots which were the faces of people who had come out to watch the battle. For a time their voices came across the water like the buzz of angry wasps around a nest. Now, as if they knew the curtain was going up on the play, they fell silent, gazing across the glassy water at the slowly moving ships.

From the masthead of the *Serapis* fluttered St. George's colors, the white flag crossed with red, with the union at the head. Suddenly it dropped down and in its place was the blood-red battle flag. Nick could see her captain nailing one like it to a staff on the quarter-deck.

Now above the *Richard's* top the American flag with its thirteen stripes and its union of thirteen stars was run up. It was the first time it had flown from the *Richard's* masthead. It drooped at first with only the stripes showing. Then, as Nick looked up at it, a little breeze caught it and he saw the stars.

He was carried back swiftly across oceans and continents to where Tupia lay dying and heard him say, "A strange flag... stars... a dark ship..."

Always before when Nick had thought of Tupia's words he had imagined a battle under stars in the sky.

American Stars, he thought. How strange that he should have seen them. And we'll soon have English stars, too.

There were already faint flashes of gold in the clear sky, but now a brighter light was dimming them. Out of the sea to the east the full moon was rising. To the people on Flamborough Head, Nick thought, both ships, still gliding silently on the still water, must be dark against it.

The *Richard* and the *Serapis* were now on the same tack, heading northwest toward Flamborough Head, the *Richard* slightly in advance. In the deep, breathless silence a hail rang out: "What ship is that?"

John Paul Jones did not answer the hail at once. He hoped to drop astern of the *Serapis*. He waited, taking advantage of every moment of delay possible. When the ships were barely more than a pistol shot apart, he called: "I can't hear what you say."

He could see the British frigate's lower deck. The gun ports were now triced up. Two complete batteries, besides those on the spar deck, were lighted up for action. In the growing darkness the burning matches glowed like red stars.

Captain Pearson's voice rasped, "Answer immediately or I shall be under the necessity of firing on you."

Fire followed at once from both ships, but where the broadside from the *Serapis* darkened quickly into black smoke, from the stern of the *Richard* came a flash of scarlet flame. Two of the old eighteen-pounders had exploded, killing many of the gun crews. The explosion had smashed the deck above into splinters and had blown a great hole in her hull.

The ships were abreast of each other now and the *Serapis* brought her lower battery into play. Her first fire had been from the guns on her quarter-deck. Jones tried several times by backing his topsails to get under the stern to rake her. (Raking is sailing across the path of an enemy ship, firing all the guns of a battery, one after the other. Raking may reach parts of a ship that might escape shots from a broadside.) Unfortunately the *Richard*, always a dull sailor, had had some of her braces shot away. She responded badly to her helm. The *Serapis*, quick to move, even in the light breeze, succeeded in raking the *Richard's* stern. Her fire killed several of de Chamillard's marines on the poop. He withdrew his men to the quarter-deck. More broadsides damaged her starboard side. Before long some of her guns were out of action.

In the tops things were going better. The Americans kept up a constant fire against the enemy. Man after man in the tops of the *Serapis* was hit and fell. The fire from her tops did little damage to the *Richard*.

"But she outsails us two feet to one," Fanning said to Nick.

For a moment the *Serapis* swung away from the *Richard* out of musket range. The tops on both ships were quiet. Nick heard the carpenter say to Captain Jones, "We've had several shots between wind and water, sir. I've patched up some but we're leaking badly in spite of all I can do."

Captain Jones said calmly, "Do the best you can," and then, to the sailing master, "Mr. Stacey, they are trying to get athwart hawse to rake us. We must close with them and get ready to board."

From the top they could see that Captain Pearson was trying to cross the *Richard's* bow to rake her from stem to stern. They began firing again—at the men who worked the topsails, at the men in the tops, at anything that moved on the deck. The *Serapis* failed to cross the *Richard's* bow. Captain Pearson ordered his helm put hard aweather. This brought the *Serapis* in line with the *Richard* and ahead of her.

Neither ship could now use her big guns to advantage. For once the wind, which had so often defeated John Paul Jones's plans, helped him. A lucky puff carried the *Richard* forward and she ran into the enemy's starboard quarter. Captain Jones ordered grappling irons out and shouted to his crew to board the *Serapis*. They tried it but were thrust back into the *Richard*. The grappling irons were thrown into the sea.

There was a strange moment of silence. The smoke from the guns drifted away. The moonlight shone down on the ships. It showed the British flag still flying but on the *Richard* the Stars and Stripes had been shot away and hung dangling from the staff. Captain Pearson must have seen it and have thought that the *Richard* had struck her colors.

Why not?

By every rule of war she was a beaten ship. There was room to drive a coach and four through the gaping hole between her mainmast and her stern. Her biggest guns were useless, her best gunners dead. Between wind and water, her rotten old timbers were so splintered by shot that they could not be patched up. Her sails were hanging in rags. She was on fire in several places. There was so much water in her hold that she had begun to settle into the sea. There were so many holes in her side, close to the water, that a wave of any size would have sunk her. No wonder Captain Pearson thought she had struck her colors.

He called through his speaking trumpet: "Has your ship struck?"

John Paul Jones needed no trumpet to make himself heard. They could hear his voice in the tops of the *Richard*, on her deck, on the quarter-deck of the *Serapis*, as he answered, "No, sir! She has not struck. *I have not yet begun to fight.*"

In writing about the battle John Paul Jones used some of his favorite long words. "I answered him," he said, "in a determined negative." Luckily, in the battle itself he used words that gave his men new courage.

Guns crashed again. The *Serapis* once more tried to cross the *Richard's* bow to rake her, but at last came the wind for which Captain Jones had been hoping. He put his helm hard aweather. His topsails were braced back. A fresh flaw of wind swelled them. The *Richard* shot ahead, swung sharply around the *Serapis*, which ran her jib boom between the starboard mizzen shrouds of the *Richard*.

Nick was putting out a fire in the maintop with his jacket. He heard Captain Jones cry out, "Well done, my brave lads—we have got her now!"

Nick looked down. He saw the *Serapis* let go her anchor. The pull of the anchor, working with the *Richard's* headway, might tear the ships apart, he thought. No doubt Captain Pearson thought the same, but Captain Jones was too quick for him.

"Bring me a hawser, Mr. Stacey," he called.

The sailing master brought it, cursing as his fingers fumbled over a knot.

Jones took it from him.

"Don't swear, Mr. Stacey," he said gravely. "We may at the next moment be in eternity but let us do our duty."

He seized the jib stay and, with the aid of the hawser, made it fast to the mizzenmast of the *Richard*. By good fortune, a spare anchor of the *Serapis* hooked the *Richard's* quarter. The two ships now lay locked fast together, bow to stern, so close that the muzzles of the *Richard's* starboard guns almost touched the starboard guns of the *Serapis*. From then on the two ships swung together with wind and tide.

The guns in the center of the ship were so close together that they could not be sponged and rammed. Farther along the sides they could sponge and ram the guns but had to run the rammers into openings in the enemy ship to make room for them.

From the tops, musket balls screamed. In forty-eight minutes by Fanning's watch the tops of the *Serapis* were silenced. Yet once, in spite of the deadly fire from the *Richard*, Captain Pearson collected a party and tried to board the *Richard*. He

was driven back. Many men were killed at the gangway, others as they retreated. Soon after, the Americans tried and were in turn thrown back.

Now Fanning led them across the yardarms. They went easily across, from the maintop into the enemy's foretop, from the *Richard's* foretop into the maintop of the *Serapis*. They took grenades with them and threw them at anyone who dared to come on deck. Soon, except for Captain Pearson who bravely kept to his quarter-deck, there was no one alive on the deck of the *Serapis*.

Still her guns kept firing. They soon silenced any fire from the *Richard's* gun deck. Richard Dale could still hear the sound from the guns on the quarter-deck above. He started to go there. The master-at-arms and the gunner ran past him shouting, "The Captain's killed."

The carpenter followed them, calling, "We must ask for quarter."

Before Dale could stop them, the three men were on deck, bawling, "Quarter, quarter. We must haul down the flag."

Dale saw them run aft, looking for the flag and heard them yell that it was gone. He raced after them to stop them.

Then he heard the Captain's voice. John Paul Jones was by no means dead. He was shouting, "Who are these rascals? Shoot them! Kill them!"

At the sound of the Captain's voice, the master-at-arms and the carpenter rapidly skulked below. The gunner was not quick enough to avoid the Captain's wrath. Jones had two empty pistols. They had been shot off when he tried to board the *Serapis*. He threw them at the gunner's head. The man fell to the deck unconscious.

Dale went below. He heard the carpenter shout that they were sinking. The master-at-arms called out something about the prisoners. Taking a party of marines with him, Dale hurried after them into the darkness below deck. He arrived in time to find that the master-at-arms had just opened the hatch of the hold. The English prisoners, more than a hundred of them, were pushing their way out to freedom.

At this moment they might easily have taken possession of the *Richard*, but they were bewildered and without leadership. Dale told them that the ship was sinking; that if they wished to escape drowning, they must man the pumps. They did so, patiently taking their turns.

So, with the help of English muscle, the *Richard* was kept afloat and fought on. Blood and water ran out of her scuppers. Many of the stanchions that supported her decks were shot to bits. The British guns had torn such holes in her sides that shot now passed through the whole ship and splashed harmlessly into the sea. The tarry oakum that calked her rotting sides was on fire in several places.

Sometimes there was a lull in the shooting on both ships while all hands put out fires in hulls, sails, and rigging. At one time, the whole starboard side of the *Serapis* was ablaze. A shot from her struck down Mr. Mease, the purser, who had been commanding the guns on the *Richard's* quarterdeck. He was carried below to the surgeon across bloody decks to a bloodier cockpit.

Captain Jones now took command of the quarter-deck guns, the only ones that could still be fired. There were only two but he dragged a third across the decks. The smoke blew clear for a moment and, from the foretop of the *Serapis* where he then was, Nick caught a glimpse of the sturdy, stooped figure, the long, powerful arms tugging at the gun.

The moon was high now, pouring down silver light. Signal lanterns had been hung on the *Richard* to show the rest of the squadron which she was. The lanterns were in a horizontal line, one at the bow, one amidships, one at the stern. Their candles were burning clearly.

With his quarter-deck guns, Jones directed his fire at the mainmast of the *Serapis*. His fire was accurate and the mast soon began to quiver under repeated strokes. He also sent occasional bursts of scattering grapeshot to help keep the deck of the *Serapis* clear. Whining musket balls and grenades from the tops also helped to keep anyone from moving on the deck.

All this time the *Alliance* had kept a safe distance from the fight. Captain Cottineau of the *Pallas*, without help from either the *Vengeance* or the *Alliance*, had captured the *Countess of Scarborough*. At half past nine, when he was safe from the *Countess*, Landais sailed out from the shore toward the place where the *Richard* and the *Serapis* lay locked together. He soon reached a spot from which everyone on the deck of the *Alliance*, as Duncan said later, could see both ships clearly. In the moonlight the *Richard*, with her high poop and stern and her signal lanterns hung in a line, was unmistakable. So was the *Serapis*, with her bright yellow stripes checked with the dark openings of the gun ports.

In the maintop where they were putting out a fire, Nick said to Fanning, "The coward's coming to help us, now he knows he's safe."

He was mistaken. Captain Landais was not coming to help them.

He came up on the *Richard's* starboard quarter and sent a scattering fire of grape into it, killing several of her crew. As he sailed past her, many voices—Nick's, Fanning's, Captain Jones's, those of his own officers among them—shouted to him that he was firing into the wrong ship. He must have recognized her high, black outline as he passed along her side but when he reached her bow, he raked her again, killing more of her men. Some of his shots may have reached the *Serapis* but the real damage was done to the already sinking *Richard*.

Yet she fought on. Her crew with pikes and lances struck through the portholes at the enemy's gunners. Her topmen kept tossing grenades. Captain Jones, hatless and powder-stained, still fired his gun at the mainmast of the *Serapis*. Captain Pearson bravely kept his position alone on his quarter-deck.

One of the British prisoners, less bewildered than the rest, escaped from the party working at the pump. He managed to cross the bulwarks, bravely made his way to the quarterdeck, and told Captain Pearson that if he could hold out, the *Richard* must certainly surrender, since she was on the point of sinking. Almost at the same moment de Chamillard was trying to persuade Captain Jones to give up the useless fight.

"You are sinking, sir. You must strike! You must strike!" he kept saying.

John Paul Jones had for the moment run out of ammunition for his guns. While he was waiting for more he had sat down on a coil of rope. He looked completely exhausted. He was resting his pale face on one of his powder-stained hands. The other hung limply by his side. He looked as if he could hardly move but when de Chamillard spoke to him he leaped to his feet, his eyes blazing with determination.

"Sir," he said, "I will sink. I will never strike!"

The cartridges he was waiting for arrived. He turned from de Chamillard and went back to firing at the mainmast of the

Serapis. The fine, new mast was still a shining yellow target in the moonlight. It was beginning to shake and tremble.

In the maintop Nick's jacket had been used as a fire extinguisher so often that it was only a smoky rag. Nat Fanning's jacket was the same.

"We both look like chimney sweeps on a busy day," Nick said.

"Or as if we'd been having a holiday in the Black Hole," Fanning agreed. "There, that fire's out. I wonder how long this has been going on."

They were waiting for ammunition. A seaman was hauling up a bucket of grenades. Fanning pulled his repeater out of his fob and held it to Nick's ear. There were ten of the silver strokes.

Fanning said to the seaman, who now had a grenade in his hand, "Throw it! We must keep the deck so dangerous they won't dare to come up. Try for that hatch. It's open—see?"

The man crawled far out on the yardarm, grenade in hand. They saw his arm move. In a moment on the *Serapis* there was a terrific explosion. Smoke and flames welled up from her decks. Groans and shrieks followed the sound of the blast. The grenade had exploded where cartridges, spilling powder, had been left by the powder monkeys. Twenty men were killed. Others had their clothes blown off and stood only in their shirt collars. Many were so badly burned that they died later.

Yet Captain Pearson still stuck to his quarter-deck. The gun crews still kept firing though the shot did not harm the *Richard* but fell into the sea beyond her. The *Serapis* could no longer hurt the *Richard* but the *Alliance* could. She appeared again out of the smoky darkness. This time her fire was directed at the forecastle where she killed several men. Shouts that she was firing into the wrong ship still made no impression on Captain Landais.

To his officers who protested, he said: "It does not matter if Jones strikes. Then I can make the *Serapis* strike to me and soon take the *Bon Homme Richard* back."

It may be that his crazy behavior did help the *Richard* in her struggle. It gave Captain Pearson, that brave, obstinate British bulldog, a reason for surrender to superior force. A little after half past ten, with his own hands, Pearson tore down the battle flag he had nailed to the staff on his quarter-deck.

The fine, new frigate had struck her colors to the rotting, blazing, sinking ship lashed to her side.

It was Richard Dale who first saw Pearson pull down his flag, and it was Dale who, at Captain Jones's orders, went across to accept the surrender. Nick saw Richard jump onto the gunwale, seize the main brace pendant, and swing himself over to the quarter-deck of the *Serapis*. John Mayrant and a party of Americans followed him. On the *Serapis* there were men amidships who had not been reached by the grenades. One of them, not knowing Captain Pearson had surrendered, rushed up and wounded Mayrant with a pike. Mayrant killed him. Three other Americans were killed at this time. They were the last deaths in the battle, yet below the guns were still fired.

Richard Dale said to Captain Pearson, "Sir, I have orders to send you on board the ship alongside, which is the American continental ship, the *Bon Homme Richard*. Mr. Potter, you will escort Captain Pearson to Captain Jones."

Captain Pearson did not speak a word but started to follow Midshipman Potter. Just at that moment the lieutenant of the *Serapis* rushed up to the quarter-deck and said to Captain Pearson, "Has the ship alongside struck, sir?"

Captain Pearson still did not speak.

Richard Dale said, "No, sir! On the contrary, he has struck to us."

The lieutenant did not look at Dale but said to his commander, "Have you struck, sir?"

Pearson said curtly, "Yes, I have."

The lieutenant turned to go below and said, "Then I have nothing more to say."

Richard Dale told him he must go across to the *Richard* with his captain.

The lieutenant, still hoping, perhaps, to collect a party and take back the ship, said, "I will go below and silence the firing of the guns."

"I must decline that offer, sir," Richard Dale said. "Please escort the gentlemen across, Mr. Potter."

Like John Paul Jones, Captain Pearson had risen to his command from a humble rank in life. Unlike Jones, he had never learned courteous manners suitable to his position. In the cabin of the *Richard*, Captain Jones, again dressed with his usual spotless neatness, greeted Captain Pearson and his lieutenant with formal courtesy. At last Pearson ungraciously held out his sword, saying in a surly tone, "I don't much like to give up my sword to a man who fights with a rope around his neck."

John Paul Jones overlooked Pearson's rude words and insolent tone. He said politely, "Sir, you have fought like a hero and I make no doubt but that your sovereign will reward you in a most ample manner."

Captain Jones was right about King George's generosity. Captain Pearson became Sir Richard Pearson for his heroic defense of the *Serapis*. The American Congress was less appreciative—Jones remained a captain.

When the news of Pearson's new nobility came to Jones, he laughed and said, "I hope to meet him again. Next time I'll make a duke of him!"

CHAPTER 19

THE TEXEL

THE BATTLE was over but there was no rest for the officers and crew of the *Bon Homme Richard*. Fire still blazed dangerously near her powder magazine. Both ships could have been blown to pieces by an explosion there. Nick worked beside midshipmen from the *Serapis*, moving powder kegs from the magazine to a safe place and putting out fires.

There was blood everywhere on the victorious ship. More than half her crew had been killed or wounded. Desperate hours were spent moving the wounded to the *Serapis*. Everyone knew the *Richard* might sink at any time. Captain Jones was determined to have her patched up and sail her triumphantly into L'Orient, but even his persistence had to give way. If she sank, she would take the *Serapis* with her.

At last he ordered the lashings between the two ships cut. As they separated, the mainmast of the *Serapis* splintered and fell into the sea with a hideous, screaming crash, taking the mizzen topmast with it. The mainmast had been held in place only because the yards of the *Serapis* had been interlocked with those of the *Richard*.

Among the wounded on the *Serapis* was Richard Dale. He was in command of her when Captain Pearson left but had suddenly fainted from loss of blood. He had been wounded in the leg, how long before he never knew, by a flying splinter from the *Richard's* side. It had pierced him like an arrow. Blood had been running down his leg without his noticing it.

He had just discovered that the *Serapis* was anchored. When the ships separated, he had tried to get the British ship under way and had found that she would not answer to her helm. One of her lieutenants told him the *Serapis* had dropped her anchor hours before. Dale ordered the cable cut and the ship began to move in the direction of the smoking, sinking *Richard*.

It was then that he fainted. Lieutenant Henry Lunt had not returned to the *Richard* during the battle. He now came back and took command of the *Serapis*. Not all Americans were heroes, even those born in America. Lunt explained that he thought it was not prudent to return during the engagement. While the wounded were being brought from the *Richard* to the *Serapis*, some of the English prisoners got possession of the *Richard's* helm and turned her toward the land. The wind was now east and carried her toward the shore.

Nick was one of a party of Americans who fought the Englishmen and took them prisoner again but they could not prevent a dozen of them from getting into a boat and escaping to Scarborough.

All that night, all the next day, as the wounded were ferried over to the *Serapis*, the pumps were kept going on the *Richard*. People still watched from Scarborough Fort and Flamborough Head. They hoped British warships might come and help the *Serapis* but none came. The American carpenters were working on her now, fishing her mainmast, hauling the mizzen topmast into place, patching holes between wind and water, calking leaks with oakum. American seamen set new sails in place of her tattered, scorched canvas. The sailmakers were patching the old ones. She was far less damaged than the *Richard* but a much larger number of her crew had been killed or wounded.

On the morning of September 25th the wind freshened. Everyone knew that the *Richard* must soon sink. Water gurgled in and out of her ports, swashed up her hatchways. By nine the water had reached her lower deck. All the living men on board were ordered to abandon her. The dead—that strange mixture of nations, English, Irish, Europeans from different countries, men from the Far East, Americans from New Hampshire to Georgia—were left on board.

She began rolling as if losing balance. She settled forward and went down bow first. For a time her high poop and mizzenmast still showed above the water. Then they were gone.

"A little after ten," John Paul Jones wrote to Dr. Franklin, "I saw with inexpressible grief, the last glimpse of the *Bon Homme Richard*."

Nick Caryl was not among those who saw the *Richard* sink off Flamborough Head. Uninjured all through the battle, he was hurt after it was over in the fight with the English prisoners on the quarter-deck. A thrust from a pike had broken his leg. He fell, striking his head on the gun that had shot at the mast of the *Serapis*. He was in the last boatload of wounded to leave the *Richard*. It was Fanning, coming aboard for a last hunt for living men, who had found him where he had fallen.

"It took six of us to carry you," Fanning told Nick weeks later. "It was the carpenter of the *Serapis* who washed your wound with sea water and put splints on your leg so it wouldn't break any worse. I swear he's a better surgeon than ours. I believe your leg is mending better than most that were broken that day. The wound has healed cleanly. You'll be walking soon."

"I don't remember anything after the pike struck my leg," Nick said, speaking slowly.

He had been lying helpless all those weeks, not speaking, knowing no one, eating only the food that Fanning or Richard Dale or Duncan fed him from a spoon. He had grown so thin that his cheekbones seemed ready to break through his skin. He raised his thin, bony hand, looked at it a moment and let it fall as if he were dropping something he did not know how to use, that belonged to someone else.

He said, pausing between the words, "I don't know where I am."

He was in a fort near a Dutch port called the Texel, they told him. They would not be there much longer because the English were angry with the Dutch for letting the Americans stay there at all. The Dutch would allow them to stay only until their ship was ready and the wind fair.

"Can the old *Richard* sail again?" Nick asked.

"No," Duncan said. "She's resting off Flamborough Head in twelve fathoms of water. The *Serapis* has been put under French colors to keep her from the English. Our ship is the *Alliance* now."

"And Landais—where is he?"

"In Paris, explaining his conduct to Dr. Franklin."

Nick smiled for the first time. "That," he said, "I would like to hear," and turned over and went to sleep.

The next day he was better, eating whatever they brought him, asking for more. The day after that, he got out of bed, using Duncan and Fanning for crutches, asking a hundred questions. They told him how a sixty-four-gun ship and three frigates had chased them all the way from Flamborough Head to the Texel, how the British were furious, demanding that the Dutch should arrest the pirate Jones and free all his prisoners.

Duncan, who had been acting as Captain Jones's secretary, said that Dr. Franklin had written to say how much pleased he was with the number of prisoners that Jones had brought to the Texel.

"There are near five hundred of them," Duncan said and added that Dr. Franklin had said that they now had enough British prisoners to free every American left in England.

The prisoners were all now in the fort on the Texel. Both English and American wounded were being cared for there. Colonel Weibert and a company of marines were on guard at the fort. There was a drawbridge over the ditch around the fort. It could be raised or lowered at Captain Jones's order.

"He must like that. How is he?" Nick asked.

Duncan said the Captain was in excellent spirits. He had been to Amsterdam and had visited the Exchange, where he caused so much excitement that all business stopped. Such a crowd collected that at last he went into an inn and appeared on a balcony.

"He greeted the people—like royalty," Duncan said with a grin. "He wore his uniform and a Scotch bonnet edged with gold. He's writing very grand letters. The words get longer and harder every day. He writes poetry, too," he added. "Nice, clean, fat Dutch girls write verses to him. They call him the Sea King. He writes back and calls them nymphs. I have to make copies—sometimes as many as five. I wish the wind would change and the Sea King would get back to the sea."

Nick laughed and said, "Oh, give him a chance to be admired on shore a while, he's earned it."

"Aye, laddie, but it's an awful thing to feel seasick on land," Duncan said. "Get out of that bed, you malingering rogue, and get back to copying letters yourself."

Nick laughed again and asked how Captain Pearson had taken his defeat.

"He says the *Alliance* beat him," Richard Dale said in his soft, pleasant voice. "So does Captain Landais. I reckon he's telling Dr. Franklin so in Paris right now."

"And I reckon Dr. Franklin knows a coward and a traitor when he sees one!" Nick said. "Is Pearson here in the fort?"

"Captain Pearson," Duncan said, "was released on parole with his officers. He is on Helder Island, rather a pleasant place, near here. He writes letters complaining about not being treated with consideration and courtesy. I made five copies of Captain Jones's letter answering him. I'll probably have to make more. He gives copies to everyone who comes in. I can tell you what it says—unless you'd rather hear a poem about turtledoves and silver lyres and sea nymphs with wreaths of coral in their hair."

Nick said hastily that he would rather hear the letter so Duncan recited part of it.

"I know not what of respect is due to rank between your service and ours; I suppose, however, the difference must be very great in England, since I am informed that Captain Cunningham, who bears a senior rank in the service of America to yours in the service of England, is now confined at Plymouth in a dungeon and fetters."

"The Black Hole... Mill Prison... Gustavus Cunningham..." murmured Nick.

He knew that dungeon—and Captain Cunningham, too.

"Poor Cunningham—that's bad," he added, shivering a little.

"Captain Jones has arranged to exchange him for Pearson," Fanning said. "Pearson has agreed, though with his usual courtesy he calls Cunningham a traitor and a pirate."

"Tell him about Pearson's plate," Duncan suggested.

It seemed that while Captain Jones was sailing for the Texel, he had used the silver plate belonging in the cabin of the *Serapis.* Instead of claiming it as part of his prize goods, as he might well have done, Jones had it packed up with everything personal of Pearson's—plate, pistols, swords, clothes—and sent to him at Helder Island.

Fanning had been among the group of Americans who had gone to deliver it. Pearson, with his usual insolence, declined to receive it at the hands of a rebel.

"If Captain Cottineau, who is an officer in the service of the King of France, delivers it, I will accept it," he said.

"So we put it into the boat," Fanning added, "and shoved off and went back to the ship. And the next day we lugged it all over there again. Cottineau, in spite of his wound, went along with us and handed it over with much bowing and scraping. Pearson thanked him, but he never sent a word of thanks to Captain Jones."

"Was Cottineau wounded in the battle?" Nick asked.

Cottineau had been badly wounded, they told him, in a duel with Landais.

"But why should he fight Cottineau?" Nick asked. Duncan explained that nineteen officers of the squadron, Cottineau among them, had drawn up charges against Landais and sent them to Dr. Franklin. The charges stated that Landais had behaved with disrespect to the commander-in-chief of the squadron many times; that he seldom answered signals and often disobeyed them.

Captain Cottineau stated that when the *Bon Homme Richard* came in sight of the *Alliance* off Scarborough Head, Landais, thinking she was a British ship, told Cottineau that if she turned out to be a fifty-gun ship, the *Alliance* must run away. He knew that the slow-sailing *Pallas* would certainly be overtaken and captured by a British frigate, but he was ready to desert her.

The charges went on to describe how, when the *Richard* met the *Serapis*, Landais stayed to windward of danger, how he fired first into the *Richard's* stern, then into her bow, and returned later and fired into her again, though she was clearly marked. It was repeatedly stated by the officers that the *Alliance* was never on the port side of the *Serapis* where the British guns could have been brought to bear on her, but that Landais always kept the *Richard* between him and the *Serapis*.

"When we told him he was firing into the wrong ship," Duncan said bitterly, "he said, 'It's no harm if she strikes. I will retake her after I take the *Serapis*.' I believe he wanted to kill Captain Jones so he could have the credit of the victory and all the prize money. He was furious with Cottineau for signing the charges. As he has enough courage on land to fight someone who isn't much of a swordsman, he challenged poor Cottineau and ripped a hole in him. Next he challenged Captain Jones. No one knows how that would have turned out—I would bet on Jones—but Dr. Franklin's orders came to arrest him. He was sent to Paris under guard, calling the Captain a coward, of course!"

"A few more cowards like Captain Jones and the war would be over," Nick said.

It was now November. All that month and most of December the English ambassador complained to the Dutch about the pirate, Jones, and the presence of his ships in a Dutch harbor. All that time the Dutch urged Jones to leave and he declined for different reasons—repairs to be made to the *Serapis*, to the *Alliance*, contrary winds. Jones had hoped to sail the *Serapis*, but, because of British protests, she was turned over to the French and he was put in command of the *Alliance*.

Landais had left her in a very bad condition. She was filthy below decks, guns, sails, and small arms out of order, cables missing, powder spoiled by dampness. Her crew were drunken and untrained. It took most of December to repair these defects.

All that month gales came from the north and west. British ships sailed back and forth outside the Texel, waiting for Jones to come out and sail for America. They knew, of course, that the *Alliance* must return to America and obviously she would take the shortest route, which would be to sail north of Scotland.

To be sure of seizing her, British ships, many of them frigates, waited for the *Alliance*. There were usually twelve ships, sometimes as many as sixteen. Once they thought Jones had gone. Forty ships hunted the ocean for him.

Lord Sandwich, head of the British Admiralty, stopped eating the sandwich, an invention of his—two slices of bread with meat between—long enough to write to one of his captains: "Get to sea at once. If you can beat Paul Jones you will be as high in the public esteem as if you had beat the combined fleets."

The British captain did not beat Paul Jones. Sandwich was criticized by the newspapers for sending against Jones "only" a few frigates and the *Jupiter*, a sixty-four-gun ship of the line.

Jones himself gravely explained to the Dutch that he could not sail because he could not fight more than three times his own force.

Nick had left the fort by this time. He could walk around on his own long legs with only a stick to help him. He and Duncan shared a cabin. They took turns copying the Captain's letters.

One day, in Duncan's hearing, Captain Jones asked Nick if he remembered the old secret code that he had learned on the brig *John* so many years before.

"Yes, sir," Nick answered. "I can write it pretty fast and read it almost as quickly."

"Which is harder," the Captain said. "You must have used it a good deal."

Nick told him about the journals of his South Sea voyage and the one written in Mill Prison in both of which he often used the code to save space.

"I wrote my journal on the *Richard*, too—up to the day of the battle," he added.

"I would like to see them," Captain Jones said.

Nick told him that Mr. Banks had promised to send him his South Sea journals after the war.

"But the others," he added, "all went down with the *Richard*, sir. Like most of us, I own nothing but the clothes I have on."

"I lost my papers, too," Captain Jones said.

"But Nick didn't, sir," Duncan said. "I never told you, Nick. After you were knocked on the head, you wouldn't have known what I said and lately I haven't thought of it."

"How did you find them?" Nick asked.

"I was taking wounded from the *Richard* to the *Serapis*. On one of my trips I found your chest floating around amidships. I could not bring the chest but I knew what you would want most out of it—your books. Your Golden Horseshoe. They're in my own chest—I'll get them."

He raced out of the cabin, leaving Nick still trying to thank him.

"What is this horseshoe?" Captain Jones asked. "An odd piece of equipment for a sailor."

So Nick told about the Knights of the Golden Horseshoe and about Caryl's Maze. He told about Pambo and the duel in the London garden, of his long journey since, always hoping to get back to Virginia, always turned aside.

The wind screamed and howled from the northwest. The *Alliance* pitched at her anchor. Duncan went on with his copying. John Paul Jones listened, turning the Golden Horseshoe over in his strong hands.

When Nick stopped speaking, Captain Jones was silent a moment, then he said, "You are a fortunate man, Mr. Caryl.

Perhaps you do not think so, tossed about here, wearing powder-smoked, salt-stained, blood-spotted clothes, cheated out of your prize money, as we are all at the moment. Your enemy, master of your estate. But—I am fey tonight, McTavish knows what that means. We Scots never quite lose our second sight, even when we become Americans, eh, McTavish?"

"I hope not," Duncan said, "but it has not visited me of late. What does it tell you tonight, sir?"

"That the wind is going to change," John Paul Jones said, "and when it does that Mr. Caryl will be on the last part of his voyage."

He stood up, handing the Golden Horseshoe back to Nick.

"Good night, gentlemen," he said. "Good fortune, a good voyage!"

They passed through the waist of the ship to reach their cabin, which was forward.

"Listen!" Duncan said.

"What do you hear?" asked Nick.

"Nothing—the wind has dropped!"

ALL IN THE DOWNS

THE DAY the wind changed was the 27th of December 1779. That morning the *Alliance* weighed anchor and got to sea.

"I am here," John Paul Jones wrote, "with a good wind at the east and under my best American colors."

The Stars and Stripes, still unknown to most Europeans, whipped sharply from the masthead and stern of the Alliance. There were no British frigates to see the flags. Some had sailed north, thinking that Jones would take advantage of the east wind to beat up north of Scotland and head for America. The ships that guarded the southern part of the harbor had been driven back to England by the same western gale that had been tossing the *Alliance* at her mooring.

To Nick, who had been writing letters for him, Captain Jones said, "We cannot sail for America yet, Mr. Caryl. The British know I do not dare sail south down the English Channel so close to their ports, so they will expect me between Holland and Scotland."

"So what will you do, sir?"

"Why, naturally," John Paul Jones said, with one of his unexpected smiles, "I will sail down the Channel."

So down the Channel they sailed with the staggering breeze, the sea open before them. On the 28th of December the Stars and Stripes fluttered through the Straits of Dover. The *Alliance* ran close to the Goodwin Sands, so close that she was in full view of the British ships anchored in the Downs. Spyglasses that were turned on the American frigate might have seen Duncan McTavish in the maintop, waving his greetings. They might almost have heard a dozen excited midshipmen singing an appropriate old English ballad, "All in the Downs the Fleet Was Moored." However, they might have failed to recognize it because Richard Dale had organized a rival chorus. They were singing "Yankee Doodle," a rebellious song, the kind for singing when Americans found themselves in the Black Hole on half allowance of moldy bread and old beef bones.

While the English ships were still windbound, the *Alliance* was cruising around Cape Finisterre. Her captain was complaining that the weather kept the English in port and that he could make no prizes.

It was February when they reached L'Orient.

The quay was almost empty when they came into the harbor, but by the time they landed it was full of people shouting, "Long live the *Bon Homme Richard*! Long live Paul Jones! Welcome Bostonians."

His tall young midshipmen had to make a guard around the Captain to keep him from being torn to pieces by the friendly crowd. The top of his gold-edged Scotch bonnet barely came up to Nick's shoulder. He had on his best uniform, the one in which he had received Captain Pearson's surrender. It was his best—also his only one. The rest of his clothes had gone down with the *Richard*. Its blue cloth and gold braid were now stained with salt water from storms between the Texel and L'Orient. His face, with the deeply marked lines between his eyes and around his mouth, deeper than ever now, was as weather-beaten as his coat. His own sandy hair, unpowdered, was tied with ribbon that had met more than one salt wave.

"Yet every woman on the quay was in love with him," Fanning said to Nick later that day. "No one has an eye for handsome young heroes like you and me. They don't even look at you, Richard."

"No," said Richard Dale, smiling, "and they never will while Paul is around."

He was the only man on the ship who ever called the Captain by this name and he used it always in a tone of affectionate friendliness.

It was the same on the streets of L'Orient as on the quay. John Paul Jones was followed everywhere by admiring crowds. When he went into an inn, they waited for him to come out. It was days before he could appear on the streets without causing excitement. After some weeks, during which repairs were being made to the *Alliance*, he went to Paris.

Duncan went to Paris with him. He was chosen partly because he could be useful as a secretary, partly because, having served on the *Alliance*, he had not lost his clothes. Even the common sailors of the *Richard's* crew had hundreds of dollars of prize money due them but no settlement could be made until Captain Jones went to Paris and came back. In the meantime he gave them money out of his own pocket. It left him very little but did not satisfy the crew. They had lost their possessions. Many of them were still wearing the ragged clothes in which they had fought the *Serapis*. There was plenty of American grumbling at L'Orient as the weeks dragged on.

At last came a letter from Duncan.

My dear Nick,

Our Captain's triumph continues. The ladies of the court all love him. They paint pictures of him on little pieces of ivory. They look as much like him as they do like you, my old one. If your French were better, I would say "mon vieux." I speak French now like a native. A native of Scotland, I mean. So does the Captain.

Houdon, one of the best sculptors here, has done a bust of him. This is more like. The scowl is very fine. When I look at it, it makes me feel as if I had been caught taking a nap in the maintop! He has ordered twenty copies made to give to his friends. Some will go to America.

The shops are full of engraved portraits of him, cocked hat, pistols and all. There is one where he is throwing his pistols at gunner Randall. The Captain is daintily dressed in a skin-tight suit—colored pink or blue, you can take your choice. He has powdered curls and a large ostrich plume in his hat. There is some smoke around him but the plume is unruffled. I will bring you a copy so you can laugh, too.

The English have sent over prints showing their idea of him. He is seven feet tall with bushy black whiskers, wears baggy striped trousers. (Could they have seen you, Nick, and confused you with him?) His hat and a sort of apron he has on are both ornamented with a skull and crossbones. He is shooting a pistol with his left hand and leaning on his sword with his right. He must weigh about 250 pounds because the sword is bent nearly double.

Luckily, he now has a new sword. The King gave it to him. It has a gold hilt and Latin on it. I will kindly translate it for you out of my vast knowledge of that tongue. It says: Louis XVI, rewarder, to the brave conqueror of the sea for his strenuous fight. (At least, that's what J.P.J. says it means.)

The King has made him a chevalier and the Queen has asked him to the opera. He loves the opera. You would think that he had been Mozart's shipmate, I mean schoolmate. He writes a good deal of poetry. I have to keep making copies of it and of his letter to the Countess of Selkirk. The Earl has at last answered the letter. He says he will accept the plate if it is given to him by Congress. Perhaps he is related to Captain Pearson, who also wanted his plate but was particular about who gave it to him. The Earl, however, sounds like an honest man, though he does not write so well as J.P.J. The Captain has bought back the plate with some of the first prize money he got from de Chaumont and the Earl has it now. We checked it all over. The pieces were all there and the tea leaves still in the pot.

When the *Alliance* sails for America, we are to take uniforms and arms and powder for General Washington. Also Mr. Arthur Lee and his family. He was one of the American commissioners here but is now going home. He wants to take his traveling carriage. J.P.J. says we are to take only weapons, etc.

We shall see you before long, bring you a few coins to jingle in your pocket and then be off for America with a yo heave ho!

DUNCAN

Nick was soon to wish he had never heard of Mr. Arthur Lee or of his carriage. There was trouble between Lee and Franklin. Partly for that reason, partly because he disliked Jones, Lee took the side of Landais, who was trying to get command of the *Alliance* again. Jones's refusal to make room for Lee's carriage seems to have been the main cause of what followed.

Jones had returned to L'Orient but was on shore. While Richard Dale and the other former officers of the *Richard* were eating their dinner, Landais and the former officers of the *Alliance* seized the ship. Dale, Fanning, and others among the *Richard's* officers and crew were thrust off the *Alliance* by a mob of armed sailors of her crew. Encouraged by Arthur Lee, angry because they knew the *Richard's* crew would soon get prize money and that they would get none, they had thrown in their fortune with Landais. In the scuffle that took place, those who stayed on the ship and resisted the Landais party were seized and put in irons. Among them was Nicholas Young Caryl, who was at last sailing to America.

The passage from L'Orient to Boston seemed to Nick the longest voyage, longer than the journey along the Great Barrier Reef, longer than the voyage from the East Indies with fever on the ship. The days were longer and darker than those in Mill Prison. The food was worse.

He was released part way through the voyage. Captain Landais showed such obvious signs of madness after the first weeks had passed that even his officers and Mr. Lee, for the safety of the ship, found it necessary to put him under restraint. The prisoners, Nick among them, were set free at this time. Yet, though the voyage still seemed endless, Nick found himself at last wandering through the crooked streets of Boston.

He saw the State House with the King's Lion and Unicorn still on it. Not far away someone had painted the cobblestones to show where the massacre had taken place. He went to Griffin's Wharf and thought of Duncan, dressed as an Indian—a red-haired Indian!—breaking open chests of tea. He saw the Old Elm on the Common, an enormous tree where they used to hang pirates.

The British would have hanged John Paul there if they had caught him, Nick thought, looking up into the waving sea of green above his head.

It was a hot day in September but a breeze from the east was blowing across the Common and beginning to cool the city. Nick wandered about on Beacon Hill. The neat red brick houses there with their white pillared porches reminded him a little of his native Portsmouth.

The voyage on the *Alliance* began to seem as if it had happened to someone else. The marks of the fetters on his wrists and ankles had almost healed now and the purple-brown scurvy marks on his legs and arms were fading. He was lucky, he thought, that they had set him free before his teeth began to fall out.

In the money belt under his shirt he still had some of the guineas Mr. Banks had given him. He found a shop and bought some

clothes. There was a small tailor there whose business it was to alter the clothes to fit the patrons. He said unflattering things about giants, but finally produced a coat almost long enough in the sleeves, and breeches to which he said he would add a six-inch band around the waist. The waistcoat, he said, would cover this extra piece and was a perfect fit, pretty near. It was actually long enough, only rather too large around the middle.

These clothes must have belonged to some dignified Boston gentleman, Nick thought. They were clean, of excellent material and of a sober shade of dark brown, not unlike his own sunburned, coppery skin. Nick bought a new brown beaver hat to go with them at a hatter's farther along the street. In the window of a shop nearby a dark-haired man in a green jerkin and a white shirt with full flowing sleeves was engraving a pattern on a teapot. Nick watched him for a while, marveling at his deftness.

Long afterwards he learned that he had been looking at Paul Revere.

The next morning he had a piece of good fortune. He paid for his new clothes and then, bundle in hand, had been visiting different wharves, trying to find a ship bound for Virginia. At last he found the *Charming Nancy*, a brig, clean and well rigged. She looked as if she would sail fast, he thought. Her captain was ashore, but her sailing master said that though they were bound for the Carolinas, the Captain might manage to land him somewhere along the Virginia coast. Nick could wait and rest in the cabin, he said. The Captain would be back soon.

Nick had not known how tired he was until he saw the bunk in the cabin.

"Lie down," the sailing master said. "Feet get tired tramping around on land."

Nick was asleep before he knew it.

Some time later he heard a voice say, "Pretty near time to start."

He opened his eyes.

The voice went on, "Well, by the grasshopper on top of Faneuil Hall, I believe it's Nick Young!"

He was looking—or was he dreaming he was looking?—at Captain Hicks, once of the *Sea Otter*, now captain of a neat little brig, carrying a cargo of—what had the master said?—English prize goods, chintz, linen, broadcloth, to South Carolina.

"Ports are far apart but men meet there," Nick said sleepily.

"About time you came along," Captain Hicks remarked. "Growed some, ain't you?"

"Reckon so."

"See any fighting?"

"Just one battle."

"Come out good?"

"Pretty good. Took a ship called the *Serapis*."

Captain Hicks was jolted out of his usual calm enough so that he opened his eyes a quarter of an inch and was silent.

Then he said, "We'd better get going. Catch the tide. See you at supper. Guess the master'll be kind of interested."

Everyone on the *Charming Nancy* was interested. The days slipped by almost too fast. To be a passenger waited on with eager respect by the cabin boy, to have even the Captain listen to every word he spoke, to have the helmsman say, "I hear you was with John Paul Jones, sir," was almost too much of a change from being in irons on the *Alliance*. Some of the time he did not feel like talking, even about the Richard, but lay on the deck, soaking up American sunshine, drawing great breaths of American air.

The clouds were different from English clouds, he told Captain Hicks, bigger, faster moving, whiter, higher in the sky. And the air smelled different.

"What does it smell of?" asked Captain Hicks.

"Liberty," said Nicholas Caryl.

The Captain could not take the risk of running into Hampton Roads. There were too many British ships about, waiting for just such prizes as the *Nancy*. He would have to land Nick along the shore somewhere, he said. The British had taken possession of Portsmouth long ago. Captain Hicks did not know if there were British troops there at present, but said he had heard Lord Cornwallis might march that way any time.

"You had better be careful in the city," he said. "There's plenty of patriots. Lord Dunmore burned most of their plantations. But there's Tories, too. And trimmers."

"What's that?"

"Folks that are patriots one week, Tories the next, according to how the war's going. With Cornwallis on the way I guess they're Tories now. Don't know's I blame 'em. Don't want their houses burned, tobacco stolen. Guess I'd be a Tory myself. Anyway, most of 'em still work for the Revolution. Maybe accomplish more that way. Plenty of the men are away in Washington's army or on our privateers. Women get on the best they can. Call themselves patriots or Tories but most of 'em are spies for Washington."

"And thoroughly enjoy it, I reckon," Nick said, laughing.

They were close enough to Virginia now to see the shore. It seemed to rise up out of the sea like a dark green wave with a white wave following it. The green was pines, Nick knew, and the white was the sand of the most beautiful beach in the world with whiter foam breaking on it.

He said so to the Captain, who smiled and said, "What, better than the beaches you used to tell me about? Coral, palms, breadfruit, beautiful girls swimming?"

"Much better," Nick said firmly.

The sun was sinking over the pines. The wind had lightened. The *Charming Nancy* hove to and a boat was lowered over the side. Nick dropped into it neatly. They tossed his canvas bag in after him. It easily held his few possessions—the books Duncan had rescued from the *Richard*, his new brown suit, his pistols and powderhorn. The books were wrapped, as his journals had been so many years, in the shirt his Aunt Dorothy made for him, for which Cherry had hemmed the ruffles. The green silk purse, green no longer but faded to gray and stained with sea water, was in his pocket.

Cherry, he thought, must be twenty-one now. He wondered if she were still the toast of the town as Richard Dale had said. Probably not. She was probably an old married woman by now with a couple of fat, pink babies. Most Portsmouth girls thought a girl of twenty-one was an old maid. He smiled at the idea of Cherry as an old maid, or as a reigning beauty, either. He could never remember her as anything but a pink-cheeked little girl at Caryl's Maze.

The keel of the boat swished into the soft white sand of the beach. Waves broke against her stern and lapped back into the quiet sea with no more noise than a sailor makes scrubbing a deck.

One of the sailors said, "Jump now, sir, and you won't get your feet wet."

Nick jumped and the white sand of Virginia was under his feet. A flock of canvasbacks with their long, rusty heads flew over, going south. He could hear the beat of their black wings and see their breasts like a fleet of new sails. Yes, no doubt this was Virginia.

The sailor said, "What will you do now, sir? Take a privateer out?"

Nick put his hand on the small anchor the boat carried and said what many sailors have said before him and many more since, "Lend me your anchor," he said. "I'll put it over my shoulder and walk inland until someone says, 'What's that thing you're carrying?' then I'll settle down."

Two of the sailors grinned and said, "Let us come with you, sir. A nice little farm, plant tobacco, corn, pumpkins, hunt wild turkeys, ducks. No sails to furl when the wind comes. That's the life, sir."

He knew they did not mean it. They rowed off cheerfully, thanking him for the shillings he gave them. They were like porpoises, gracefully jumping through waves, clumsy or helpless ashore. He watched them for a moment.

"Don't take any Continental dollars," one shouted.

Nick waved again. He picked up his canvas bag and stood still looking at the boat and at the brig and at the quiet sea.

His voyage was over. He had no more idea than the men out there what he was going to do now!

CHAPTER 21

CARYL'S MAZE

THE TALL YOUNG MAN in the brown suit, who was reading an old copy of the *Virginia Gazette* as he ate his dinner, was a mystery to the other guests who came to the General Washington Inn on London Street in Portsmouth. Any stranger might be a British spy and this man did not talk exactly like a Portsmouth man. He did not talk exactly like an Englishman, either.

By the way he ate the good Virginia food—the greens with a ham hock cooked in them, the first pickled oysters of the season, the spoonbread—he certainly seemed as if he had lived along Tidewater sometime. The English officers from the ships in Hampton Roads were always asking for saddle of mutton and half-cooked beef. They criticized the oysters for being too large to swallow. The young man in the brown suit had no difficulty in swallowing Virginia oysters. He had already eaten two dozen and had asked if there would be more for supper. And how many beaten biscuits had he eaten? At least ten. And three melons!

The landlord did not grudge them to him. He liked his good food to be appreciated, especially by a young man who had paid his reckoning the day before with an English guinea and who had taken the change in Continental notes—practically a basketful of them—instead of demanding hard money, as he had a perfect right to do.

Prices were high, Nick noticed, as he read the *Gazette*. He was putting off deciding what he would do by reading every word of it.

Then, when there was nothing left to do, he went to his room. For a while he wrote, covering two sheets of paper with his small, neat writing. Then he tucked his pistols into his flapped pockets, brushed his new hat, smoothed his straight black hair, retied the brown ribbon that held it, and pinned the Golden Horseshoe into his shirt under his waistcoat.

There was a small looking glass on the wall with a curlicued frame and a gilded eagle at the top. He looked into the glass gravely, almost sadly. No one in Portsmouth had recognized the face he saw there. Yet it had not changed greatly. Even when he was twelve there had been those high cheekbones, the nose like an Indian's, the coppery skin, the four smallpox scars. A pretty plain face, he thought. He did not realize how he looked when he smiled, with his dark eyes full of fun and his white teeth showing.

His height must have disguised him, he supposed. He had seen plenty of people he recognized—friends of his uncle's, boys he had played leapfrog with, Negro mammies who had presided over birthday suppers, ladies who used to be rowed out to Caryl's Maze to take tea with Aunt Dorothy. He even knew some of the girls, though this was harder. They were now young ladies with powdered hair showing under flowered hats, as fashionably dressed in their chintzes and calicoes as the ladies of the French court in their silks and satins. Still the old Portsmouth names—Stuart, Purcell, Watts, Armistead— began to come into his mind. He thought he could fit one or two names to the right girls.

Being unknown was in a way convenient, yet it had its drawbacks. Tories no doubt thought that he was a patriot spy so they did not talk freely before him. Patriots probably thought he was a Tory. The few questions he had asked met with answers either brief or evasive. Sometimes both.

When he asked what had happened to Mr. Sprowle's marine yard at Gosport, he was told simply that it had burned. It was some time before he learned that it had burned at the time Lord Dunmore bombarded the town in '75. Later someone mentioned that General Collier, who took the town in '79, had burned a hundred and thirty-seven ships, some of them at Gosport. These facts were dealt out like cards from a pack. You could take them or leave them. Nothing was said of how anger at having their houses used as targets for British guns had stirred the men of Portsmouth to violence, so that they had burned the marine yard because Sprowle, the owner, was a friend of Lord Dunmore's.

In speaking of Sir George Collier, the landlord said that he had been good to the town and that they were sorry to see him go. He seemed to regret that there was no British regiment in Portsmouth at the moment. Yet his painted sign showed George Washington commanding his troops. This was confusing to Nick, who was also puzzled by the fact that no one seemed disturbed by remembering a hundred and thirty-seven ships burning at the docks. Nick thought of the outcry when John Paul Jones burned one ship at Whitehaven and shrugged his shoulders wearily.

He had not mentioned Captain Jones's name. Captain Hicks had warned him not to.

"There are still British soldiers enough on ships in Hampton Roads to haul you off as a pirate and put you in jail again," he had said. "Did you hear about Captain Cunningham?"

"Gustavus Cunningham?" Nick asked. "Why, I knew him when I was a boy and I saw him again at the Texel after he was exchanged for Captain Pearson. Why?"

"You didn't know he was a prisoner in Portsmouth?"

"Cunningham a prisoner again!"

"Yes, he joined the Army about as soon as he got home and he was captured again by the British. I heard they were planning to send him back to England and really hang him as a pirate this time. Perhaps he's been sent back by now. It was some time ago I heard it. The talk in Boston was that they would hang him and any of Paul Jones's men they caught. If you want to join General Washington, as you said you planned to do, don't say too much about Jones. You can't serve America in irons in some Black Hole with a rope around your neck."

That was true, Nick knew, and he must be on his way, the way that led to General Washington with only one more stop —at Caryl's Maze.

He put his papers into his pocket, picked up his sword, and belted it on. There was a knock at the door. Nick spun around, hand on sword.

"Who's there?" he said, sharply.

The door swung open. Sunlight from a window across the room fell on a dark bronze face that broke into a smile of complete happiness.

"Good evenin', Mistoh Nick Young," said Pambo.

They got into Pambo's boat at the end of Ferry Street. They had walked there separately.

"Better not talk here," Pambo had said. "Come to the end of Ferry Street. I'll be waiting."

A dozen men with boats for hire crowded around Nick on the wharf. He told them gently that he had already engaged one. Now he and Pambo had left the city, with its poplars and mulberries and elms planted along the sides of the squares, behind them.

They had passed Richard Dale's house and what had once been Uncle Nicholas's house. His uncle had died, Pambo told Nick. The house had been left to Sandy. He had gambled it away, throwing dice and betting on horses with the officers of Lord Dunmore's fleet.

"Only it wasn't really Mistoh Sandy!" Pambo added.

Nick only nodded. He and Pambo did not need to discuss who the present owner of Caryl's Maze really was.

"How are things at the plantation?" he asked.

"Pretty bad, I reckon, Mistoh Nick Young. Mrs. Ashton died—of a lung fever. McFarland's a good overseer. He and your Aunt Dorothy and Miss Cherry keep things going some way, I hear. But there's not much use making a crop of tobacco if someone bets a thousand pounds of it on some horse that runs mighty slow on account of having only three legs."

"How do you know these things, Pambo? I've been here three days and have learned nothing."

"One medium-sized colored man's not so noticeable as a seven-foot white man," Pambo stated. "You know how white folks are. They figure colored people don't have good sense. They'll talk their business in front of you in your boat as if you're carved out of some little old pine tree and painted up like a figurehead. You hadn't been in the General Washington two hours before I heard there was a seven-foot—"

"Six-five and a half," corrected Nick.

"—won't argue about half a foot," Pambo continued calmly. "A mighty tall white man, part Indian, talked English or Yankee or something, at the inn. I'd have come sooner but I had to watch my chance. Wanted to see you alone. White folks think you might be a spy for that Lord Cornwallis or for Mr. George Washington. But half the Negroes in Portsmouth know

Mr. Nick Young Caryl's home. They wouldn't tell any Tory or trimmer Negroes, of course, but I reckon the men hiding in Dismal Swamp know you're home. Like Captain Cunningham. He's in the swamp."

"Cunningham escaped then? How did he do that?"

"Well," Pambo said, "they had him in a right strong prison. They built a stockade around a house on Crawford Street. There were forty-fifty men on guard. Of course, there were other prisoners, but they were mostly guarding the Captain. One day he said to a visitor he had, 'I will see my wife tonight or perish in the attempt!' When they changed the guard, he dashed out of the house. Maybe there were eighty-ninety redcoats, stacking arms, moving baggage, parading up and down. The Captain goes through them like a cannon ball—*pow!* There's a little old British sentinel walking to the gate. The Captain butts him with his head—*Bamm.* Englishmen run into each other in the dark. Shotguns go *Bang! Bing! Wheeeee!* Captain isn't there. Runs to the navy yard. Into the water *whoosh*, swims half a mile, gets home. Colored boys have his horse saddled. He kisses his wife. Rides off into the swamp."

"How did the boys know ahead so they could get his horse ready?"

"They put it on the drums—" Pambo said. "He gets the news the same way. You know, Mistoh Nick Young."

Nick nodded. He remembered hot evenings in his boyhood when the drums sounded through the Dismal Swamp where escaped slaves had their hiding places. So now both white and colored men would be hiding there. It would be no different.

The river was the same too. The oaks and sycamores and beeches had grown a little bigger, he supposed, but most things—houses, boats, wharves, trees, even the James River itself—appeared smaller than they had to the twelve-year-old boy who had sailed down the river thirteen years before.

"You haven't told me how you got back here, Pambo," he said after a few minutes of silence.

Mr. Banks got a letter from Duncan McTavish, telling him that Nick had sailed for home on the *Alliance*, Pambo said. Mr. Banks arranged for Pambo to go on an English ship bound for Portsmouth as valet for the captain. He had sent money for Nick and had given Pambo enough so that he could buy his boat and start in business. Also a paper with seals on it and writing that said Mr. Banks had freed him.

"Paper's not worth much in Portsmouth. Mistoh Nick Young—I still belong to you the way I always did, but it makes good reading for white folks. And none of my passengers has known me yet. One colored man looks about like another so long's he got his legs and arms, I reckon. Of course, I always talk mighty grand and English. I say, 'Yes, sir, I had the honor to be in the employ of Mr. Joseph Banks, President of the Royal Society. Mr. Banks set me free and I determined to seek my fortune in the New World. It is the land of opportunity, sir.' Then they say, 'What's this Royal Society?' and I say, 'It is an association of gentlemen interested in the advancement of scientific knowledge in various fields, sir. Botanical and astronomical studies were Mr. Banks's chief interests.' Then I tell them about the transit of Venus and the breadfruit trees. They think I'm as English as a little old boiled cabbage."

"I don't wonder," said Nick, who had been laughing so that he almost fell out of the boat. "So he's President of the Royal Society! He must like that."

"Yes, sir! They had his portrait painted. He's sitting there dressed in black velvet with this big gold club in front of him.

They call it a mace. That's what the President of the Society keeps order with, knocks those scientific ideas into their heads, I reckon."

Nick laughed some more at this method of advancing learning.

"Here's the letter he sent you, and the money," Pambo said, pausing in his rowing long enough to pull them out of his pocket.

Nick read the letter. It was like the one he had read in Mill Prison, a letter from a just, sensible, generous, honorable man. A man, Nick thought, as English not as boiled cabbage but as roast beef and Yorkshire pudding. There could not be many men like Mr. Banks in England or anywhere else. But there had been also all the good English people whose names Nick would never know, the ones who had given more than £16,000, some of it in shillings and pence, to help the American prisoners of war. The only man Nick had ever known in America who made him think of Mr. Banks was George Washington...

"I'm going to join General Washington's army as quick as I can, Pambo," he said. "I've had enough of the sea."

"I reckoned you would, Mistoh Nick Young," said Pambo.

The sun was going down in a sky of purple and gold when they came to Caryl's Maze. There was no wind. The leaves of the paulownia trees hung quietly like the ears of lazy elephants. The sun made mirrors of the polished leaves of the magnolias and warmed the old bricks of the house to a dozen shades of rose color. From the maze came the scent of box, still warm from the hot day.

"Dickson's here all the time since your uncle died. You'd better see him first. He knows you're coming. I came up when

I got Mr. Banks's letter. I waited till I saw that Gilbert with the pointed ears in town. I told your Aunt Dorothy and Miss Cherry, too. They're mighty happy, I can tell you. Just about couldn't speak."

"What did Dickson say?" Nick asked.

He remembered the butler, a tall Negro of great dignity, who had once caught him and Cherry eating grapes out of a dish of fruit arranged for a company dinner. Dickson had said what he thought of such behavior in a way that Nick had never forgotten.

"Said it was about time," Pambo said. "Said you'd better get on up to the Maze before the Snake Brother swallows it all."

"Snake Brother?"

"These plantation Negroes who have never been out in the world," Pambo said in his most superior tone, "have some ideas that are right *old*-fashioned. One is that Mistoh Sandy had a snake brother he was supposed to feed. He didn't feed him enough so the Snake Brother killed him and took his place. They claim it often happens if anyone's snake brother gets hungry. They all know that's not Mr. Sandy up here."

"They think the same thing in Java—only they call it the Crocodile Twin. Don't you remember?"

"Don't make much difference what you call that cousin of yours," Pambo remarked dryly. "Up here they say never let a snake brother in the house. I reckon they're right."

There were two men on the float. One looked a little like Dickson, only smaller, stooped, gray-headed. The other was McFarland, the tall Scottish overseer. As the Negro moved toward the end of the wharf, Nick realized that the small man was Dickson himself. Only like everything, like McFarland and even the leaves on the paulownia trees, he was a little smaller than Nick remembered.

"Good evening, Mistoh Nick Young," Dickson said quietly. "Happy to see you at Caryl's Maze, sir."

"You know me, Dickson?" Nick asked, looking down at him.

"Certainly, sir."

"And Mr. McFarland—do you know me, too?"

"Your height changes you, of course," McFarland said. "Otherwise you are like the boy I remember."

"I have the Golden Horseshoe," Nick said. "It was among Sandy's things when he died—or was killed."

He unpinned it from his shirt and held it out.

The overseer glanced at it briefly.

"Your face is an even better passport," he said. "You are very like your father. We had better not waste time talking," he added. "Dickson told me the whole story last night. I knew at once it must be true. There was always something strange, something not like Sandy, about this man. But your uncle and aunt accepted him. It was natural for them to do so—but we shall have plenty of time to talk of all that later. At present you had better get on up to the house and stop Gilbert Caryl—if that's his name—from gambling away Caryl's Maze as he did the Portsmouth house. He had out the title deeds from the lawyer's lately. And the list of slaves. He owes great sums to the British officers who are here this evening. Only yesterday, he demanded so much tobacco from me to pay his debts, you couldn't grow it from here to North Carolina."

He turned and said to the butler: "Had they finished dinner when you left, Dickson?"

"Yes, Mr. McFarland. He rang for candles in the library. I carried them in just before I heard the boat."

Like everything at Caryl's Maze, the library was smaller than Nick remembered it. Still, the greenish blue of the woodwork, the arched bookcases with the busts of Homer and Socrates above them, and the rows of brown and gold books were the same. So was the old desk of red lacquer and embroidered bell pull like the one at Caryl's Mount. Nick could see them all as he stood at the door that opened onto the terrace.

There were four men around the mahogany card table.

The evening was hot and they had made themselves comfortable. There were scarlet coats and white waistcoats and powdered wigs tossed on chairs and sofas. Candles were lighted in the great crystal chandelier and in the brass candlesticks on the mantelpiece. The light shone on the polished gorgets at the soldiers' throats and on Gilbert Caryl's bald head.

He was facing the door, shaking dice in the box, calling for doubles or quits. He had changed more than anything in the room.

Sandy would never have been like this, Nick thought.

Gilbert had grown fat as well as bald. His cheeks were flabby. There were pouches of fat under his eyes, rolls of it on his wrists, but his ears were still pointed. Yes, Nick thought, this was the Crocodile Twin—or Snake Brother—whichever you liked to call him.

"Go in and announce me," Nick said to Dickson.

He saw Dickson cross the room in the old-fashioned, stately way, heard him say, "Mr. Nicholas Young Caryl is here and would speak with you, sir."

Gilbert Caryl dropped the dicebox. He turned a strange color, a sort of ashen purple, as he looked up at Nick. He put his hand to his throat and tried to speak, but no sound came out. The Englishmen had leaped to their feet but he still sat there, choking.

At last he said to Dickson in a hoarse tone, little above a

whisper, "What do you mean, you black rascal, bringing this impostor, this giant out of a traveling show, here? Boy died years ago. Buried in the garden in London. Next to his brother, I mean my brother."

"You mean *my* brother, Gilbert," Nick said, quietly. "Gentlemen," he added to the officers, "this is a family matter. I do not think it is necessary to trouble you with it. Mr. Caryl will be returning to London by the next ship. Perhaps you can continue your game, which I am sorry to interrupt, there. If he has staked land or slaves or tobacco against you, I must, in fairness to you, tell you that he owns nothing in America. I have ordered your boat brought around. May I escort you to it?"

Gilbert Caryl struggled to his feet. "Don't leave me, don't leave me!" he gasped out, clutching the arm of the man nearest to him. "He'll kill me. It's all a cowardly lie, made up to get the plantation away from me. Keep off, you coward, you dirty pirate. I swear you're a pirate. Don't touch me!"

"I hope not to need to," Nick said.

"Don't leave me!" Gilbert repeated, wildly. "I tell you, he's a pirate. Kill him, fight him. He's not my cousin—my cousin died of smallpox in London."

McFarland was just behind Nick.

To the officers Nick said, "This is Mr. James McFarland, the son of the former overseer of Caryl's Maze. He was born here and has been assistant overseer or overseer for more than twenty years. Will you tell these gentlemen who I am, McFarland?"

The overseer said, "Your servant, gentlemen. This is Mr. Nicholas Young Caryl, the younger son of John Caryl, of this place. Mr. Nicholas became heir to the estate when his brother, Alexander, died in England. His cousin, Gilbert Caryl, as we now know, took advantage of a striking resemblance between him and Mr. Alexander and got possession of the estate. Mr. Alexander was killed in a duel by Sir John Desmond in 1768. We have reason to believe this was part of a plot in which this man here, Gilbert Caryl, was the moving force. We all thought Mr. Nicholas Young Caryl had died, too, but he is evidently very much alive. This is a matter for lawyers, gentlemen, not for swords."

Gilbert said hoarsely: "I swear he's one of Washington's officers. He's sneaked in here to meet Cunningham. I warrant he knows where he is. Put him in irons, get it out of him. Think of the reward you'll get. You owe me something for all the work I've done for you."

The soldier whose arm Gilbert was clutching shook him off, saying contemptuously, "I do not think we owe you anything,

Mr. Caryl. Shall we go, gentlemen? This seems to be a private matter." He put on his wig and his coat.

"Take me with you, Captain," Gilbert said, still in that hoarse, gasping whisper. "You'll need me when Cornwallis comes. More than ever. Fight them—there are four of us."

"Fight your own battles, sir! And if you expect to continue in your trade of spy, learn to keep your mouth shut," the Captain said. He turned to Nick and added, "I'm not at all sure that four of us—I mean three—could take care of this gentleman. I'll do my fighting where I belong—on the battlefield. It isn't the business of His Majesty's soldiers to murder civilians. I take it you are not one of General Washington's officers, Mr. Caryl?"

"No, sir. Not yet," Nick said. "But I hope to be someday," he added frankly.

The officer laughed.

"Perhaps we'll exchange shots, then. You would make an excellent target," he said. "Come, gentlemen, goodbye Mr. Caryl."

"Goodbye," Nick said. "Come see us after the war's over."

They went out without speaking to Gilbert, who had slumped back in his chair and was staring helplessly after them, his face gray-green now, rather than purple.

Nick could hardly bear to look at his cousin.

This fat, cowardly spy—he thought—reminds me of the bald green caterpillars that crawl on ash trees, sucking the life out of them. He's sucked life out of everything he's touched.

"Don't kill me," Gilbert Caryl gasped.

As an answer Nick tossed a paper on the table in front of him.

"I have no special desire to kill you," he said, "but if you ever set foot on Caryl's Maze after tonight, I will make it so dangerous for you to do so that you will be sorry you were ever born. The Negroes here know that you had my brother killed and took his place. They loved him and they call you the Snake Brother. They have a way of dealing with snake brothers."

Nick paused and looked down at Gilbert's shaking hands. From somewhere he heard a faint sound of drumming that grew louder, died away, grew louder again.

"It begins," he said, "with drums... you had better sign that paper," he added. "You will? Good. Shall I read it to you? Dickson, tell Mr. Gilbert Caryl's man to pack his clothes and whatever else belongs to him. Cards, dice. Books, Gilbert?... No books, Dickson... wigs, perfumes, dressing case. Whatever he needs for the journey. Mr. McFarland, please get your assistant. We shall need two witnesses to Mr. Caryl's signature. Pambo, have the barge brought around. There's a ship sailing for England with the morning tide and we will escort Mr. Gilbert to it. In the meantime, Gilbert, I'll read your confession to you."

He began reading: "I, Gilbert Caryl, of Caryl House, Bloomsbury, London, England, do hereby confess..."

It was all there—the plot against Sandy, the resemblance, the duel, the scar made on Gilbert's forehead after Sandy's death, how old Nicholas Caryl, who was already growing deaf and blind, had accepted Gilbert as the heir, how Gilbert had gambled away ships and goods and houses, how he had sold information to both American and British soldiers.

There followed a promise, in return for some of Mr. Banks's guineas, to leave Virginia and never return to Caryl's Maze.

Gilbert recovered somewhat during the reading, his hands stopped shaking. The scar on his forehead turned pink instead of purple.

He said in a wheedling tone, "Now, Nick, you know that's

all nonsense. Gilbert's dead and buried in London. I'm your kind brother Sandy, who used to carry you on my back through the maze, who taught you the paths through the maze, who used to let you play with my Golden Horseshoe. Don't you remember the Golden Horseshoe, Nick?"

"Yes," Nick said, quietly, "and I remember the maze. Suppose you show me the path through it now. The moon's up and bright. And first tell me what the Latin on the sundial means. We can read it together if your memory needs refreshing."

Gilbert stammered: "I—I wouldn't go into the maze alone with you. You'd kill me."

"And you've never been really sure of the paths, Gilbert, have you? Dickson told me you screamed your head off because you were lost and had to be guided out of it when you first got here. But I know the maze and I know what it says on the Golden Horseshoe, too. I'll give you an extra guinea besides those I promised you if you can tell me."

Gilbert Caryl said nothing. In the silence Nick heard the steps of McFarland and Jim Brown, his assistant, on the bricks of the terrace and in the distance again the booming of the drums.

"I'll read you what it says," Nick said, unpinning the horseshoe from his shirt. "It's in Latin, but I'll still give you the guinea if you can translate."

Gilbert stared at the gold and garnets sparkling in the candlelight, but still did not speak.

Sic juvat transcendere montes.—

"Thus it was pleasant to cross the mountains," Nick said. "And for your motto, Gilbert, why not say *sea* for *mountains.* Here's the pen and ink."

Gilbert Caryl wrote his name at the bottom of the confession. He sat, grinding his teeth in anger, as McFarland and Brown added their signatures as witnesses.

"You'll be sorry for this, Nick Young," he said.

Nick said quietly, "Don't call me Nick Young, please. That is a name I keep for my friends. See Mr. Caryl to the barge, please, Dickson, Mr. McFarland. I'll follow in a moment." They were gone, but a voice from the hall seemed to echo, "Nick Young—Nick Young."

A little old lady—but it was still Aunt Dorothy—was standing there and, behind her, the most beautiful girl Nick had ever seen.

Chapter 22

LETTERS FROM ABROAD

So NICK and Caroline Ashton, whom he still called Cherry, were married. And Nick had his wish to become one of Washington's officers. "I was never more than a midshipman in the Navy," he used to say.

Cherry would add, proudly, "Well, you were a captain in the Army!"

He took part in the siege of Yorktown. On the 19th of October, 1781, he saw the British troops surrender their arms. They marched through the lines of American and French soldiers with the band playing "The World Turned Upside Down."

Lord Cornwallis, [Nick wrote to his wife] was less proud than you say he was when he had his headquarters at Portsmouth. He did not even show his face but sent a message to General Washington by General O'Hara, saying he was not feeling well. I can well believe he was not! O'Hara carried out the surrender most politely but when the British officers received orders to ground their arms, many of them threw them down in a very sullen way, as if they intended to injure them. Our officers soon stopped that, however.

Our French allies made a grand show in their uniforms. Our troops made the neatest appearance they could but we were not all in uniform. They never could find one big enough for me. I was still wearing my old brown suit. Though I had some gilt buttons on it then and new facings.

Our General behaved throughout with his usual courtesy and modesty, giving the credit for the victory to everyone but himself, though everyone in the Army knew that the whole scheme was his and without him it could never have been carried out.

Cherry read Nick's journals over and over again while he was away. And when letters had come from his old friends, she was as interested in them all as Nick was.

There was one from Nathaniel Fanning on board the *Ariel* with John Paul Jones. Captain Jones had started to sail for America in the *Ariel* on the 7th of October, 1780. Unfortunately, a great storm came up soon after they left L'Orient and the ship was almost driven on the Penmarque Rocks.

Fanning wrote that Richard Dale said that throughout that night they were in more danger than they had been even when the *Richard* fought the *Serapis* and that no one but John Paul Jones could have saved them.

Richard would write to you about it himself [Fanning said], but he says to tell you that you knew he never could spell and besides he doubts if letters will get through to Portsmouth. We are sailing again soon. He says he will tell you everything when he sees you.

We are almost ready. It took two months to repair the damage caused to the *Ariel* in the storm. Yesterday the Captain entertained our friends here on board the ship. The quarter-deck was turned into a ballroom and banquet room by spreading awnings over it. From the awnings hung curtains of pink silk with mirrors and pictures fastened to it. Also wreaths of artificial flowers, and the rigging was all hung with flags. Cooks and waiters from the shore got a splendid dinner ready. Three boatloads of us in our best uniforms with French and American cockades in our hats went on shore to escort the guests aboard.

They were persons of rank and distinction, both ladies and gentlemen, all splendidly dressed. Captain Jones received them as they came over the ship's side and conducted them to their seats with ease, politeness, and good-nature.

At half past three the company sat down to an elegant dinner. We did not rise till sunset. The officers and crew went to their stations to exhibit a representation of the capture of the *Serapis*. At eight o'clock the moon rose. The evening was much the same as the one you and I remember. A gun was fired as a signal to begin. A tremendous explosion of guns, muskets, rockets, and grenades followed. In the tops, as we did against the *Serapis*, we kept things in a complete blaze. The scene was splendid but the ladies were terrified and screamed to John Paul Jones to stop, so at the end of only an hour, he stopped the action. The band then struck up—lively French airs—and the dance began. This the ladies enjoyed more and the dancing went on till midnight. Then the company got into their boats again and we escorted them to their own doors. You will gather that the Captain got some of his prize money—and has spent it! I have received a part of mine and I hope you will get yours. The *Ariel* will sail without me and by the time you receive this, my dear Nick, I hope to be captain of my own privateer and annoy the British a little. I think I have learned a trick or two from the greatest captain who ever sailed the seas. I only wish you were going to be with me, but wherever you are and wherever I am, I shall always be

Your sincere friend

N. Fanning

On the 27th of February, 1781, Congress met and paid. tribute to the distinguished bravery of John Paul Jones, especially in his victory over the British frigate *Serapis*, and gave permission for him to be decorated by the French minister as a Knight of the Order of Military Merit.

On April 17th, Congress passed more resolutions thanking Jones for his services. They did not, however, pay him the money they owed him. He was given command of a fine new frigate, the *America*, which was being built in Portsmouth, New Hampshire. Before she was completed, Congress, however turned her over to the French Navy to take the place of a French ship that had been wrecked.

"In fact," Nick said to Cherry, "this Captain Jones never had command of a ship that was worthy of his talents. When I think of what he did with the little *Providence*, with the *Ranger*—only a sloop of war—with the *Poor Richard*—poor indeed in every way—I wonder how much the war might have been shortened if he had been given even one of the ships that other commanders threw away."

When the war was over and there were no more battles to fight for America, John Paul Jones, the Scottish gardener's son became an admiral in the navy of the Empress of Russia. He won a brilliant victory, the credit of which went to others. He died in Paris in 1792 at the age of forty-five.

Richard Dale came often to Portsmouth, where he and Nick would fight the battle of the *Bon Homme Richard* and the *Serapis* over again. Models of both ships were on the mantelpiece of the dining room at Caryl's Maze. On winter evenings when the wind off the James River sounded loud in the chimneys, and a sea fog was blowing inland, they would sit around the big mahogany table after Pambo had cleared away the walnuts and raisins and wine and put the two ships through the correct maneuvers.

Some years after John Paul Jones's death, Commodore Dale had a chance to buy the gold-hilted sword with the Latin motto that the King of France had given to the captain of the *Bon Homme Richard*.

For a while Richard Dale and Nicholas Caryl were in business together, sending ships to ports all around the world. Later Richard Dale was a commodore in the Navy, but Nick never went to sea again. He did not have to go far enough inland with an anchor over his shoulder so that people would ask him what that thing was. He liked the sound of tidewater lapping against the wharf at Caryl's Maze, but he had had all he wanted of strange lands and seas. His ship captains were often surprised to have him write instructions telling them about foreign ports: where they could find the best water or the best anchorage, where wild celery grew, how the crew must have lime juice or lemon juice to prevent scurvy.

The old giant—that's what his captains called him—was crazy on the subject of scurvy. However, it was a fact that there was almost never a case of it on the Caryl ships.

It was a long time before Nick heard about Captain Cook's death. After the surrender of Cornwallis it became easier to get letters to and from England. Nick wrote to Mr. Banks to congratulate him on having been made a baronet by George III and to thank him for the help that he had been to him at Mill Prison, and again in sending Pambo to Portsmouth. Nick had set Pambo free, he told Sir Joseph, but Pambo grew tired of his ferry business and had come back to be butler of Caryl's Maze after Dickson's death. He and Pambo both wanted to know about Captain Cook.

Sir Joseph wrote that Captain Cook had been killed by the natives on the beach of one of the Sandwich Islands. He had succeeded in getting most of his men away safely but stayed until the last and was killed. The natives, who had first welcomed Cook and treated him as if he were a god, now carried off his body and cut it up into pieces, dividing it among different tribes.

Perhaps [Sir Joseph wrote], they thought that it would give them some of his courage and wisdom. Our officers succeeded, though, through one of the native priests, in getting most of the body returned to them, and it was buried at sea. His hands were easily recognized because of the large scar, which you will remember. So died this wise and good man who had always, in dealing with native tribes, used the greatest patience, kindness, and understanding. He was one of the best friends I ever had and I shall always regret his passing.

You asked about my scheme for transporting breadfruit trees to the West Indies. It may still be carried out. I had always hoped that Captain Cook would be in command when the time came. Lately I have talked with Lieutenant Bligh who knows the South Seas, having served under Captain Cook on his last voyage. Perhaps the scheme can be accomplished with Bligh in Cook's place, though I doubt if such a man's place can ever be filled.

Thank you also for the seeds you sent and the beautiful painting of the camellias from your garden. I did not know they would grow so far north. I am glad you are working on your book on American flowering trees and shrubs. You must come to England and publish here. I know a good engraver who could make fine prints of your trees. I hope to see them growing in Virginia someday."

Sir Joseph Banks never came to Caryl's Maze but there was one visitor who came every time the brig *Caroline* sailed into Hampton Roads and up the James River and tied up at the wharf of Caryl's Maze. This was Duncan McTavish, partner of Caryl and Company, who never lost his taste for faraway places and faraway names.

Duncan always brought unusual gifts with him—a tea set with emblem of the Cincinnati on it for Nick, because Nick had been one of General Washington's officers and belonged to the Society, a beautiful chocolate pot with the Golden Horseshoe on it, and an ivory chess set with red and white elephants with castles on their backs and a white king dressed like Louis XVI of France. The Queen, Nick said, did not look at all like Queen Marie Antoinette. Better than any presents were the stories Duncan used to tell. Cherry and Nick's four sons sometimes wondered if all his stories could be true.

"Certainly," Nick would say. "Duncan was always a model boy."

"And what was the greatest adventure you ever had, father?"

"Coming home," said Nicholas Young Caryl.

www.ingramcontent.com/pod-product-compliance
Lightning Source LLC
Chambersburg PA
CBHW060802190726
48285CB00002B/518